The Home for Wayward Girls

The Home for Wayward Girls

a novel

Marcia Bradley

HARPER

NEW YORK • LONDON • TORONTO • SYDNEY

HARPER

THE HOME FOR WAYWARD GIRLS. Copyright © 2023 by Marcia Bradley. All rights reserved. Printed in the United States of America. No part of this book may be used or reproduced in any manner whatsoever without written permission except in the case of brief quotations embodied in critical articles and reviews. For information, address HarperCollins Publishers, 195 Broadway, New York, NY 10007.

HarperCollins books may be purchased for educational, business, or sales promotional use. For information, please email the Special Markets Department at SPsales@harpercollins.com.

FIRST EDITION

Designed by Jen Overstreet

Library of Congress Cataloging-in-Publication Data has been applied for.

ISBN 978-0-06-327604-8 (pbk.)

23 24 25 26 27 LBC 5 4 3 2 1

With love
For my parents
Frances and Emily always,
Joanne and Tom, my strength,
And our sister and brother gone too soon

You gain strength, courage, and confidence by every experience in which you really stop to look fear in the face. You must do the thing you think you cannot do.

—ELEANOR ROOSEVELT

Contents

ONE

New York City

Loretta was an independent woman. She was cautious about shadows yet her hunger for the future was distinct, subtle as fine jewelry, strong as her prairie roots. The silk scarf around her neck was not meant to hide her scars, although she covered the wounds she'd carried to New York. She wasn't sure why. Even her hair was a mixed message, streaks of auburn, brown, and gold.

"Hey, Siri, play my sunrise songs." She paused to listen, to mark time, to affirm what came before and what was to come next. A singer's husky voice, slight as a feather, floated toward the walnut floors of their Manhattan apartment. If it was a different morning, Loretta might have canceled her appointments and lingered over coffee with last Sunday's *Times*, headed to Trader Joe's, and made a stop at her favorite thrift store to scout for unexpected treasures. Had hers been a different life, perhaps this would not be the long-awaited Tuesday, a day of critical importance.

Loretta stood by the window. She watched the hustle of the city eight stories below; the sounds of horns rose to greet her, an ambulance sped down Broadway. Her heartbeat raced, even her freckles trembled. The feelings of anxiety were too familiar. She wanted to hold herself in check, to keep her secrets bound to her soul, to tell the world off but also hug it close. Born on the cusp between Gen X and Millennials, she was now, at age thirty-five, tempted by the opportunities the twenty-first century presented. She felt close to unstoppable, she'd worked hard to prepare, knew to breathe, to find her center. It was a coerced strength, an internal muscle she'd trained. No giving in to fears today.

"You ready?" Clarke called from the kitchen.

"Almost," she said. It was unlikely Clarke could hear her, but she was sure he was counting down the minutes as she was.

"Nervous?"

"Nope," she said, although he'd know better. "Maybe I am. About talking to the reporter."

"You don't have to, you know." Clarke appeared in the bedroom doorway; his lucky tie hung from his shoulders not yet knotted. "Don't let it mess with your head."

"No. I do have to. I'm committed. I must. It's gonna help others."

"I knew that's what you'd say." He stopped long enough to catch her eye and offer his pep talk smile. "Come on. Coffee's ready."

"Be right there."

Her friends asked how she stayed so calm. They didn't know the skills she'd learned when she was a child, that hiding nervousness can give one a sort of strength, and that years of always keeping a safe arm's-length distance wasn't necessarily good for your spirit.

"Do you meditate? Are you never anxious?" some asked.

"I try not to let things get to me," she winked and told those closest to her, the people she trusted with her sticky incontrovertible past where she'd both cowered and prevailed, led and fled. Her thoughts debated what she owed the decades that had fostered the person she'd become, those days and months when she would do anything, right or wrong, to get by. Is victory deserved if the journey included errors in judgment and turns that might have been avoided? These questions were the squatters that claimed space inside her head.

"How is it that you are nothing like your parents?" Clarke had asked when she finally broke her silence and told him about her childhood and her life before New York. "It doesn't seem possible. You're not similar, not even close to how they sound."

"But I am," she told him. "I grew up with William and Mama, worked on their ranch, cleaned the chicken coop, raised their rabbits. We had rabbit stew many times. Take a moment and think about that." Loretta frowned as she remembered skinning and gutting the rabbits. "I've shot a gun—more than once. I stole things."

"You also read books. You were a great student. You were good to the other girls."

"Ha! You believe the best picture of me. But really?"

"Really, what?"

"I wasn't always good. I was jealous of them. Especially when I was a kid. Like eleven or twelve. Those girls came to the ranch from nicer homes in bigger cities. And they got to leave. I didn't. Then I realized who the real enemy was. That's when I started to change. I really did—I'd do anything I could for the girls after that, and I began to hate William and Mama. I still do. Especially William."

"With good reason."

"Hmm. Sure. Yet although I don't go to church, I know hatred is a sin." Loretta scrunched her lips tight, her mind off to its private thoughts.

Loretta slipped her arms into the brown corduroy blazer she'd worn to important meetings since grad school. Embers of jasmine and citrus perfume resided in the seams. A speck of dust beckoned from her western boots, leather dark as ripened avocados. She brushed it away with fingers manicured burgundy, straightened her worn extralong 501s, and urged waves of auburn hair behind her shoulders.

"Choose life." She whispered one of the few biblical quotes she clung to and grabbed the ancient satchel she'd rescued from a store on Seventy-Second Street.

It was almost time to go.

TWO
West of the Rockies

What Loretta longed for growing up at the Home for Wayward Girls may seem an odd lot. She was a scrawny seventeen-year-old with hair a messy blend of red and orange and brown, her skin far too freckled to mark her as pretty. Not that Loretta had a good picture of herself. She lived in a house that never had a camera, and their only mirror was on the small medicine cabinet door in the bathroom at the top of the stairs.

"I'll not have conceit in this home. Vanity of vanities, all is vanity," her father, William, yelled when he heard her asking for something from the Penney's catalog that arrived in the mail.

"Yes, sir." Loretta closed her mouth and didn't say another word. Her father could shift to anger in a split second; there were days when his face suddenly became enraged, eyes bulging, his hands weapons. She didn't argue. She wore the Home's boring wrap-around denim skirt, pocketless by design because who knew what evil trinkets could be hidden within, and a white blouse or T-shirt with William's No Foolish Sinnery mantra printed across the front despite how peculiar it made her appear at the local school.

"I'll just put this away." Mama carried the Penney's catalog off, hid it somewhere, gave Loretta a flicker of her eyelids, the meaning of which she was never sure. Did her mother know her daughter dreamt of teen girl clothes, that she yearned for a friend? Was she aware how desperate Loretta was for freedom?

Whether Mama knew or not didn't matter near as much as that February afternoon when the best part of Loretta's life began. It was no different from any day before, but it was the day the new resident arrived. She was the exact kind of girl Loretta would have ordered if catalogs mail-ordered friends. The new girl didn't know her, but she would become Loretta's everything—her confidante, a partner in her plans, the kind of friend girls yearn to have and dread ever losing. Girls don't need to be told who is invaluable. Girls know.

Loretta spent her first seventeen years landlocked on her father's ranch—a residential home for immoral young females. Uncontrollable teens. In high school, the realization ate at her insides. People paid her father to lock their daughters in his bunkhouse. Girls who were forced to work for him.

"Wayward girls," he called them. "Need be fixed."

"Yes, William," Loretta's mother, Bess, agreed. Loretta had lost hope; she wasn't sure she ever had hope that Mama would speak up, fight, become a hero instead of the collaborator she appeared to be. Mama always agreed with William.

Loretta's most courageous act when she was growing up was to hum Paula Abdul songs—her voice buried beneath her breath. Her father, William, would not appreciate pop music about cold-hearted snakes; this was too close to his own existence in the town west of the Rockies. On the bus from school, Loretta listened to Billboard hits and news reports: it was the 1990s, a man

William despised from Arkansas was president, something called Super Nintendo had been released, and *Clueless* was playing in theaters. Loretta had never been to a movie. She wanted to understand everything but didn't dare ask. William would go ballistic if he learned Loretta had stolen a radio from the G&A, and anything about Democrats was best left unspoken.

G&A, Guns & Ammo, was a sort of 7-Eleven for weapons found on the main street of every town for miles around the prairie lands where Loretta lived. It was filled with hunting paraphernalia, no-questions-asked gun permits, and camouflage fashion as well as pawnshop loans, gun silencers, pocketknives, and freeze-dried food for campers. Fathers in western wear, moms with babies clutched to their breasts, and kids in camo roamed the aisles with plans to hunt deer, scavenge elk antlers, face off with bears, taxidermy animal heads, and use BB guns for prairie dog target practice.

Sometimes Loretta snuck into the G&A when school got out early. In her long denim skirt, she was sure the clerks and townspeople knew she was from William's ranch. It was the uniform worn by every resident of the Home for Wayward Girls. Her orange-red-brown hair in the standard ranch ponytail. The lace-up boots on her feet were weathered. The clerks must have seen she was stealing—it was possible they felt sorry for her.

"Hey, I can help if ya need anything," a guy named Roger behind the counter told her a few times. He wore a black cap with the words THIS IS A RIFLE embroidered beneath the image of an AK-47, a full-on assault weapon. He smiled in her direction, and though his hands held a pen and pad, she'd never seen him write anything.

"Thanks. I'm fine," she said. Roger glanced a different direction, a purposeful turn of his head, a silent promise not to watch whatever she was doing.

Loretta wondered if he knew she had to get away. That she had dreams that might seem lofty, but they weren't to her. She longed to see an ocean, watch actual television, read magazines like girls at her school did, and she imagined opening the pages of books she didn't yet know existed.

"Oh my God, I love Target," one of the residents, Gayle, moaned when she heard a commercial on Loretta's radio the night before.

"What's Target?" Loretta asked, sitting on the floor of the bunkhouse.

"You've never been to a Target? How about Walmart?"

"Nope." Loretta was embarrassed. She didn't know most of the stuff the residents knew about. "But there's a Walmart in town. William goes there." She always referred to her father as William, hated that he demanded they all call him Papa.

"There's a Target back home. Where I *used* to live before here, I guess," Gayle said.

"At least Loretta gets to stay in the house. Not in this awful bunkhouse. You have a bedroom," Crystal said. The youngest resident had told Loretta she missed her fluffy dog and closet filled with pretty clothes. Loretta wanted to tell the girls that life in "the house" was close to miserable.

"Turn it up, oh my God, this song is the best," Tanya squealed.

"Who's singing?" Little Crystal look confused.

"It's Jewel. Turn it off. I think I see your father coming," Gayle warned. If William found them listening to music, oh Lord, someone, probably Loretta, would have hell to pay.

Loretta fantasized about shopping at the stores they mentioned, like Target—the radio station said one was opening the next state over. Loretta wanted to walk around town in jeans with friends. She yearned to be free and very, very far from guns, church folks, and threats that manipulated the meaning of Bible passages. The paying residents at the Home had past lives—they'd grown up outside the ranch—they'd worn pretty dresses and been to Target and Walmart. Loretta had not. Loretta had never shopped for clothes, or stood in a cosmetics aisle, or subscribed to a magazine, and she desperately wanted to.

"Stop your daydreaming," Mama sniped at her the next morning, a very particular February morning. "Get the bowls for breakfast." Mama, with a Brillo pad of barely brown short hair, wore her pink-green-red plaid apron and snapped her chin toward the cabinet where stacks of dishes were stored.

"Yes, ma'am." Loretta knew her duties. Ladle servings of oatmeal, hand out pieces of toast, pour a glass of milk for each of the ten residents.

"Well, whatcha waitin' for? Get a move on." Mama grabbed the towel from her shoulder and swung it at Loretta's face.

Loretta ducked and hurried to the stacks of dishes. Mama's towel slaps were intended to hurt. How she wished it was summer, August, her eighteenth birthday. She needed to make it to eighteen to be legally unbound from Mama and William. Loretta stared at the frozen land outside their windows. Although she avoided the organized religion of her father, she caught herself praying.

"Dear Lord, help get me to freedom." She added that if she was supposed to run sooner, if she dared take the risk, would the Lord please tell her now? No easy answer descended from the heavens.

Outside the kitchen window, beyond the ranch and into the distance, unreliable glimmers of warmth teased the prairie lands. Temperatures had hovered in the high 30s for days, a warm spell for these parts. Snow that blizzarded in weeks before had eased. At school Loretta had watched overheated young men toss their heavy jackets into the cargo beds of their fancy pickup trucks. Girls in Dixie Chicks and Ace of Base T-shirts gazed at sunlight that drenched the far-off mountain peaks. Students and teachers and ranchers alike held dear the promise that spring would soon bless them with its bounty. Winters in this state were brutal but not without hope.

Loretta watched from the window when the transporters delivered the new resident. Transporters had brought girls many times before. Steely-edged people hired to do a grab and go of teens, the transporter team would march into a house, find the teen, and barely nod to the parents who paid them. Loretta searched them in Yahoo! on the computer in the library at school because there was no technology at the ranch—she learned that transporters were akin to military dropouts who made their living hauling supposed miscreant teens to awful residency programs. They were licensed to carry Glocks and authorized to use them should the adolescent try to make a getaway.

"Oh no, not them." The words slipped too quick from Loretta's lips.

"Shut your mouth." Mama gave Loretta her *this is how we make a living* frown, her *you best quiet yourself or I'll tell William* threat. Loretta knew how her parents made money, that there was nothing of merit to William's work. In elementary school, William had been cruel to her, but it wasn't until fourteen or fifteen that she realized his meanness was what he sold. His skill was drawing hard lines, using biblical threats, and making girls accept meekness as their key strength. Loretta wasn't meek and wouldn't ever be. Somehow she knew which side she was on—and it would never be his.

Outside, the black four-door zipped up their private dirt road and came to a skid, which was unnecessarily dramatic. A stern man and woman in leather jackets emerged wearing metallic sunglasses as if they thought themselves incredibly cool. Given the chance, Loretta would have reminded them that delivering girls to the Home for Waywards was not a classy business.

The woman opened the rear passenger door. Made a motion with her hand. Gave a command. "Now," it seemed to Loretta, but she couldn't be sure.

Out moped the first girl in some time who looked close to Loretta's own age. In the past, most had been a few years younger. Loretta felt an instantaneous connection to her. A young woman with hair so blond it was almost white. She was kind of fragile looking, but Loretta could tell she knew her mind because the girl didn't jump on command, and wow, credit to her for holding her own despite the shit show she was entering. Her backpack dragged alongside the soles of her Keds. The collar of her checked gingham shirt stuck out of her jacket. She wore fancy jeans of the sort Loretta had seen in magazines at school.

It was then that Loretta thought how she did have some good fortune in life; for one thing she got to attend the high school a few miles down the state highway. Elsewise, she'd know nothing about the real world. She'd never have gotten the radio. Never known a soul not on the ranch.

"Finish those dishes." Mama again whipped that towel at her and made a grumbling effort to hurry outside to welcome the new girl. Mama's blood didn't flow very well. "Poor circulation," she said. She wore old-man corduroy slippers, her steps were slow, her hands flailed about wiping sweat from her forehead, all manner of physicality needed to help propel her forward.

"Yes, Mama." Loretta gave the required response. The same as she'd said far back as she could recall. Yes, Mama. Yes, Papa. Very few no's allowed. Saying no to Mama might pass but said to William there'd be anger that Loretta worked to avoid.

Through the window, Loretta could see that the new girl was

in no hurry and that she'd already accepted this near destitute piece of prairie as her destiny. The Home for Wayward Girls west of the Rockies and far east of the Pacific bordered on barren. Lonesome land, difficult to cultivate much in the way of crops. Winds swept off most efforts. Thankless soil would be one way to put it.

The jackpot for William was that nobody ever-ever-ever passed this way by chance. Not like there were tourist shops with souvenirs for sale. The small town discouraged outsiders—local citizens were happy with their school and a couple church ministries, gays simply not allowed, very few people of color, some Mexican ranch hands. There was one watering hole, the Saloon, with stuffed moose heads, snakes, and prairie dogs mounted above its bar. Loretta had heard that even God-fearing men like William downed a shot of whiskey there on occasion.

"Loretta!" Mama yelled.

"Comin', Mama." Loretta scurried through the kitchen, out the door, jumped the two steps to stand by her mother's side.

"This here's Elsie. Our new girl," William announced. Him very tall next to the black car, him making his power play sort of stand. Starched old-man Levi's, the belt pulled too tight around his thick waist. His palm rested on the pistol strapped to his thigh.

"Welcome, welcome," Mama said, a hand raised to shade her eyes from the already bright sky. She might have been the nicest old auntie ever, wrapped in her apron that covered an ankle-length denim skirt of her own. Except Mama wasn't ever nice.

William talked to one of the goons for a minute. Took a card from the guy before he slid back into the Dodge. Car doors slammed. They reversed down the dirt road, dust flew, them off to pick up another unsuspecting teen. William waved, held his arm high, his authoritarian this-is-my-land pose. Ownership such an ego boost. Not that anyone would want his paltry ranch with its decrepit vegetable beds, rabbit hutches ahead, chickens pooping in their coop to the rear. William wasn't much of a rancher, no money for the cattle that neighbors had, but he was shrewd. Each season's residents provided the labor, gathered eggs, cleaned the chicken coop, cared for his bunnies, sold them in the roadside stand, and did Mama's chores in the house. There were worse tasks assigned when girls didn't follow the rules. William kept the profits.

"Elsie, this is our Loretta." William's voice was boastful, his rancher's welcome. "She'll get you settled. I'll be up shortly." He turned his mean glare to Loretta. His message was clear. Same as many times before. Loretta understood that she was to say as little as possible. Make nice. The furthest thing from what she felt.

"Be careful, girl," Mama whispered.

"Yes, Mama."

"Tell her the rules. Remember your father will be watching," Mama said.

"Yes, ma'am," Loretta mumbled, and as she had for as far back as she could recall, she wondered just whose side Mama was on.

Up close, Loretta saw that Elsie was William's type, very white-skinned, pale as a cloud. This wasn't good. It had been some time since William had commandeered a girl to his private office; still, Loretta kept watch. If it were possible to help Elsie flee right then, Loretta would have done it in an instant. Instead, she let a few ideas gel inside her head. Maybe Elsie was the friend she hoped for. Maybe the two of them could escape together. Possibly—and she knew this was a big ask—but maybe they'd find Charlie perfume, new jeans, and the highway that led far to the east.

"Hi there. Come this way." Loretta swished her hand ahead, gave a small lift of her chin. She knew better than to appear friendly. Any sort of fraternizing would be noticed.

Elsie followed.

On a girl's first day, William taught them the what for. *What for* meaning discipline and punishment, meaning actions render consequences. Loretta had seen it many times over. She tried to warn girls, but it was hard to talk on the ranch where even a hushed voice interrupted the silence of prairie land, a place so quiet the wind announced each day's weather. When the earliest signs of morning broke through the skies, Loretta could hear it from her bed. If her windows rattled, it was fair warning a front or storm was on its way. If it was a buffeting, same as how she figured a boat's sails might sound, she could be pretty sure it was gonna pass. But what will descend next—always a question on this land.

"Those goons do anything to you? You know?" Loretta, eyes forward, used few words but enough to be understood. They were on the snow-muddied path to the bunkhouse. Loretta waved the girl to her side but kept her own head straight up like a string from a cloud held her taut. No leaning in allowed. Any show of fellowship would be cause for separation.

"They hauled me from my bedroom. My father stood in the doorway the whole time. My ma didn't appear until they dragged me outside. She mighta been crying. I think she was."

"But did they—"

"Nope. Didn't touch me after they threw me in the back seat of the car. Handed me a bottle of water and told me to shut up. Four-hour ride in silence."

"Well, welcome to here." Loretta knew she sounded kinda stupid. "I mean. Sorry you had to come."

"I understand. It's not your fault." Elsie took a quick glance in Loretta's direction.

"William, that's Papa, so you know," Loretta said, although

she herself hated to call him anything, least of all that. "You got to call him Papa, understand?"

"Okay. Call him Papa. Got it," Elsie said.

"Don't act friendly. To me. To the others. Especially not to me."

"Others?"

"The residents. You'll meet them. They're in the bunkhouse now."

"What else?"

"Avoid eye contact. Don't talk to the girls till later. They're anxious, everybody's nervous and scared here, but they have your back. We all do."

"Okay."

"He's gonna start off real scary. Do your best to go with it." Loretta aimed to warn her.

"Will you be there?" she asked. Her voice tried to get Loretta to face her, to connect their eyes. Loretta wanted to turn, to give Elsie the smile the girl needed, except she knew better. William had eagle eyes; he might be on the porch watching them or inside spying through a window. He had his ways.

"I'll stay if I can. And I'll come back later. Promise."

"Please. Promise. I feel like I know you."

"You got anything important in that bag? He's gonna take it from you."

"My journal for sketching. I can't live without it."

"Okay, as soon as we get in the door up there, pull it out fast. I'll hide it under your cot."

"I will. And thanks, really. I mean it."

"I know." Loretta tried to offer a small smile. "Here he comes. Don't talk." Loretta knew then and felt pretty certain Elsie knew, too, that the two of them were starting a real friendship. Even before they became regular old laugh-and-have-fun friends. Still, on this day, the whole idea frightened Loretta. She'd read enough

Brontë and Alcott at school to know that real friendship was most assuredly accompanied by responsibility.

"Pile them slut jeans and that shirt right here. The backpack as well," William announced to Elsie in the bunkhouse where residents lived until such time they'd become cleansed and disciplined young women. "You be changing into Mama's clothes right quick. No talking. Follow the rules. Underwears, too."

"What?"

Loretta saw Elsie's shock. She'd watched many others' same reaction; she'd been at this for some time. She recalled that somebody famous had said that humans are blessed with a memory for forgetting. She took that to mean that if we had to remember everything we'd ever experienced, wouldn't that be a horror? This here, watching her new friend whose eyes had gone wide, and the way Elsie drew her hand to her mouth to keep from sputtering a profanity, this was a repeat of a scenario Loretta had tried to forget many times over.

The residents sat on bed cots around the room. In ones and twos. Tanya with her long maple syrup brown hair. Little Crystal biting on the collar of her white blouse. Redheaded Gayle. The girls halted their whispering when William entered. Heads lifted, and their stares jumped from Loretta to the new arrival and back. A few frowned, not at Elsie, but they didn't want more residents; they were praying the home would be shut down, that they'd be freed by a warrior like Boadicea, whom Loretta considered a personal hero. It was unlikely.

"Deuteronomy 22:5," William declared, not yelling, using his preacher's voice, him on a pulpit of his own making, the residents, including this new girl, his congregation. "A woman must not wear men's clothing, nor a man wear women's clothing, for the Lord your God detests anyone who does this."

"Not my jeans," Elsie whispered.

Loretta agreed with her so much. She stared at the Guess logo, the red triangle with its question mark. She understood Elsie's loss.

"Silence." William slapped a hand on the Smith & Wesson strapped to his thigh. "You—" He pointed to Elsie. It was time to give her a lesson, her first, fast and right away. *They see, they learn* was his standard go-to.

"What?" Elsie's words were clenched somewhere between her throat and her mouth. Loretta worried the girl might cry, that the ache sure to be festering in Elsie's stomach might cause her to burst.

"Get those denim slut clothes off your body this instant." Large, harsh William stood before her. His legs parted. A stance from old shoot 'em up movies. Despite the earlier warning about eye contact, Elsie glanced to Loretta, then to the other girls, but they lowered their gazes, unsure what to do, still uncertain how they'd ended up on this sad piece of land with barely a tree or bush and no other dwellings in sight.

"Change? Where?" Elsie raised her chin. Loretta saw how the girl fought off its quivering, that she was in trouble but still proud. Loretta could almost see the wheels whir in Elsie's head, and she was sure her mind was racing to figure out how to deal with William.

"Here." William grabbed the pile that was waiting on her cot. Threw it at Elsie, a knock to her gut, a hard throw that startled her. "Take everything off. And tie back that mane."

Loretta stared at the floor, also unsure what to do. The lower she hung her head, the greater her own desperation. It's one thing to peel off jeans and a shirt, but William would demand all her clothes. Make her put on old lady cotton briefs, an undershirt. Loretta had seen it before, how shame layers itself onto a girl. She'd been that girl too many times. William took particular joy in making one feel they were the sinner and not the abused.

"I'll stand here." Loretta jumped in front of Elsie. Not the best curtain but she could try. William's eyes narrowed, him both perplexed and angered by her effort.

Elsie banded her hair behind her ears. Tried for privacy. Pushed her jeans to her ankles. Held the skirt up to hide her polka-dotted thong then quick-tied the faded blue wraparound about her waist, pulled the thong off, and slipped into the horrid elastic-waisted white cotton briefs, the undershirt, and an awful tee.

"Now get to your knees." William pointed to the floor. He did this with new girls. Made them examples. Elsie's lot had been cast. He'd sell her jeans but keep the thong for Mama to store in a sandwich bag in case the girl ever ran—his dog Bull would need to sniff it for tracking.

"You're kidding me." The words peppered out of Elsie's mouth probably before she thought better. Her regret rippled slow down her cheek. She swiped the tear away. Loretta wanted to go to her, to be her guide, to tell her to let it pass, this was only the first day, that they were friends now, that she would help her through her stay on this god-awful ranch.

"You wanna test me, girl?" William's voice rose, a hill of threats within each word.

Elsie was silent.

"I said now."

She dropped to the wood floor.

"You stay there. Don't speak. Don't move."

Loretta knew and hated that William would teach Elsie as he

taught all girls to clasp their hands in prayer, to cower, and that their true natures must be put asunder. Her father who so understood true natures. Put asunder they would be.

Not for the short term. Forever. Let go and let God?

Girls learn quick to do as told. But Loretta also knew that they did not let go of their wild spirits . . . not by a long shot. Girls who'd been caught having sex. Drinking alcohol. Smoking marijuana. Girls kissing other girls. Dancing till dawn with the reckless and feckless. Exhibiting anxiety, acting out, or vomiting curse words from their mouths. William and Mama might try to cure every bit of a resident's sinful ways except Loretta believed way deeper than in her heart that girls are far better at waiting than changing.

Loretta had learned to bite her tongue. Some kernel inside her promised that William and Mama's day would come. As would hers. The promise of escape was sublime, it filled a mind with grandeur, it had settled within a small place of safety within Loretta's soul. She didn't know why but she was certain that this new friend, Elsie, was key to her next steps.

"Follow me." William raised his voice, turned to the girls on their cots, those who'd watched with scant expectations that maybe, just maybe, he'd forgotten them. "You, too," he said to Loretta.

Elsie's knees remained glued to the floor. Loretta wanted to kneel with her and assure her she'd be okay.

"Don't think about moving an inch," William warned Elsie. "I'll be back for you."

A thin line of paper doll cutouts in blue denim skirts and fresh laundered STOP FOOLISH SINNERY T-shirts followed William outside in silence to do their chores.

In total silence. Required at the Home for Wayward Girls.

THREE

West of the Rockies

Days later, Papa charged into the kitchen before Loretta could flee to school. His mad dog self spewed inexplicable anger. He surveilled the room, his eyes heat-seeking missiles on the hunt. Loretta recognized his mood—when someone, most likely her, was certain to be on the receiving end of his fury.

"You're bustin' outta that shirt," he accused in a flat tone, not a yell, an insidious challenge to his voice, a double dare to see if Loretta would have the audacity to reply. He stepped closer, playing hopscotch with her nerves.

"Huh?" she asked, startled, never surprised, but anxiousness made her stiff, afraid to move. What had she done, what now, what, what, what?

"You some kind of whore, girl?"

"What?" Loretta had no answer. She was in a hurry to get to the roadside gate by the mail stop where the bus picked her up each morning. Residents were homeschooled by William. She alone was allowed to attend County District High. Mama told her she was "damn lucky" the state inspector had convinced William to let her, that it wouldn't look right if Loretta was cast in among the paying residents, "the sinnerly girls," as William called them, girls of supposed questionable reputations.

"What you mean what?" Papa's voice made a quick rise in volume, a threat hidden within, his bellowing a sure warning there was more to come. Loretta knew the signs.

"I don't mean—" She didn't cower. Couldn't. Not anymore. She was desperate to fight back but he lurched, thrust his hand at her, right there by the potbellied stove.

Mama's sweaty swollen fingers held fast to the sink's edge; she didn't do nothing, not a move on her part. Mama laid claim early on to her role as an observer. She watched William whip Loretta from near the warm stove to the old wood chair on the other side of the room. Loretta about flew into that chair. The one that wobbled. The chair no one used. He grabbed her white cotton collar—and buttons flew, the blouse ripped open, Loretta gasped, her hand went to her breast, she froze in place, on the chair where she'd been flung, other side of the potbellied stove.

Mama all the while observing.

Papa dragged the crisp ironed collar down her shoulders, more buttons rolled across the kitchen linoleum, the sleeves bunched to enslave her wrists. He pushed her against the back of the chair. The chair that wobbled. Left her there. Half naked except for her white pointy bra they'd ordered from last year's catalog. Mama twisted her whole self away, the tie of her plaid apron backside to Loretta, her eyes affixed to something outside the kitchen window.

"You sit!"

"Yes, sir."

"Think about your actions."

"What?" Loretta's voice was a whisper. She had no idea what he meant. The girls would be headed over for breakfast. Please not Elsie. She prayed her new friend wouldn't see this. *Please, please, don't see this. Please don't see the man who is my father treat me this way.*

"Devil's in you, girl. You're gettin' ideas. I can tell. You best pray for your soul." Papa bent in very near her, his large body a menace, too close, too near her neck, her shoulders, herself. His smell was old and mean, his breath sprayed onto Loretta's face. He eagle-eyed her with a stare so downright cold she felt hatred—not shame but scorn.

"Yes, sir," she mumbled wanting to hold her hands over her face, to wipe away the tiny droplets of spittle that had landed on her right cheek. Getting ideas? Would he rob her of Elsie? Could he possibly already know that, yes, she had ideas and hopes and plans? She kept her stare glued to the floor. Watched his boots cemented in front of her, didn't dare raise her eyes, thought to grab the Smith & Wesson strapped to his thigh, but knew that such an act, brave though it might be, wouldn't end well for her.

"Not a word." He again spit the words, on purpose might be, and sneered. Her presence in his life was vile, repugnant, dirty, and she did not know why.

"Yes, sir, . . . yes, sir," she said over and over until his heavy feet marched to the door. She saw the Winchester 94, the hunting rifle by the coat hook, and thought better than to make any move, heard the door slam behind him, him headed to the bunkhouse to check the residents were on their way.

Loretta wobbled on the off-kilter chair in a state of penance, her shoulder blades pinned back by her blouse, sorry for that which she couldn't have done. What sin had she this time committed? Was it the mere glance she and Elsie had exchanged the day before, or the many why why why's she might never comprehend? She heard the rustle of the residents outside, their feet on the path, William lecturing, admonishing their evilness, citing the Lord, the sins of women, vanity and lust, them poor girls just hungry for their oatmeal and dry toast.

"Get on." Mama waved a hand her way, *get out, get out of my sight, be gone*, an implied guilt arced through the air. "Go to your room and don't come back." She twisted a knob on the stove. The clicking noise accompanied the hiss of the flame, the thwack of a pan set on top to warm. Loretta was certain Mama was angry at the loss of her breakfast helper. Her mother unable to commiserate with her daughter's confusion, her pain, the defeat of never having been innocent of any crime here on this ranch.

"Yes, ma'am," Loretta whispered, jumped to her feet, heard the echo of one lone button that fell and rolled across the weary floor.

"Humph. Pick those up, you hear me?" Mama's tone worse than the slap of her towel. She slammed another pot onto the stove.

Loretta grabbed the few buttons near her feet, couldn't see the rest. She hurried to her bedroom at the top of the stairs in the cabin, past the glare of the woman in the kitchen. An awful thing must have happened. Something that serrated Mama from her forever. A blood tie splattered. She wondered same way she had far back as she could remember why her mother's eyes breathed nothing onto her being, no pride, no responsibility. Certainly not love. Nothing. Only eyes worse were her father's. They brimmed with anger. An unexplained hatred that never abated.

Loretta didn't take the school bus on that not yet spring day. She pulled on a T-shirt, certain William would leave her in her room or dish out some awful chore. She was disappointed because a book report was due. She'd written about *The Outsiders* and S. E. Hinton's novel left her wondering less about Ponyboy and his sad life, and more about how it was possible that the author, a woman close to her own age when it was written, could have accomplished so much so early. How had S. E.'s world allowed her the downright freedom to write a book? What did the gloriousness of that sort of freedom feel like when S. E. awoke each morning? This led Loretta to the fleeting hope that life beyond the prairie dogs must hold promise. Life on the other side of the sunlit, snow-capped mountains . . . had to be better. The freedom to wear a simple morning smile would do fine. To receive one in return a true blessing.

Loretta was filled with anxieties, fears for sure. She listened to the bark of the dogs outside. Bull's was the worst, a rottweiler, her father's partner with teeth bared day to night. Loretta's own mouth forced into silence. Despite the daily dreads that left her fingers clenched and numb—she would not yell, would not, would not. Loretta was desperate as ever to reach her eighteenth birthday where escape awaited. The thought of a runaway's life, adrift and alienated, offered more solace than any fears her father could shoot her way.

"Morning. Morning, Mama." She overheard Elsie and the others arrive from the bunkhouse.

"Where's Loretta?" Tanya asked. If Loretta was down there, she'd have given the girls her *don't say a word* face where she bit her lips, made a quick nod, a well-understood part of their silent language.

"Mind your business," Mama snapped. Loretta recognized Mama's *shut up and eat your mush* tone, the best-be-quiet warning or Mama would find some unsavory chore to assign them—like shoveling chicken poop or scooping up dead winter mice in the cellar. The walls absorbed the girls' voices. There was barely any sound. She heard "Yes, ma'am" and "No, sir" and listened to the muted scratch of benches shoved close to the table, bowls plunked down, spoons scraping for the last bit of oatmeal.

Loretta was expert at gauging this kind of quiet. She sat cross-legged against the bedroom wall, her door open, knew Papa for sure was in his seat of honor—the glint in his eyes enough warning to keep the residents' mouths closed. Heard Mama's old-men's corduroy slippers—*shuffle shuffle*—near the big metal pot on the stove before she reached to the broiler for burnt toast: three slices for Papa, one for each of the rest of them. Walmart Great Value Margarine to spread on top. No jam. Theirs wasn't a house big on sweets or second helpings.

"Elsie, come take this toast. Now!"

"Yes, ma'am. Yes, ma'am," Elsie said. She'd learned quick to do what she was told.

It helped that Loretta and Elsie already had a pact. They'd agreed within days of Elsie's arrival.

Loretta reviewed the map stored in her head. Her mind traveled to places about which her father had no curiosity, the destinations she aimed to see. She had read books in school, on bus rides home, novels hidden under her jacket on those occasions when her father banished her to a log far beyond the prairie dogs on their land. She'd borrowed the See the USA Atlas from the school library and memorized highways and interstates she knew would lead to her destiny.

"You sure like them maps," Mrs. Barry the librarian told her. "I set aside this new one for you special." A yellow Post-it note stuck to the cover had "Loretta" written in red pen script.

"Thank you," Loretta said, almost a whisper, words afraid to be spoken. Mrs. Barry's kindness brought minuscule teardrops to her eyes that she quickly wiped away with the sleeve of her army jacket.

"Don't you be stressin'," the petite librarian added. Could be she understood the girl's life or was gifted with insight or felt a kinship since they both had hair the color of dry autumn leaves. "When you're ready, your journey will await you."

"Um, yes. Okay." Loretta gave a lackluster smile, much of it in her eyes, her lips not prone to happiness.

The thing was Loretta already had the plan ready, even if she kept it to herself. There were times when believing in it was the only thing she did have. She promised herself that she'd survive no matter how black and blue her spirit nor how bandaged her heart. She memorized red and green lines with highway numbers on them, knew an inch indicated this many miles, and could well read the compass she'd also stolen from the G&A to guide her east. These were the treasures that ensured her future.

For now, she sat on the floor in her bedroom and listened to the kitchen cleanup.

"Yes, ma'am."

"Dry those bowls, Crystal," Mama ordered.

"We'll be cleaning the chicken coop today, young ladies," Papa said. His generous use of the pronoun *we* was simply not true.

Loretta began to strategize. Not much else to do on the floor in her room in her denim school skirt with no school bus ride to occur. She unlaced her worn boots, knew it was best to wait a few days, let things settle, and then sneak over to huddle with the residents. Spend late-night hours with them after Papa had gone to sleep—and when she was sure he'd gotten over whatever had riled him this morning.

She needed to check on Elsie. Make sure she knew how to survive this place. Elsie was far too much the kind of girl Papa inclined toward. Maybe that was why he hated Loretta—her dark hair, her many freckles, her own skin never quite the pale of others these parts. Loretta had to give the residents fair warning. They listened to her. She'd advise them what they could do and what they should never try, not ever. Especially the braver girls, those whose eyes filled with joyful glee at the thought of running.

She'd tell them about foraging bears and the wolves that hide on the land. Gray wolves that crouch in the farther away, a true distance from the road, in the bushes and crevices that rocks so aptly provide. The wolves you need to be prepared to stare down. Not unlike her father. All of which made her tremble and shake as well. What awaited her? She knew the animals near the ranch but in the beyond, what then? How would she survive?

FOUR

New York City

"I can get a car to take you," Clarke offered while Loretta retied her teal-and-gray scarf, checked her antique satchel, ready to leave for Hunter College.

"No, I've got this. I'm happy with the Crosstown." She leaned against the kitchen counter, taking her last sip of coffee from a delicate rose-colored cup. One sugar and lots of cream mixed in. Having grown up with only chipped and cracked beige ranch dishes, her cabinets held a delightful mix of pottery and fancy china bargained for at New York street fairs and in secondhand shops.

"It's a big day. Important. You sure?" Clarke asked. He was the spouse who took care of their day-to-day worries. Organized, a person who kept tax records years longer than required; at this moment, if he'd had his Mets cap on, she knew he'd be adjusting the lid, his one nervous tic.

"I absolutely am." Loretta was certain her husband wanted to help. It was far more than that. He tried to protect her even when she didn't need it, to be on call because he knew more about her past than anyone else.

"You okay?"

"I am."

"You don't have to be, you know," he offered.

"Thanks for reminding me." This was one of their rituals. Checking in with each other, letting each other know they could fall apart, and it would be okay. That they were there to pick each other up when they fell—both their jobs offered plenty of opportunities to fail and more than justifiable human frustration.

"Except . . ." Loretta rinsed her cup, stared at the faucet as if it might have answers for her. "Well, it sounds foolish—" She began to strum the counter, her fingers up, down, tapping.

"I doubt that. What is it?"

"He warned me. He said he'd find me. What if he's not at the ranch? Am I being crazy?"

"You don't really think William would be lurking around New York City, do you? After all these years?"

"I don't know. It's just that today is so important for me. I know it's a day, only one day, only one speech, but it's everything. To me, you know? My future. My plans. But what if he ruins this, too."

"I'll call them. I'll make sure they've got eyes on him. I'll let you know when he's in the state's custody."

"Yes, please. Please do." If this moment weren't truly serious for her, she'd laugh at Clarke's police lingo, how he'd go into lawyer speak, cops and robbers, legalities, and such. She was, after all, the spouse with a lighter side, who saw no problem as insurmountable, except perhaps when it came to William.

"I could go with you?" Clarke said, more a question than not.

"I know. But no, I've got to do this." Loretta raised her amber-brown eyes to his, no message, no hidden meaning, her chance to give a nod, to let him know she appreciated his understanding. It was unusual for her to be so anxious, except when it came to her past.

"You'll text me the moment you hear anything? Right?" she asked.

"Of course. This has been a shadow at your heels. For too long. You weren't supposed to be down to the wire."

"I know. But it's William who's down to the wire. I'd like it to be over. I'm still sorry—"

"You know it's taken me a long time to understand . . ." Clarke tightened the knot on his blue tie patterned with small green shamrocks. She knew it was how he stalled while he considered his words. *Scrunch scrunch*, the knot got tighter, more scrunching. "But I think I get it. I wouldn't have wanted to talk about my past. Not if it was like yours."

"Except I hid it too long. I hated to talk about it. Even to you." Loretta's hand went to her neck. Her safe spot. Where so much was locked away.

"It's almost over now. Today is your day. Yours."

"Right. And I should get going." The idea of "almost over" felt impossible. Loretta ran her fingers down the sleeve of Clarke's navy suit jacket and reached to hold his hand, not for long, a short linger to feel his warmth, what they meant to each other.

"You do know I'm very—"

"Proud. Me, too. Finally. It's all coming out." Loretta finished his sentence in the way one of them had done for the other for years. "You know what I heard some actor from the Harry Potter movies said?"

"Nope. But I bet you're gonna tell me." Clarke waited for a quote from the trove of them his wife stored inside her head.

"That there's something inherently valuable to being a misfit." Loretta paused, her mind lost in memories of the many girls she'd known on the ranch; the girls she'd since tracked down, those she still hoped to learn were okay. "And I'd add, today us misfits get our fifteen minutes."

"Your Honor, I must object." Clarke threw his hands in the air and turned as if to a jury. "This woman is not a misfit."

"But I was."

"All right, I withdraw my objection." They shared a quiet laugh. Not a big ha-ha. Tender understanding spread to their eyes and no further words were needed.

"Good morning," their doorman called to Loretta in the lobby.

"Yes, it is a good morning." Loretta grinned at the acknowledgment between them. She felt she was a favorite tenant, that there was a recognition of their shared space, a mutuality, that they mattered to each other. Although she knew she was one of twelve floors of co-op dwellers. Maybe everyone felt as special.

Giorgio straightened his shoulders when she approached. He used his palms to unwrinkle his gold-buttoned overcoat, opened the heavy glass door of the apartment building on Sixty-Ninth near Broadway, and tipped his uniform cap to Loretta. Often, Loretta stopped to have a word, ask about his wife or ailing father. It was these small familiarities that bonded residents and staff, neighbors and curbside vendors in the grand metropolis Loretta had adopted as her home. The closest people she had to a family were around her every day.

"Hey, you got the Powerball tickets yet? I'm waiting for our big win." Loretta donated to a weekly pool that Giorgio managed for everyone in the building who wanted to chip in. She hoped they won—more for his sake than for her own.

"Going for tickets at the deli on my break." Giorgio winked. She winked back. It was a thing they did.

Loretta began the short walk to hop onto the M72, the East-side York Avenue Crosstown bus. She listened to the hard taps of her boots on the pavement, how her angled wood heels were solid and emphasized each of her determined steps. With a hand raised to swish away her hair, she enjoyed the scent of her jasmine perfume, the hint of citrus. She was grateful for her city, perhaps today more than ever for busy, crazy, often startling yet oddly comforting Manhattan—this was her world.

"Ma'am, look here!" On the corner, Estelle held up a perfect orange persimmon from her vegetable stand.

"Beautiful. I'll see you on my way home."

"It will be my son later. You come by. Please."

"Yes. Definitely." The melody of Loretta's voice was reassurance to people. She knew it would be Estelle's older son Henry when she returned. "He doin' better?" she asked.

"Yes, yes, thank you for asking!"

Loretta made it a point to be connected to her neighbors, to Estelle who hand-shined perfect orange persimmons, stellar green apples, and the reddest of fresh tomatoes. Loretta waited for the green light at the crosswalk and wanted to nudge others nearby and say *hey we're alive together and isn't that wonderful?* She might add that knowing Giorgio and the street vendors gave her strength, settled her nerves. Maybe it was that they saw her, that they'd return her smile . . . that if William or anyone were to accost her, they'd help. In a quiet reverie, she simply crossed when the light changed and walked farther along Broadway.

"Morning, Miriam!" She waved to a woman setting out buckets of flowers on the corner.

"Hi there, sweet lady." Miriam raised a bunch of pink, yellow, and red blossoms into the air.

At last and, Loretta was sure, at exactly the moment when it was meant to happen, everything was falling into place. Her goals had taken years. But she believed in signs. Her own being Leo. And there'd been a full moon the night before. That had to mean something. She'd even caught Venus, the morning star, after 3 A.M., when unable to sleep she'd stared out their eighth-floor windows and felt a chill.

"It's pretty late. Need this?" Clarke had appeared with her favorite heather-green blanket.

"I'm scared." She'd given him her *I know it's foolish, but I am* face. After all, Clarke was the one who'd told her that in the law he'd learned to never assume an outcome. That the one time he had, he'd been regrettably wrong.

"Me too," he agreed.

"Okay, I'll take the blanket."

Clarke wrapped it over both their shoulders. Loretta offered him a lopsided smile before they plopped onto the couch and watched the night sky, a favorite hobby of theirs. She dropped her head onto his shoulder, fears shoved aside. It was one of her well-honed skills, appearing calm, yet anxieties she'd carried for years hovered, never far afield.

Almost at the bus stop, she neared her favorite street vendor. It was fall. Obama was due at the United Nations, causing unbearable traffic delays in Midtown, and she had no fear to speak of him or any politician. *Hamilton* had opened on Broadway and all things historic were in vogue—Loretta expected to see men wearing knee-length britches any day. As for Loretta? She had stayed with her favorite corduroy blazer. No new outfit despite how much the day mattered to her.

After today, I will have so much to do, she told herself. Her propensity to plan took over. Making lists was a favorite use of her time. Her mind went into overdrive. *Guns. I have to call the folks in Newtown, check in with them.* She knew the opposition they faced. Not here so much but the rest of the country was different. Growing up where Loretta had, guns were as common as dogs, blustering winds, and the blue-and-white cans of vegetables loaded with salt stored in every pantry. She looked to the faint gray sky over the city, a prescient warning that any possible weather pattern might emerge. If the stars were gonna align, it had to be today. Everything she'd prepared was ready, and at last it was almost the moment she'd anticipated.

"Hello, my friend." She waved to Joe Demir, who wore a black fedora and matching turtleneck outside the Starbucks.

"Morning, Mrs." He pointed to an array of plaid, faux Burberry scarves displayed on his sidewalk stand.

"I'll stop by later," she added.

"Please do, Mrs." Joe clasped his hands in prayerful hope.

Loretta paused and gave him a kind nod. Clarke told her she had "I'll rescue you" amber eyes. She couldn't help it, for some reason these folks made her remember the girls she'd left behind on the ranch, and how much she wished she could have done more for them.

"Hi! Right on time!" She hustled up the steps of the bus that arrived exactly when her MTA app had estimated and tapped her MetroCard. Her enthusiasm took Daisy, the driver, by surprise.

"Well, someone's havin' a great morning."

"I am," Loretta agreed.

"Okay then." Daisy shook her head. Ringlets of long hair bounced about her happy face. She hand over hand turned the big steering wheel, swung into the morning traffic, and drove east.

Loretta dropped into a window seat. Gripped the top of the leather satchel on her lap and watched Central Park unfold before her. Her park. The truth being that it belonged to many. Yet every New Yorker believes it is theirs alone.

As she often did while riding the bus, Loretta thought about the many steps she'd taken within the six-mile perimeter of New York City's Central Park. She could navigate its paths, inlets, and hidden spots the same way other people know the streets, alleys, and shortcuts of their childhood neighborhoods. Central Park was her backyard.

She had led friends inside telling them to "come this way, there's a secret trail." She relished the chance to see Balto, or Strawberry Fields, the mosaic-tiled Imagine memorial to John Lennon. Friends did the same for her. Central Park lent itself to a harmless game of one-upmanship with its glorious open land that apartment dwellers are prone to think of as their own. As far as Loretta was concerned, this was as it should be. Her park, everyone's park, in the largest city in the country. From her seat on the M72, she knew the exact location of the carousel—not far off to her right. Where Clarke first said he was "pretty sure" he loved her.

"Let me know when you decide," Loretta had tossed back at him. She hadn't been one who would accept anything less than full commitment.

"I take you to my carousel and you—"

"Yours. Not hardly," she'd countered. "It's mine now, too." Another thing transplanted folk did—adopt the park as if they'd always lived nearby.

The bronze statue of Balto, a Siberian husky, was off a ways to her left. She knew he wasn't the only hero in the story of getting serum to children with diphtheria in Alaska a hundred years ago. A brave husky named Togo ran a lot farther and should be in the park, too. Still, Balto offered one of her favorite stopping places over the years . . . and she did love his big dog face. Probably because he wasn't Bull, the angry ranch dog she'd never forget, the dog that had lunged at her on that last day on the ranch.

"He's my friend," she said, pointing to Balto on a jog with Clarke during their dating days. Muscular and thin, an Adidas early adopter, Clarke used to do marathons. Now they both preferred short runs and longer walks. Clarke mostly wore his Mets cap when he wasn't sailing—he had a thing for underdogs—and it covered his balding head. Loretta stuck to khaki hats embroidered with the word *Compass* in script, the name of her nonprofit devoted to helping the homeless and runaways seeking new lives.

"Really? He's your friend? You know Balto is a long story, don't cha?" Clarke's lawyerly instincts kicked in during many of their intense side-by-side dialogues while jogging.

"I do know. But he's a transplant. Like me." Loretta plopped her Nike-clad sweaty self onto one of the park's large mica-flecked boulders that Balto guarded, big rocks that sparkled as if infused with diamond slivers.

Balto's rocks became Loretta's personal Zen garden where she went if perplexed, angry, or downright lonely. Especially during her first years in New York when friends flew home, but she remained behind in a city that emptied like a drained pool come holidays. Clarke once asked if she'd be going west to see her parents for winter vacation.

"No such folks. Left them behind ages ago," she'd answered, her voice monotone as she tossed her auburn hair over her shoulder. Clearly, she wasn't offering more information. Loretta could be brusque—it was a sort of pride she clung to. Yet the inquisitor within Loretta's murky dreams remained inside her head, an ever-invasive voice that harassed her with accusations. She knew that letting go of her past wasn't anywhere near as easy as a walk in the park.

When they first met, sharing bits of her prior life with Clarke made Loretta anxious in a manner that was both fraught and optimistic. Is that possible? To be scared silly at what the future might portend and at the same time filled with thoughts about the incredible what-ifs that might await? Back then she discovered Jones Beach east of the City—a bit of a hike on the Long Island Rail Road but quickly one of her favorite destinations. At last, she'd found the ocean.

The Atlantic!

She went each fall in worn jeans, a school sweatshirt, and a thick wool scarf from a thrift shop. She'd walk to the jetty, stoop to the shore, and grab hold of a fistful of sand until it drained through her fingers. At those moments, she worried if she'd made enough of the summer, saved enough of her earnings?

Which was oddly also how she felt about the past.

Her past was her bank account. The trembling she felt when she got scared, the anxiety attacks when someone sat too close on the subway—each of these moments reminded her that she'd survived. She didn't want to share her story with just anyone. She wouldn't let it slip away like sand on the beach. Her life on the ranch had to fuel her future, and she clung to her memories like a purse clutched close to her side.

During early days in the city, Loretta had watched crowds of very pretty people wearing stonewashed high-waisted jeans, grunge, Ozzy Osbourne tees, and Velcro-strapped shoes. She was a naive young woman in worn lace-up boots and a tired green camo jacket. Women in Jennifer Aniston blow-dries and Mariah Carey ripples of curls made her nervous. Confident young adults she passed left her doubting she had any chance for survival.

"Do you need some help?" a woman in a very businesslike gray suit asked her on Lexington Avenue the first time Loretta stood outside Hunter College too nervous to venture inside.

"Help?"

"Are you lost?" The lady carried a briefcase and hesitated, caught in stay-or-go mode. Loretta could tell she had places to be.

"No, I'm fine. But thanks." Loretta forced a brave smile onto her face. "Thank you," she said again and hurried toward the street corner pretending she knew where she was headed. Truth was she'd felt both lost and found. The big city scared her and at that point she'd only been brave enough to stare at the college entrance. She'd needed courage to go inside. Her first job working in the kitchen of a diner near the youth hostel helped a little.

"You've got this, babe," Louie, flipping burgers, told her.

"I'm not sure," she said and pulled hard on the hot water sprayer to clean off plates littered with the remains of egg sandwiches and leftover pickles before she loaded them into the dishwasher. "I mean, me? Get into a college like that?"

"Won't know unless you try." He shook his head at her. "You're smarter than most. Give it a try, why don't ya?"

"I'm going to," she said, but her fingers on the sprayer shook more than usual. Her stomach ached. Many what-ifs abounded. The biggest always was what if William appeared, what if he sent goons in a black car to get her, what if she was dragged back?

"It's a deal then?" Louie cocked his head and waited for her to agree.

"Okay, okay, I will."

Loretta never forgot Louie, or the woman in the gray suit who had taken a moment to bend a smidgeon closer to Loretta, had asked *are you lost?* in a quiet voice, who had been kind.

Do you need some help? Are you lost? Such simple, easy words. Never gratuitous.

In a city of more than seven million people, a huge metropolis made up of five boroughs that sit where the Hudson meets the Atlantic, with the Statue of Liberty, the Empire State Building, the Metropolitan Museum of Art, Central Park, and the tempting allure of hot dog stands everywhere, citizens stopped to ask, *Do you need some help? Are you lost?*

What Loretta discovered on her journey from west of the Rockies was that someone would always assist, that more people cared than not, and that being lost is but one step before you are found. She'd traveled along highways with stops for bad coffee, met some jerks but more people who cared. She made friends like Louie who helped her find her way.

He applauded the day she told him she'd been accepted to Hunter. He was not surprised when she moved in with a few friends on the Lower East Side.

"You're a good egg," Louie said when she quit dishwashing for a student job at the college. "Make us proud, babe."

She did. She hadn't traveled the many miles between her past and future to stop midstep.

FIVE

West of the Rockies

"You've seen a wolf? For real?" Tanya asked from her cot, legs crossed, eyes wide, braiding and unbraiding her long maple syrup–colored hair.

"Sure have. A few times."

"How'd you get away, Loretta?" Skinny Crystal pulled her thin army blanket to her chin, bent close to hear, and said her stomach ached. Crystal was thirteen, a recent arrival, with massive twisty curls, the youngest of the bunch. "I couldn't ever run through the prairies and past rocks where who knows what might hide." She'd told Loretta that she missed her mother, her daddy's house, didn't care anymore if he felt he had no choice but to take his belt to her. She'd give anything to return home where she had a bed with a real mattress and a choice of hair ties. Loretta understood except for the whippings—she'd had enough of her own. The luxuries, well, she couldn't imagine ever having those in her own life.

"I'll tell ya"—Loretta put a finger to her lips—"but shhhh, come closer. Hey, turn that light off. Can't let William figure I'm out here."

Their circle grew tighter. Loretta in her long denim skirt under her green army jacket. The residents in flannel nightdresses, thick work boot socks pulled over their cold feet, half-moon shadows below somber eyes; their skin so pale one might think they had the flu or fevers, but Loretta had told them, "Don't worry, you're not sick, it's a malaise from the lack of leafy green vegetables. I looked it up at school."

The girls scooch-squished to the ends of a couple of the cots, a few sat cross-legged on the floor near Loretta. Elsie couched herself next to Loretta and held one of her hands. Gayle tied her bright red hair into a ponytail and rested her head against Loretta's opposite shoulder.

"How'd you get to wear that black T-shirt?" Elsie asked, her translucent blue eyes a beautiful question mark.

"William didn't see it." They laughed. "From the free bin at church. Had to have it." Black clothing was not allowed on the ranch—such was the color evil teens wore so they could scatter into the darkness of night.

Loretta felt a debt to these girls. She was old enough to understand the awful situation her parents capitalized on. She knew that true sinnery had nothing to do with the residents. Her parents breathed an immorality that foisted a cargo load of pious accusations and punishments in ways that didn't compute with the goodness and love often proclaimed at church.

"So when I'm gone—" she began.

"Gone? What do you mean gone?" Tanya's wide eyes about jumped out of her head. Her braid fell apart and waves of hair cascaded down her back. "Please say this isn't happening." The one constant that made the Home bearable was the older sister Loretta became to each of them.

"Oh, Tanya." Loretta reached to push a straggle of hair behind the girl's ear. "It's almost time for me to go. I've told you before. Once I'm eighteen, I can't stay. You know that."

"I do know. But not now. Not while I'm still here. Please."

"I've taught you most everything I can," Loretta continued. "But if you get stuck out there in the backcountry, you know where I mean." The girls nodded. "You must be prepared. Don't worry about coyotes. They don't give a shit about us humans." The girls giggled. Nervous but trying their best to be as grown-up as Loretta.

"I remember you said to keep a good-sized stone in our pockets. What else *should* we give a shit about?" Tanya asked, hair rebraided. She had a mental filing cabinet where she stored every one of Loretta instructions. Tanya was smart and tougher than she looked.

"No rattlers this time of year," Loretta said. "Just don't lift up any big rocks. Definitely don't go perusing under them. Not that you would. Snakes hibernate for a time yet. Till the warmth of spring lasts past the afternoon sun. Still, mind you, rocks are always best left undisturbed. Watch out in summer. Got that?"

"Yikes."

"Sure will."

"Won't catch me touching rocks." Tanya was adamant.

"How about grizzlies?" Elsie asked.

"Oh, them. One comes near you, drop some food. Maybe they'll go for that. They're just scrounging for dinner. Mainly around campsites. Don't make eye contact and back away."

"Okay, got it."

"But wolves. Well, they are smarter. Cunning. Gotta give them credit." Loretta lifted herself off the floor to glance outside, made sure no lights had gone on in Mama's house. "Thing is, wolves *don't* hibernate. Always out there. But they want deer and moose way more than any of you skinny things. Remember that."

"But, what if?" Crystal bit on the edge of the musty green

cover she held to her shoulders to hide the still fading bruises received from her father before she came to the Home for Wayward Girls. The blanket smelled of mothballs and worn-out leather, a dank wet that never quite disappeared.

"Crystal, you're scrawny. Pure bones. No way any wolf would even notice you." Tanya cross-legged on her cot hooted. The girls laughed.

"Okay, okay. Listen up. This is serious." Loretta waved her fingers for the group to come even closer to her. Their inner circle formed, heads close together, the youngest holding on to one another's knees, or hands clasped with the girls to each side. "Let's say you take off from here. Or Papa banishes you for a night. You're stuck in the prairie. Better hope he gives you a bedroll. You're sitting on a log or by a tree. And it happens."

"Banishment? And then what happens?" Gayle's head swished around, and her ponytail bounced off Loretta's shoulder. She waited, silent, her quiet stare in urgent need of an answer.

"A wolf comes moseying near you. Let's say that happens."

"Moseying? Do wolves mosey?" Elsie held back a chuckle and poked Loretta in the ribs.

"Hush. I'm trying to downplay it," she whispered to Elsie. "So, everybody, it's worse late summer. But wolves are out there all year. If you see one, here's what you must do."

"Must do?" Crystal draped the army blanket tighter over her shoulders, so scared you'd have thought a wolf was in the room before her.

"Yep, take these steps. First, don't turn your back. Maintain eye contact. You got that. Don't take your eyes off the creature."

"Really?"

"Bears, no eye contact? Wolves, eye contact?" Tanya asked. "Oh my God."

"Back to wolves. Think that it's some mean guy at school. Give your best mean stare. Now, toughen up, you all. Be fierce. Let's see you glare."

"Like this?" Tanya lowered her eyebrows, wrinkled her nose, and burst into laughter.

"Except no giggles." Loretta tried not to smile. "Next, don't run. Hopefully, the wolf will turn around and head the other direction. But if not."

"What? But if not? If not, what!" Gayle bolted farther upright, crossed her arms; she was a strong young woman, but she was clearly petrified.

"Then take a step toward the damn thing, clap your hands, yell, scream. Throw anything you can. Jump up and down. Don't run!"

"Toward the wolf?" The fear on Gayle's pale face worsened.

"And then what?" Tanya asked; she could well be taking notes.

"Stand your tallest—wolves don't know what to do with us humans on our two feet. They're after four-legged creatures. So even you, Crystal, be tall."

"Me? How would I do that?" The thin waif, shortest in the group, chewed harder on the edge of her smelly blanket.

"Again, I ask, and then what?" Tanya's face was serious.

"Only one thing left to do."

"What?" A couple of tired residents popped up from their weak pillows.

"That would be pray." Loretta bit her lip. Caught each girl's line of sight. Hoped she was right. Waved them back to their pillows and cots. "Not much else to do but pray."

"Right, pray." Voices around the room hushed their way to sleep.

The bunkhouse was silent, an occasional rattle of a window, a hiccup from one of the girls. Elsie stayed by Loretta. Squeezed her hand tight. They had become quick best friends. Already had signals they shared, particular expressions they understood. A shared determination had taken root and they'd made an agreement. Not one without the other.

"You know, you haven't asked—"

"Asked what?" Loretta nudged Elsie with her shoulder.

"Why they put me here."

"It's not my business."

"I want you to know."

"I figured you'd tell me if you wanted to." Loretta sat quiet. Having a real friend was the pot of gold for her. Nothing Elsie had to say would change that.

"I ran away." Elsie bent in, eyes close to Loretta's. "With a boy. Lee. He said we'd never go back."

"Oh dear." Loretta bit her lip. She'd barely ever had a conversation with a boy much less the chance to try such a breakout.

"Worse, I took my pa's gun. I don't know why. It was there by the Mr. Coffee in the kitchen. I took it with me. I did. Got no excuse."

"That was brave."

"Or stupid. Didn't use it or nothin'."

"I'd never think you would." Loretta found Elsie to be the most peaceful soul, her new friend whose very presence made Loretta optimistic. "I know that feeling."

"Whaddya mean?"

"William's rifle. In the kitchen. I've reached for it. Once or twice. Then backed away. But it's called to me."

"Exactly."

"So, what happened?" Loretta made an earnest turn to Elsie. A listening turn.

"Sheriff caught us. Caught me. Brought me back to my folks. My father said I needed to learn my place. That night, four A.M., the transporters arrived."

"Those goons?"

"Yep."

"Do you know what happened to Lee?"

"I don't. I sure hope he's okay."

"Me, too."

"I don't pray much. But I do for him." Elsie reached under the cot for the sketchbook and pencil she kept hidden. "Thank you for rescuing this. William said no drawing. But I can't help myself."

"Because if you don't draw, that's like you not breathing."

"That's true." Elsie nodded and opened her book to a drawing of a peregrine falcon in the sky, a tall pine nearby, a log empty beneath.

Loretta took quiet soft steps to the door of the bunkhouse. The girls had fallen asleep with her last word on their lips. *Pray.* Something Tanya did each time she braided or unbraided her hair, as did skinny Crystal. Redheaded Gayle, the resident Catholic, whispered Hail Marys every waking hour of the day. The few other girls were mostly quiet and scared. It didn't matter that each of them knew better than to conjure up false hopes; they still wished that the good Lord might find a way to set them free, which was as unlikely as winning any lottery.

"A no-star night," Loretta whispered and pointed out the door. Elsie hurried to her side, the sketchbook gripped in one hand; her other grabbed Loretta's. Funny, but not, how quickly their friendship took hold. The sky was painted black; it was the deep of night when you can't see in front of your face nor any pockmark in the dirt path that waits to trip your foot and spill you to your knees.

"I'm scared." Elsie's words breezed between her lips. Her eyes squinted, her few freckles joined forces—the bridge of almost invisible spots across her nose a sure sign of fear—her creamy white-blond hair tied back like the others.

"Of?"

"Everything."

Loretta went still, her fingers on the rusted door latch, her face as worried as a mother-sister-friend could be. She and Elsie needed to be confident. To believe. They were each other's guardian angel if such a thing were possible. She reached inside one of her army jacket's many pockets. Her fingers slipped past her knife and the metal compass she kept close. She found one of her buttons.

"Here, hold on to this." She handed it to Elsie.

"A button?"

"It's important," Loretta told her.

"How so?"

"Emily Dickinson said something. I read it at school." Loretta opened the bunkhouse door. Zipped her bulky jacket tight, its army-green color spotted and faded with combat memories. Dawn would break too soon, and she needed to return to her room in Mama's house. "She said to dwell in possibility."

"Nice, but what does that mean?" Elsie's eyebrows lifted with curiosity, certain that some special wisdom was headed her way.

"I think"—Loretta stepped into the night, then turned to Elsie, whose hand cautiously released hers—"well, truth is, I'm not positive. But I'm pretty sure it's all we have. Possibility. You and me. We dwell in the chance."

"The chance of what?"

"That we'll escape. I'm holding on to that notion . . . and buttons." Loretta hugged her first and only best friend. Sleeping girls lay in the cots just beyond. Loretta wished she could do something more noble than sharing wolf warnings or how to best clean the chicken coop while drenched in the smell of vinegar.

Elsie squeezed her back. They only had each other.

SIX

New York City

Loretta's bus jolted to a stop at Sixty-Seventh and Madison. She jumped up and grabbed the metal bar to catch her balance. Twelve minutes had passed, exactly as the MTA app had predicted.

"Good job," she whispered to the tech gods and hurried to the door. "And thank you," she said to the driver, who shook her head but smiled. With the handle of her satchel clenched in one fist, Loretta checked her phone with the other. No messages yet—it was far too early. The four-minute walk to Hunter would help calm the anxious energy that zinged from one side of her brain to the other.

"Therefore, choose life," she again reminded herself. "Always."

She walked with confidence, in a hurry to get to the glass and chrome entrance of the college where she had earned her BA, fifteen stories of gray concrete that angled toward the street offering affordable education to everyone. A man brushed by her too fast, caught her off guard.

"What the!" Loretta almost tripped; she pulled her bag to her chest.

"Sorry, sorry." The man stared quick her way, his eyes not sorry, not a bit.

Loretta stopped. He hadn't looked anything like William, but her heart pounded with fear. What if, what if? She scooted away from others, counted and breathed and counted again. *You're fine*, she told herself, tried to laugh but that would be hard. At last, she hurried to the school's front doors not far from the subway stairwell and waited for Annie.

She stood very still, remembering her early days in the city, that time the businesswoman had asked if she was lost. Now she knew most every corner in Manhattan. The streets belonged to her. She felt both accomplished and inexperienced, an apprentice, ready yet too, too nervous. So much had yet to unfold. Loretta remained rooted to the corner of Sixty-Eighth and Lex, continuing the effort to breathe out and in and out again, her eyes latching onto the bright round sun peeking from behind the curtain of clouds above the East River a few blocks away.

"I'm grateful," she whispered. The early light of day had to be a positive sign.

Each of life's details popped around her. Women wearing sleeveless gosh-I-hope-it's-still-fall dresses, others in fashionably ripped T-shirts and sweats, and health fanatics sporting designer running shoes raced by. Students in black jeans and thick-soled boots, with metallic face studs in noses and lips, pushed through the glass doors on the way to their classes—cultures and genders redefined daily. Loretta believed it was long overdue. Enough of categorizing people by checkmarks in boxes on forms. She'd counseled too many young people whose families had forsaken them over that which made them unique and incredible.

"What the fuck," a man at the curb yelled at a huge Escalade that zipped past the corner too close for comfort. Nearby, a medley of honking cars lodged dead center in the intersection daring one another to proceed.

"Bagels, warm pretzels," a vendor called from the window of a red-and-silver aluminum hutch and waved his tongs midair. "Hot dogs!" Loretta smelled the aroma of the rotisserie already at full throttle in anticipation of a long, profitable day and thought it had been years since she'd enjoyed one. With mustard.

"I told them no. Not going to happen. My calendar is full till next week," a millennial in heels too high for comfort instructed the cell phone glued to her ear and hurried past.

"Oh my." Loretta praised all that is good for her comfortable worn western boots. No one on this busy morning would care that she, Loretta, a lone woman in a blazer and Levi's near the door to Hunter College, wanted to yell, "New York is my home!" She'd yet to find a quote that succinctly summed up the joy of relocating to where she was meant to be, but she was certain it would appear in time. She was also positive that today would be a success, yet another beginning, the fulfillment of her own dreams seeded years before when she so often had meditated in Central Park. She just had to stop worrying.

Her phone beeped. No message from Clarke yet. It was Annie. Annie was her right arm at Compass; once a runaway, she'd become an earnest champion for the rights of women, always ready for their next endeavor together.

2 & 1/2 min away. Almost there.

I'm outside the subway, Loretta texted back.
Set for the reporter? Annie asked.

I must be, right? Conference good to go?

Of course, followed by a laughing face from Annie. Heard from Clarke?

Not yet, but soon, I'm sure

Annie ended with praying hands, a peace sign, and a smiling face. Loretta smushed her grin; she was more happy than anything else. Today was big. She wondered how she appeared to passersby—standing her ground on the corner, thrilled with everything, and grateful that life would afford her a full reprieve from the fears she'd carried with her since her former life, the life spent west of the Rockies. At last, at last, this day was here. Oh, dear God, and she found it hard to believe she would use these words, but oh, dear God, her big some-thought-impossible plan was about to be made manifest. This day was real.

Annie ran from the subway stairs.

"Don't hurry," Loretta called. "We're early. And ready."

Annie rushed anyway, her vintage yellow leather purse slung over her shoulder, phone in hand, long hair the color of fresh straw trailing behind her like angel's wings.

"I made it," Annie gushed. "From Brooklyn. The F to the 6. Oy!"

"We've made it." Loretta adjusted the scarf around her neck. She was ready to go.

"Yes, we have."

"At last." Loretta dared to say the words out loud.

When Loretta first settled in New York, she had three main activities in her life while she figured out how to get into college. If she wasn't washing dishes at the diner or hunkered down at a table in the New York Public Library, she'd take walks in Central Park, which wasn't quite as picturesque or ice-cream-sundae sweet as it can be today. Nor as safe. Back then, eighteen-year-old Loretta watched city life with a critical eye. She noticed similarities to when she wandered the prairies out west. She figured out the unspoken rules, what to be on the lookout for and how to be on watch for wolves and hunters even in the big city.

Warm weather or cold, local citizens and tourists sauntered through and jogged along the park's paths. Loretta hadn't then been able to consider *running* a hobby—her memories of fast getaways were too painful. In Central Park, she had stared at horse-drawn carriages that offered couples romantic rides. She'd passed the Whispering Bench, the Shakespeare Garden, envied family picnics, and enjoyed the cheers of soccer players. Yet an anxiousness that mirrored her own winged overhead near the end of the twentieth century and apprehension simmered within the park's dark corners and hidden trails.

"Don't step there," she heard a jogger yell to a friend who jumped over a putrid mess.

"Watch out." Cyclists alerted each other to off-leash dogs who darted onto the main thoroughfare that curved throughout the hilly grasses. Loretta had never been on a bicycle and the almost-crashes she witnessed startled her.

"Pooch alert!" Cyclists pointed and swerved around pets and strays.

"This way!" Mothers grabbed children's hands and hurried to avoid nefarious characters.

"No tunnels," fathers warned teens who raced from Frisbee games venturing on their own.

"Hold on to your purse. Your purse!" friends admonished each other. Loretta didn't yet have friends but that was okay. She was an immigrant of sorts. A newly arrived citizen with rituals and rules to learn. A culture to adopt that she hoped would adopt her. A college to be her favorite stomping grounds.

On weekends, the streets that surrounded Central Park offered an eclectic collection of local artists. Sketches of cityscapes were ten dollars each but three for twenty-five. Charcoal portraits were on offer for those willing to sit for a while. Beguiling city sights seduced. The Pierre on one side, FAO Schwarz with its toy soldier guard, and the grand Plaza Hotel on Fifty-Ninth stood at attention. New York City royalty on display.

The park was free and irresistible for anyone with limited funds. A place where Loretta could roam, buy a hot dog or a warm pretzel like others who sauntered about. Central Park, the economic equalizer where no one was locked out. She walked for hours envisioning a better future, sat on benches, read books from the library, and then plowed farther into the park.

"With mustard," she told a hot dog vendor one Tuesday.

"How're you doin'?" The guy in a Yankees tee smiled while he pulled the hot dog from the steamer. "You visitin'?"

"No, I've decided to stay," she said. The not-quite-sure words popped from her mouth. She hadn't thought them through.

"Then this one's on me. I'm Ahmed." He reached outside his metal stand, shook her hand, and refused to let her pay.

"Wow," she said before thanking him perhaps too profusely. "I'm Loretta."

"Nice to meet you, Lorrr-etta." He smiled, both amused and pleased.

On that day, energized by the nice vendor, she hiked farther than usual. Reached an intersection where the park was less crowded and made a wrong turn. Happens to most newcomers at least once. There was a narrow trail ahead and she thought *why not*, words many vagabond hitchhikers are reticent to use. She wasn't worried until she was.

"Where the fuck am I?" she moaned when the late-day sun slowed its breath.

The sky shifted from the lightest blue with big fluffy friendly clouds to evening gray. No one, not one person, crossed her path, and she was certain she'd wandered too far from the more crowded areas of the park. Still, Loretta was sure she knew her way. She passed the Loeb Boathouse and the fine folks who were being served inside its restaurant, saw late-day rowboats straggling on the lake, trekked up a path, and went right when she later realized she should have gone left. Loretta grabbed her compass from her army jacket pocket. It was easy to see which direction was north—except this didn't help. She trekked what she thought was west, an eye on the last dribble of the setting sun, its light subservient to the darkening sky.

The arrow on the compass bounced about. Even it seemed unsure where to guide her. The temperature dropped and cold chilled her bones, an expression she understood more in New York than on the ranch where she'd known to wear layers. Loretta tried to head toward loud street traffic, but the sounds of cars faded, more distant than near. A heavy silence hovered when she arrived at a tunnel. She'd heard about tunnels. Avoid them!

She leaned to one side and tried to see within its blackness. Behind her was night and in front only the tunnel. A small yellow light flickered inside. She entered despite the smell of mold and uncertain puddles—maybe urine or muddy remains. Her boots sloshed. She found herself returned to the prairie west of the Rockies, banished, as William had often done this to her, the echoes and noises not unlike those she'd grown up beside. Was it an owl? she wondered when something flew by, but she knew better. Unable to read the compass in the darkness, she slid it back into her jacket and grabbed her red pocketknife, gripped it tight, and listened to the splashes of feet approaching from the other side.

A few steps beyond was a shadow, perhaps a pair of eyes, an arm reached out.

"What?!" she screamed. Suddenly, she could see hungry wolves back on the prairie in the dark of night. Remembered the instructions she'd given the girls. Jump up and down, yell, throw anything, *they hate two-legged creatures.*

Loretta yelped and yelled. She jumped three times. Pointed her switchblade at the stranger. "Don't come closer. I've got a knife," she warned.

"For sure, yes." The man lurched away. "Do you need help, miss? You okay?"

"What?" she asked again, her voice a little quieter.

The man froze in place. A blanket hung from his shoulders. Hair was long and gray. A duffel dragged alongside inches from the muck puddled on the ground. He again reached out, didn't touch her, a soft physical move, his hand extended, his open palm offered a question.

"Are you lost?" he asked.

"Yes." Loretta began to cry. "So lost."

"No, you're not, lady. Follow me."

She did. Through the darkness, one way, then another, out of the park. He didn't stop. Asked which subway and led her there. At the top of the stairs to the trains, she stood before him.

"You okay, miss?" he asked again.

"I will be now," she told him and lowered her head. Her wet laces had come undone. She bent to retie her boots.

When Loretta raised her eyes, she stared up the street, across it, too, but the man had gone. That night rooted itself within Loretta's heart, entwined its branches to her soul, and she long nurtured its soft, budding petals that would become her life's work. She hadn't been merely rescued by the man who wore a tattered blanket across his shoulders, she'd been given what she searched for, the gift she had yearned to find, and again she'd heard those questions.

Do you need help? Are you lost?

Far beneath the city streets, in the subway waiting, Loretta had prayed. "Dear God, please." She didn't have much faith in laying one's hopes before the Lord. However, the wind of the approaching train whooshed and startled her. She found she couldn't help herself. "Please God, if you're there, please help me survive this glorious city."

Loretta had found her destiny. Or the arm of destiny had reached out to find her.

Loretta learned her way around. She didn't find herself lost as often. She had favorite hangouts. Central Park was her personal rec room. She quit dishwashing to attend Hunter College, part of the network of the city's public universities, and she rented not a whole room but a small nook in an apartment on the Lower East Side. A fourth-floor walk-up. A pink-and-orange batik curtain separated her from three roommates. One bathroom, no AC, the heat was accompanied by the melody of banging pipes. A young virtuoso next door played extraordinary keyboard in the middle of the night. It felt luxurious.

She discovered a city where people believed in opportunities the way folks where she was raised put their faith in church-speak about sinnery and the roles of women. The difference was that, in this city, success was contingent on personal elbow grease, busting your butt, and going for it. God was the grill cook—he stayed behind the scenes and enjoyed the show.

"Coffee Boston? Your regular?" Joey, a twentysomething at the corner deli on Tenth and Avenue A, would say before he lifted the metal cream dispenser's handle twice for extra cream. That was how Loretta liked her coffee in the days before lattes controlled the universe. Each morning, she stood in the line of folks that stretched beside a glass counter filled with cheese Danishes and chocolate-frosted donuts worth every calorie.

"How do you remember?" she asked him. Joey handed her the blue-and-white paper cup used by almost every deli across the city.

"Practicing." He grinned but there was mischief in his eyes.

"For what?"

"Not sure yet. But it's gonna matter."

Loretta liked that mantra. *It's gonna matter.* She would continue to stop to say hi to Joey after she finished college. Maybe it was the approach of the new millennium that made success possible. Women were happening. Janet Reno was the first woman attorney general of the United States. Madeleine Albright, an immigrant from Czechoslovakia, became secretary of state. The loudspeakers of colorful tourist shops with green foam Statue of Liberty hats for sale blared Madonna from their doorways, urging everyone to move to the music. Loretta was safer than she'd ever been in her life. She didn't know anyone with a gun or rifle and that was fine by her.

She didn't want to. It was a rule she made clear. No guns. Not in her life. Never again.

At Hunter, she'd found a caring adviser, received scholarships, and studied nights at the 150-year-old Pete's Tavern on Irving Place, a decades-old local haunt of famous writers and thinkers and actors. Legend was O'Henry wrote *The Gift of the Magi* in the early 1900s at one of its tables. Loretta became a hard-core New

Yorker, landed in a social work master's program with Sarah Law-rence and NYU, and took up a cause that mattered to her.

Returning to William and Mama's was not part of her plans.

"How's grad school?" her adviser asked at one of their regular cof-fee dates that continued after Loretta finished her BA. The adviser wore Hunter College black—turtleneck and slacks, a black coat on the back of her chair.

"Great."

"The job?"

"Devastating," Loretta confided. "So many women need help."

"That's why you're here. It's fated." The adviser didn't blink when she said this. Her words came from a place of true gravitas. It was how people in New York talked, conversations over coffee as serious as world politics. Loretta's eyes became question marks, sincerely perplexed, but the adviser ignored her and bit into a toasted bagel. She'd been the one person far more certain than Loretta ever was of her skills.

"Fated?"

"Yes." The matter-of-fact reply without explanation was an-other New Yorkism.

"But I can only do so much. Maybe I won't be able to change the system. Do great things? The stuff I want to do." Loretta sipped her creamy coffee. "The thing is, I'm out of ideas."

"You'll figure it out," the adviser said. The same words she'd said time and again when Loretta visited her office at Hunter over the years. The adviser didn't say more, offered no thoughts; if anything, she enjoyed Loretta's bewildered state.

"You're doing that thing you do." Loretta frowned across the table.

"I know," the adviser agreed.

"Okay, I do have an idea." Loretta spoke in a hushed tone, pushed her hair over her shoulder, and leaned far forward. Her paper cup of coffee almost fell but she grabbed it in time.

"What's the big secret? You think someone's gonna steal your brilliant thoughts on how to raise money for another shelter?" The adviser laughed but her eyes listened with seriousness.

"You never know." Loretta pretended to scope out the seven adjoining tables for spies. "But it's more I have to dot my i's and cross my t's. Make sure I'm ready. You know?"

"I know that you think you do. That's why you won't fail."

"You sound so sure."

"Come on. What's the idea?"

"After grad school, I'm gonna start my own foundation."

"I knew it." The adviser tried to appear bored and shook her head like this was old news.

"You did not."

"Loretta, I always knew it. I get it. Somewhere that will let you be in charge. In other words, you get to be the boss."

"Okay, today you win."

"Of course I do," the adviser said in her most professorial voice. "By the way, how's that guy?"

"Guy?"

"The bartender?"

Clarke was the cute, trim bartender at Pete's. Loretta told her roommates, "The guy just feels sorry for the girl from somewhere west of the Rockies."

"But you go there all the time," a girl from Albany said.

"He's the one, isn't he?" another from Florida asked.

"Maybe." Loretta was unwilling to say more.

"West of the Rockies?" Clarke asked on a slow night. It was

snowing outside, and Loretta sat at the bar with her books open next to a mug of Pete's 1864 Ale. She'd gulped down the free burger and fries he told her had been a kitchen mistake although they both knew better. "You want me to guess where?"

"I'd rather you didn't." Loretta pointed her yellow highlighter at him, her eyes direct but also staring into the distance, a thing she was mysteriously able to do.

"Got it." Clarke wiped clean the ancient wood bar. Said nothing more. Until the song "Closing Time" came on and Loretta slipped her books into her backpack.

"Finished for now." She winked at him.

"You look like you're in your heavy thinking mode. You okay?" he asked.

"Maybe. Probably." She sat on the stool, hands patting the bag on her lap. Five fingers up, five down, pat, pat, pat, her lips tight, a straight line across her face, not a frown, not a smile.

"You don't have to be okay," he said.

"I know. Thanks for reminding me," she agreed.

He waited. She nodded. This became the first of their many rituals, asking each other if they were okay, simple words that started with a glance between them that they understood, or a few words that they knew meant *time to leave this party* or *please save me from this boring conversation* when they were out with others. Their own personal rituals that began at the bar near Union Square when they both studied hard and worked at low-paying jobs, but it was fine because they had bigger dreams.

"Walk you home?" he asked.

"Sure." Loretta's fourth-floor walk-up above Chinese Restaurant Number 7 and a Dunkin' Donuts wasn't really that much of a home, but she appreciated his company.

"One sec." He threw a towel into the kitchen and grabbed his REI fleece.

Loretta slipped her arms into her worn army fatigue jacket. Hoisted her backpack over her shoulders.

"I can take that for you," he offered. Clarke lagged a few steps behind.

"No, you can't. I need to carry it." Loretta smiled and headed out to Irving Place, an Early American street hidden within the big city. A collage of tiny eating establishments near historic red-brick row houses. A tavern patron told her the writer Washington Irving had lived in one of them, although Clarke said it was more urban legend than true.

Loretta threw her arms up. Flakes of snow big enough to catch in their hands fluttered and drifted through the bright streetlight that glowed on the corner. Windswept piles collected on the sidewalk. After bending to the ground, she turned and landed a snowball on his chest.

"Hey!" He hurried over and reached for her.

Which was the moment it happened. Loretta felt it. In a dramatic slo-mo way. The exact minute when she let down her guard. Without any hesitation. The very second she fell into him without any gosh-awful remorse or thinking first.

"Oh my God!" She jumped into the air and pumped a fist.

"What—?"

"It's all good!" she yelled because for the first time ever in her entire life she was more comfortable with someone than without them. Except, of course, for Elsie, who was double-stitched to her side forever. Loretta gasped and bent over giggling because it was too early to let Clarke see the depth of her joy. Heaven forbid he realize the lifelong commitment to him that raced through her soul at that instant. "It's very good," she added.

"Well, I sure hope so." Clarke grabbed her hand, and they ran across the slushy street, their hair covered in snowflakes. Such a cascade of laughter poured from them both that a passerby wouldn't have been able to sort one voice from the other. It was that night, after studying for a sociology exam she would ace, when Loretta thought, *Oh goodness, oh goodness, I'm happy*.

Which transformed itself, slowly but quickly, into their kind of love.

"Perfect, don't cha think?" Clarke asked on a Sunday morning not so many years later, after they were married, and before her foundation became a reality.

"It's unbelievable," Loretta said, her stare locked on the marina near Jones Beach. She dangled a hand over the port side of the sailboat and watched foamy water run between her fingers. They'd set off for a day's outing on Clarke's big purchase at the time—a nine-year-old used Beneteau Noema, which for them was better than any summer home.

"You know, Noema, it's Greek for—"

"A thought." She beat him to it.

"Well, I have one." Clarke's eyes remained moored to the sea.

"Only one?" Loretta raised an eyebrow. She knew better. It was never just one.

"Okay, you got me. But for starters, I think we should take a trip. Get away from my firm. From your job." He pulled his white captain's hat lower on his forehead, embroidered on front with MARIGOT BAY, WEST INDIES. Clarke had flown there to pick out the boat. Loretta knew he longed to make a return journey to the islands in the role of captain of his small vessel.

"The thing is, I have so much to do." She zipped her windbreaker, pleased with the willowy scent of her jasmine perfume that mixed itself into the sea breezes. Strands of red-orange-brown hair blew away from her face. She couldn't disagree with Clarke. The idea of taking a break took hold of her often but then there'd be a new influx of homeless women, or some illness would ravage those on the streets.

"Bad timing, right?" He said the words they both knew by heart. With the sea behind him, and the shore to her left, she saw in his eyes that he understood.

"Afraid so."

"Soon though? Soon maybe?" he asked.

"Oh you." She laughed because theirs was a bond that was not so oddly knitted together. She wondered at times if they were more partnership than romance, which she didn't mind—she couldn't imagine anyone else who'd have understood her heavy aspirations. Clarke could have worked for a big New York firm; he'd had offers after law school that included invitations to dinner cruises and fancy weekend getaways. He'd passed on them, and instead, he and three friends hung their own shingle where they mixed representation of rich clients with pro bono cases, some paying for the others without necessarily realizing it.

"We could put a date on the calendar. How about December?"

"Okay, I'll check." Loretta stared far over the water, unsure of herself at that moment and wanting not to ask too much of her husband ever. "Do I whine too much?"

"You? Whine?"

"Or not whine . . . but do I ask you to understand too much?"

Clarke's laugh rose in the breeze while the boat crested on a small wave. Drops of water christened them both. "Well, we could talk about that for hours."

"Okay, anyway." She was closer to what she was trying to say. The thing was she wasn't as practical as he was. She didn't have clients from the 1 percent echelon to resource her plans.

"Anyway?"

"Here's what I've been trying to tell you. Really." Loretta winked at him. She had a feeling he'd already figured this out. "I'm going to leave my job. I have this idea. For a foundation."

"I'm not surprised."

"I have some funding."

"Of course you do."

"And a name."

"You gonna make me guess?"

"The Compass Foundation. Just Compass for short."

"Like yours? The one you brought with you?"

"Right. And from a poet who wrote about the compass of one's offering. I think it's time. My offering. I'm going to do my best to help women on the streets, all kinds of women, runaways, the abused, find better lives."

"Sounds good."

"It does."

SEVEN

West of the Rockies

Loretta would have stayed in the bunkhouse with Elsie and the others if she could, if doing so wouldn't lead to more of her father's fury. She wasn't supposed to be there at night, yet she was pretty sure Mama knew. Sometimes Mama gave her a funny stare, her nose twitched a little, and that was a warning. On those nights, Loretta didn't leave Mama's house.

She did a turnaround to stare at the girls in their cots. She wondered if she should wake them and yell *Run, follow me, run.* She knew what trails to take to avoid the wolves, and she'd told Elsie how they would head out when it was time. Except it wasn't time.

Not yet, she told herself, although she'd read that failure is like gym class. You've got to fall down a few times before you're good at something. This scared her. She doubted there'd be much chance for a second attempt. When she fled, she'd have to get it right.

Making her way along the dirt path back to the house, eyes skyward, Loretta longed to see the morning star. It would be a good omen. But Venus was hidden behind the pitch of the night's darkness. Loretta well knew Venus was a planet, not actually a star, but the idea of its many roles in the solar system tantalized her.

Venus serves three purposes. Morning star, evening star, and the earth's planetary sister. What a thrill to offer greetings to the world each day and stand guard over the final curtain call every night. For Loretta, the thought of a planetary sister was so wrenching it tugged at her soul. What she wouldn't have done for a sibling, another person who'd grown in height with her, who could have had the same vantage point she had.

Someone with whom to have shared this captivity. To have laughed alongside a sister who would have understood. Someone like Elsie.

Loretta took slow, tepid steps, one foot forward, the other trickling behind, the sure sign of a hesitant journey. Hands in her pockets for warmth, her fingers played with the ridges of the few remaining buttons she'd salvaged from the kitchen floor—after her father's rage had instilled in her a cold-as-stone defiance. Loretta's father should have considered this outcome when he accused her that day in the kitchen.

"You some kind of whore, girl?" The words skulked from his mouth before the buttons flew. His voice quiet, sly; Loretta knew it was so very him, thinking he knew more than her, an accusation hidden within each syllable. The word *whore!* lashed at her, *whore!* doused her with shame, *whore!* foisted guilt and the vengeance of penance onto her soul.

The spittle of his words left her certain she must be. *Some kind of whore!*

But what sin had she committed? A blouse too tight? A smile she gave Elsie? William wanted to tame her, to hear her unconditional atonement, which that day, in that instant, immersed her with a power she hadn't realized she'd been given. She would never again cower, nor would she capitulate. Never. As clear for her as the map that led east.

Loretta paused at the raised vegetable beds, wished for a Marlboro but couldn't risk a cigarette's orange glow in such darkness. She rested her boot on the wooden frame, then kicked at the rusted nail in need of a good hammer. She felt guarded by the shadows of the night, a feeling sure to be disavowed come the light of daytime. In the morning, or later in the afternoon when she'd return on the bus from school, she'd have lost her bravest notions. Or not lost, not so much, but put them on hold. Because courage can cloak itself in fears that demand dismantling. Anxieties can sweater you, bring a standstill to your plans, leave you feeling lucky to breathe. Loretta knew this the same way she understood things of greater significance, even though she'd yet to sort out the many whys and wherefores . . . and the therefore of her life.

A foot pounded on top of the ground behind her. She felt the presence of a weight heavier than her own.

"You havin' fun out here?"

"What?" Loretta could barely speak, so startled her words glued themselves to her throat, his arrival an unwelcome surprise.

"I asked you a question." She heard her father's voice before she felt the sting. Far too late she caught the glint of the Smith & Wesson on his thigh, the whites of his eyes not even visible until the very second he leered at her, his mouth too close, his words spewed their assault. "How many times . . ."

Whack!

A branch swung at her. Then swatted again.

"I've told you . . ."   .

Whack! The tree limb hit her wrists, her arms. She heard Bull's growl. The dog she didn't trust. The animal always close to her father. The rottweiler who assaulted on command.

"To stay away from the bunkhouse..."

Whack! The knotty rough branch ripped at her cheeks, across her skin, swung into her arms and legs. Blood dribbled to her mouth and in between the fingers raised to her face.

Grrrrr.

Bull's teeth were bared, his flanks quivered in anticipation of his master's orders, and Loretta's hands flailed, flailed, flailed into the night sky hailing Venus, the unseen morning star, the guide she sadly needed.

"Please, please..." Her whimper became a plea to keep Bull's pointed teeth away from her body, to prevent-delay-stop, please please please stop the branch that dug deeper into the rips in her skin, digging and dragging in attack. William slammed the branch into her spine, her waist, then whacked behind her knees. She heard Bull's growl, close and mean.

Loretta buckled in desperation. Sad and tired and not near strong as William, she crumpled to the ground. Her knees spilled to the hard dirt so infertile it could well be concrete.

Time choked, it too stumbled, like her laggard steps on the path from the bunkhouse. Loretta's head zigged, auburn hair flying. Her head last to fall, it fell so slow. Later, she'd swear she'd seen her own self, her head zagging down down down until she hit the rusty nail sticking out of the wood frame of the vegetable bed that bore no leafy greens.

The nail! The nail! she tried to scream.

"Please," she cried. "Please." The words struggled from her mouth.

Her father dragged her to her feet. That bent old nail, rusted, it ripped right through her long, mountain-strong, not so pale-skinned neck. Blood drooled to her chest, across her very white cotton bra ordered from the catalog last fall.

"You are not their friend. You do as I say. You hear me, girl!"
Each word a chastisement.

Loretta did not answer.

She heard nothing more for days locked in her room. Her sleep
interrupted by dreams of greedy predators in the woods who exist
by capturing living prey.

"Beware of false prophets for inwardly they are ravening
wolves," the minister at their church had bellowed. A service they
rarely attended but she remembered enough.

For two days after the pitch-black night with no stars in the sky,
after her father had branded her neck forever with the scar from
an ancient, rusted nail that protruded from a worthless vegetable bed, seventeen-year-old Loretta remained in her room in the
cabin at the ranch, barely waking. Night terrors plagued her. At
first it was leering faces, each moment of sleep freeze-framed
within bruised blues and murky yellow shadows. Eerie voices
scorned her whimpers until at last her breathing was normal and
her dreams took refuge in maps and the inch-by-inch scale of
miles she was determined to travel. Finally, she dreamt of bill-
boards she'd never seen and roadside cups of coffee and shopping
and reading many, many books.

"RFD says school's closed." Mama relayed rural radio farm
news on day three of Loretta's confinement. The weather outside
had digressed to bitter cold after another end-of-winter storm
plowed snow onto the roads and prairies. "You won't be missin'
nothin'."

"Uh-huh," Loretta mumbled.

"But good thing you finally woke up."

Mama's appearance was some kind of too-late Clara Barton
scene. Mama did not sit on the edge of the bed but reached over

to dab a washcloth on the rip the vegetable bed's nail had torn through Loretta's neck. It had already begun to heal but would take long to scab, itching until it left a rough track mark that scarred and never would fade over time.

"Stop moving." Mama's cloth dabbed at the crisscrossed trails of dried clots of blood on her nose.

"Uh, sure." Loretta shifted her body farther from Mama, distrusting the woman whose minute acts of kindness were so unexpected . . . and seldom.

"That's better."

Loretta lay still in her single twin bed. Unlike the residents' cots, it was one of the few luxuries afforded Mama and William's daughter. A narrow dresser was lodged against a wall, each of its drawers not close to full. Five pairs of once thick socks hovered next to a few T-shirts her father disdained, and white cotton briefs she hated were stacked nearby. A brown cross hung above her bed. Loretta would have pulled it down but for the wrath this would have foisted upon her. She'd built a makeshift desk by the window. Two-by-fours with a thin plank of wood hammered to them, a mason jar set on top that held a few pencils, a Bic pen, and a yellow highlighter she found left behind on the bus. A couple of spiral notebooks her father allowed her for school off to the side.

"You're almost good as new, daughter. No sense bein' angered." Mama smelled of onions and bacon grease. "Good you been asleep. Pretty much fixed now."

"Uh-huh," Loretta whispered and dragged the army blanket above her shoulders closer to her chin. *Fixed? Not in the way her parents sought.* She closed her eyes, wanted Mama gone, wanted the snows melted and school open so that Ms. Del, her English teacher, would take note of her absence and worry about her. But she'd been robbed of being missed.

No one outside the ranch was concerned about Loretta. Not one single person.

Taped beneath her wood plank desktop was a manila envelope where she kept things. Stuck between her bed and the wall were books Ms. Del had lent Loretta that she was keen to read when she was alone—*Wuthering Heights, Rumble Fish, Brave New World*. In the small closet were a few white blouses, her two denim skirts, and empty hangers that clanked when they swung back and forth each time she reached inside. There used to be some journals hidden in back until William found them. He tossed her precious notes into the potbellied stove and declared "wickedness burns like a fire," quoting Isaiah to lend credibility to his evil actions.

"He won't let you be a layabout for long, you know." Mama placed her hand on Loretta's shoulder. It seemed she was accusing Loretta of faking an illness. "You hear me?"

"No lyin' about. Sure. Got it." Loretta shrugged her mother's hand away but lifted her head. She must have had a fever. Damp, reddish-brown strands of hair stuck to her forehead. A sharp pain shot through the jagged rip in her neck. "Don't cha care? Did ya ever?" she asked, begging Mama for any answer, something to bring some sense to this moment that might align her with the woman she barely knew.

Mama stopped. No movement. Probably not thinking but her mind gone to that place she went when her eyes glazed over. Her feet in corduroy men's slippers ready to slink through the bedroom door. She folded the bloodstained washcloth in half and half again. Slipped it inside the pocket of her pink-green-red-plaid apron.

"Care?" Mama's eyes glanced not at her daughter but outside to the far-off peak she often set her sights on through the kitchen window. "Don't much know about that kind of thing."

"What the—?" Loretta caught herself. She'd almost used

the blasphemous word *hell* but went silent, rolled over, kept the smelly army blanket near her face, pivoted to her mother who was a beaded mess of sweat despite the cold, her eyelids well into a sagging that would last the rest of her days. "You don't know much about caring?"

"Not really. Never part of my dreams."

"What kind of dreams do you have?"

"Nothing good. Lessons."

"Like what?" Loretta went quiet. Hoped for any answer.

"That my sins will extract their penance while I'm on Earth." Mama stared far beyond the window's glass. A stillness rarely seen by Loretta.

"What does that mean? Sounds more like nightmares to me."

"Enough said. I don't say a lot, daughter. You should know that. It's not news." Mama retied her apron's strings nice and tight behind her back and blew some air from her mouth up to her forehead, which didn't wither the steamy drops hunkered below her short graying hair.

"I guess it's not," Loretta whispered. No last chance revelation from the mother who shuffled away and dragged the bedroom door shut, taking her few thoughts with her.

Over the years, the battered house had settled a little to the left, and a bit the other direction—nothing inside closed without a scrape, a good strong pound, or a slam. The click of the knob was followed by the sound of her mother's heavy steps back to her kitchen, to her chair by the stove where she could raise her swollen ankles and rest a spell.

When there was silence, Loretta sat up in bed.

Certain her mother had retreated downstairs, and her father was in the bunkhouse with the residents teaching them his life lore, which bore witness to nothing, Loretta took root on the antique ladderback chair at her desk. It was painted with blue and yellow flowers. Her family's singular piece of pretty furniture. The final pristine snow of the season blanketed the prairie—flattened like a bleached white bedsheet by the harsh winds outside. The window frame shook. A cold brew of whines and shrieks stirred side to side of the tired house. The world beyond her little room might seem an artist's rendering. So perfect, clean, with sunlight casting a saintly glow across the mountains that were the insurmountable border to her world.

"Not yet," she said. "Hold on. Your moment is coming." Serene as the prairie might be in a photograph or wildlife magazine, Loretta knew the dangers that awaited any attempt at escape on such a cold day.

The snow looked soft. It wasn't, not even crisp as piecrust. Frozen white flakes joined forces, could be slates of stone, some pieces tough shards of ice. To trudge through the prairie in less than ardent gear and tough winter boots would have a person regretting the stupid idea that fleeing would be. The windchill was duty bound to bring on frostbite in less than thirty minutes; tips of the nose and fingers first to go, then body temperature would drop. Hypothermia sure to deliver shivers and mind-boggling disorientation.

Wear mittens not gloves, Outdoor Life *magazine at the school library advised.*

Skin next to skin. Fingers on fingers. Wiggle them. Hold on. Digits save digits.

Loretta was a patient young woman and running away on this day was not an option. She'd withstood her life for seventeen and a half years. The remaining months until her August birthday would not defeat her. She couldn't dare leave before she reached legal age—she needed to be certain nobody on Earth could be ordered to haul her back to her father's sorry-ass idea of a home. She'd heard stories from residents about older sisters and brothers who'd been caught on the road and sent to worse places.

There were gradations, some called troubled teen homes, others therapeutic programs, crisis centers—the pain and torture a matter of degrees. Lucky teens would be returned home in a pale, quieter state, and others, well, those teens weren't seen again, not ever. There had been whispers in school about a young poet named Bryson, a too-pretty boy with beautiful eyelashes. He died in wilderness therapy, emaciated, hungry, after a long, grueling hike. Loretta had no intention of letting that happen to her.

She reached under her desk and felt for the edges of the tan manila envelope, pulled it free, and set it on top. Got a jolt of immense expectation when she turned it over. There was a pleasure in undoing its clasp. She lifted the tiny metal tab on one side, then the other. Pulled the flap open and rummaged within her secrets, the belongings she had that mattered. Digits save digits.

"All right, students, pack up. Don't forget your reports are due on Friday. And, Loretta," Ms. Del had announced near the end of class a few weeks before, "stay after for a moment."

"Yes, ma'am," Loretta answered; she kept her eyes downward and tapped five fingers up then down, her effort to appear calm. She wasn't in trouble, that was a certainty. Still, she didn't trust some of the other students in the room. She couldn't. Many of their fathers knew William. Never could be sure what some kid might say over dinner, maybe not meaning to harm, but word could get back. Being friendly with a teacher would not be considered acceptable, not in her house.

"You doin' okay?" Ms. Del asked when Loretta approached the teacher's desk after the classroom emptied.

"Sure." Loretta crossed her arms, head bent toward the floor, her hair hiding her face. She surveyed Ms. Del's desk trinkets: a geode close to pink velvet in color, a small globe that doubled as a pen holder, a box of Kleenex, and a crystal vase that held a sprig of lavender.

"How about at home?" Ms. Del waved her hand to the chair beside her desk. "Sit for a bit. You've got time. Bus not for fifteen minutes yet."

Loretta stepped around to take the seat, hunched her shoulders, dropped her book bag by her feet. She folded her hands in her lap and said nothing.

"Gettin' by?" the teacher asked.

"At William and Mama's house?" Loretta never used the word *home* and tried to avoid the name Papa unless she was faced with him. "I guess." She pushed her hair behind her ears; her eyes caught Ms. Del's and she saw layers of concern within the teacher's compassion. She wanted to stay with the woman forever. She yearned to pour her heart out to this teacher who was the only person in the town, in the whole state, in the country who had offered tenderness to "the poor girl" with *those parents*.

"They run that awful home and lock up girls," Loretta heard kids whisper when she passed through the school hallways.

Perhaps worse than being bullied is being shunned for someone else's actions.

"I worry for you, Loretta," Ms. Del said in her serious teacher voice and placed both her palms flat on the desk. She had short brown hair cut in a practical style with bangs. She wore a sweater and a sherbet-green wool skirt. No pants were allowed for women in their school district. A charm bracelet dangled around her wrist that included the letter *A*, a tiny typewriter, a quill pen, a silver miniature of the book *Wuthering Heights*. Tangerine lipstick was her most flamboyant fashion statement. She smelled of violets and the pink Johnson's Baby Lotion she rubbed into her palms and fingers throughout the day.

"Please don't worry. Not about me." Loretta's voice sounded more pleading than she'd intended. She wanted to reach onto the desk and take her teacher's hand. She had an urge to grab the bottle of lotion and hold it to her face.

"How can I not be concerned? You're a brilliant young woman. You read. Do you know how significant that is?"

"No." Loretta was a girl without friends except for residents who came and went for a season or two on the ranch. Her commitment to Elsie was a new experience, one she'd never had before, and she wasn't sure she could live up to whatever being a best friend might require. The idea of being critical of another's life was unsettling if not altogether incomprehensible. The only plan she had was to put a hefty distance between herself and William and Mama.

"I have something for you." The teacher pulled at the drawer in the top of her desk. Loretta watched it slide open, no harsh scraping, the ease with which Ms. Del's fingers felt around inside, how she reached for something behind a collage of pens, rulers, and pencils and beneath a rubber-banded bunch of index cards.

"What is it?" Loretta asked when Ms. Del handed her the small white envelope.

"It's my home phone number. Not my name. The number. Memorize it and then please destroy the piece of paper. I want you to have it, but no one can know. You can call me at any time."

"Call?" Loretta had not shared her plans. She was too afraid to tell anyone, even Ms. Del, a teacher so filled with goodness it overwhelmed her.

"Yes. Call me. Collect."

"Collect? Really?" Loretta knew about this but had never even considered she'd have anyone to call.

"Dial zero for the operator. Say it's collect. They will place the call. Free. From anywhere. Next week or in the future. I am here for you. Doesn't matter if it's years from today. I am not just your teacher."

"You're not?" Loretta's hand shook holding the envelope.

"I'm your friend. Friends are there for each other. Friendship has no expiration date."

"Oh, Ms. Del . . ." Loretta couldn't speak. Nothing she could think to say would carry enough meaning. "Friendship has no expiration date. Is that a quote?"

"Well, it's one of mine."

"I like it." Her teacher had an endless supply of quotes, each a hug of words.

"You know what Virginia Woolf once said?" Ms. Del asked. "She's a famous author. You'll read her."

"What'd she say?" Loretta waited.

"Not exactly this, I'm interpreting here." Ms. Del winked. "But she wrote that we each have a past shut away like the leaves of a book and—" The teacher stopped.

"And what?"

"Well, this is important . . ." Ms. Del paused a moment longer for emphasis in the way teachers do. "She said that our real friends only know the title."

"What does that mean?"

"I think she was saying there's always more to a person's story."

A young pronghorn the color of butterscotch with a white furry rump raced through the prairie outside Loretta's window. Some think they're antelopes, or even deer, but Loretta knew better.

Pronghorns have long horns that curve like backward *C*'s and rest above huge romantic eyes that rarely close, not even when pronghorns sleep. The fastest land mammal in North America, pronghorns stay on guard against predators. Able to outrun coyotes, wolves, and bears. Enviable animals.

If Loretta wasn't a daughter with no legal choice, forced to reside in this residents' ranch hell, if she could be something different, she'd be one of her favorite prairie creatures. Loretta watched the falcons every summer. Each time, she was filled with a sad envy that snuck into the corners of her eyes and left her near tears.

Fast was a skill Loretta had given much thought. She longed for speed. For her time to present itself. A moment of significance, that's what it would be. She, too, kept her eyes open more often than not.

Because when the door to freedom unlatched . . . they'd best count her gone.

EIGHT

West of the Rockies

Certain Mama was back downstairs, Loretta searched inside the crisp manila envelope on her desk. It held bits of paper, notes in Bic pen blue ink, treasured quotes from Hinton, Alcott, Le Guin, and Ms. Del. She'd added the one about leaves of a book. She pulled out a poem she'd written that she thought was parochial and childish, but Ms. Del had said it was special. Found the small white envelope her teacher had given her. She traced the indentation on its flap. Ms. Del had stamped a circle of burgundy wax with the impression of a feather pen crossed over a sword.

"It's secret wisdom." Ms. Del had winked. "Drop the 's' from sword. You'll see. Words are our strongest weapon."

"You sure?" Loretta asked.

"It may seem there are easier ways to win. But not for the long term."

"Not?"

"Wouldn't be honorable." Ms. Del offered her serious smile. She meant what she'd said.

"I'll keep that in mind."

At her makeshift desk, on her ladderback chair, Loretta held the square white envelope close to her face. It smelled pink, of Ms. Del's lotion, and she hoped the scent would last. It almost took away the pain that throbbed from the wound in her neck. Words are our strongest weapons? She wondered. Countless times, she'd considered grabbing the rifle by the kitchen door, taking off, and shooting anything that got in her way. Loretta worried the day might come she'd have no alternative.

She pulled out Ms. Del's slip of paper. Repeated the number, ". . . - . . . -3026." She'd memorized it the day Ms. Del gave it to her. She hated to give up the note, but time had taken on an even more fragile feeling. She might have to run and couldn't let this be found. Finally, she ripped the sheet in half and half again. She stared at the uneven edge, held on to the envelope, which she'd save; it had a pretty liner of light green paper imprinted with a bric-a-brac of yellow circles and squares. She ripped again. The note became shards, fragments of fine stationery fell to her makeshift desk.

Ripped it again.

One by one, she slipped stationery sheet crumbs of paper into her mouth. Chewed them a little. Swallowed. Chewed some more. Held the last corner in her hand and stared out the bedroom window. She wished she had a glass of water.

Loretta heard a light tap. She slid schoolbooks on top of her treasures. The knob turned. What would Mama want now? William never knocked on any door he owned. He was a rare visitor to her quarters, and she'd not seen him since the night she felt his presence before his wrath in the pitch black—the near dawn when his eyes were so near hers. She had never before realized that the white surrounding a man's iris could cast as much fright as the meanest glare.

"It's me." Elsie slid inside and closed the door with one quick shove. She stood, her pale fingers on the knob, those freckles across her nose all tight together, her stare solemn, she, like Loretta, unsure what a best friend was to do in this here situation.

"How?" Loretta bounced off the chair and hurried to her friend.

"Mama sent me. Gave me the key." Elsie reached out her arm. Loretta grabbed her and pulled her to the bed.

"Can you sit with me? Please, please."

"Mama said five minutes. To check you're doin' okay."

"Mama said that?"

"Well . . ." Elsie's nose relaxed. Spaces between her freckles reappeared. A piece of her hair like spun silk fell from behind an ear. "She didn't say that exactly."

"Probably more like go check and tell her the layabout is coming to an end."

"Yes. That's it." Elsie laughed. So did Loretta. Then both girls put palms over their mouths, afraid to be heard. "You in pain? Those are some nasty cuts."

"I'm alive. Don't worry. Anyways, how're the girls?" Loretta snuggled closer to Elsie. "Is everybody doing all right?"

"So far. *He* hasn't been around much. Papa—"

"I know who you mean." Loretta frowned with one side of her mouth, shook her head. Papa being the only *he* on this ranch.

"Anyway, *he* had to go to town two days in a row. Gave us a break."

"The bunnies?"

"They're worried." Elsie made her concerned face.

"The bunnies are worried?" Loretta scrunched her eyes and looked confused.

"They know Easter's coming. Dinnertime."

"Spring. Yep, it's close." Loretta didn't want to think about Easter week when she'd have to cut off the heads of rabbits, skin them to fill the orders from people in town. "Look—" Loretta pointed to the lone pronghorn outside in the snow. "Probably lost its family for a bit."

"Lucky, aren't they?" Elsie set her forehead against the glass.

"Elsie! Get down here to help now!" Mama yelled from the kitchen.

"I gotta go."

"Don't worry," Loretta whispered.

"It's just—"

"Just what?"

"It's your father. Did something. When he came for the morning check-in. Gave me a bad feeling."

"What?"

"He touched my hair. For a second. Said, well—"

"What did he say? Tell me exactly."

"Said he had to go to town. Then looked right at me and said see you tonight. Right at me."

"Elsie!" It was Mama again.

Elsie jumped off the bed. Stopped at the door. Her hand gripped the doorknob. Loretta wanted her to stay. They turned to the frozen shut window. If she and her friend could escape somehow, Loretta would never leave her side.

"I'm not gonna use this." Elsie held the key in the air. "I couldn't lock you in anywhere."

"Doesn't matter. I can't leave. Not yet." Loretta hurried closer to Elsie. "But promise me. Don't go in that office with him."

"But how—"

"Be sick. Make yourself vomit. Anything. Do not go."

Loretta stared at the sky, imagining what she might find beyond the mountains in the distance. Alone again, she sat on the pretty chair. It was dainty, which didn't fit this house. The seat itself was woven from straw. She was unsure of its history. It was part of the collection of uncomfortable red horsehair furniture in the front room that had belonged to a grandmother she'd never met.

The pronghorns had scooted far away. The prairie outside her window was frigid with cold. A graying sky won its battle with the sunshine. The voice of condescension in her head berated her, accused her of evils and misdeeds, reminded her she'd entered this world a sinner and these sad circumstances were fair retribution. She didn't dare tell anyone, couldn't share her worries with Ms. Del or Elsie. She feared it was possible she deserved nothing but more years of struggle on this damn ranch.

She hated. HATED. The truth was that simple. Her heart hated, and hatred was a sin.

"Whoever says he is in the light and hates his brother is still in darkness," the minister had preached.

Sometimes at school, Loretta wondered about secrets and fate and hatred. Especially when a student didn't have their homework to turn in, if they stammered, eyes to the floor, or stared anywhere but at the teacher. If they offered no good excuse, Loretta became suspicious about their homelife. What might have kept them from finishing an assignment? Were they like her? Did they, too, hide truths far too awful to share?

Did they hate?

Her hand snaked to her neck, tentative, scared. Her fingers reached for the dried blood that would be found, the crooked rip that raked through her skin. At first, she didn't find any cut. Such is the sneakiness with which scars hide. A trickle of almost glee bubbled in her heart. Perhaps it had been a bad dream, unreal; maybe there was no wound. Her outstretched fingers stroked below her chin, traveled farther down two inches, three, until she touched the broken trail of blood—like scat droppings in the prairie. The discovery she had sought not to find.

The wound hesitated from one side of her neck to the other. Her fingers moved with caution on top of and over not a straight line but a scar that would heal into a kind of a Z that would hover beneath her chin forever, the cut raw, the false healing of a wound with no plans to vanish. Still, Loretta hoped it might; could it possibly fade and disappear? She reached for her school backpack. Found the small mirror she'd taken from the G&A.

"Oh," she whispered, scared for what she would see. Then, "Ohhh" again, a small gasp.

She held the mirror near, far, and closer still. Ran her finger over the skin. It oozed. Not blood but the oily ooze of wounds indecisive regarding their future. Some skin was cracked open. Remembering the rusted nail's sound—*rip rip rip*—made her cringe again. The cut was nowhere near healed. She wished Mama were still beside her with the cloth to offer some weak form of cleansing.

Loretta couldn't get Mama's words out of her head. *No sense bein' angered*. Loretta stared at the cold outside. Placed a hand on the window that shook with the prairie winds. A late-day lacework of frost spread across the glass. If she didn't have anger, didn't hold it close, she was afraid she'd give in, let fear win, allow this life of imprisonment to become her fate.

All fixed? Loretta had a deep-boiling not-fixed vat that sputtered breaths from within her being. Drastic scenarios rehearsed in her mind. "Fixed?"—the word shot from her mouth. In school, none of her scars had ever been visible. No one knew. Now the other students would know the truth. They'd see it on her neck. That she, too, was kept locked inside the Home for Wayward Girls.

For years within books she'd read, Loretta had seen how people come to do strange things their better selves might never have fathomed. A moment arrives, uncalled-for actions are thrust into reality, and drastic measures ensue, especially during times of worrying concerns, even more when pain has been well inflicted. People rise up. She had no choice. And thinking on this gave her a sliver of a smile. Maybe not today, nor tomorrow, but the day was near. It was certain. As was she.

She returned the mirror to the book bag. Ran fingers over her new scar, a habit that would become natural to her, like flipping her hair behind her shoulders or pushing a loose strand behind an ear. The practical voice in her head told her to let it go. *Nothing she could do about it. A scar is a scar for life.* Little tears grew into bigger tears and fell from her eyes. They weren't for the loss of beauty, not due to a mere cut that oozed with syrupy pink not quite blood.

"Let it go," she told herself.

But another voice, the one she kept most hidden inside, begged her to contemplate opportunities that might lie in wait. Questions pounded within her aching skull. What would she do when the chance came? Was she brave enough? Did she have what it takes to risk everything?

Loretta remembered the book by the French writer she'd borrowed from Ms. Del. She would finish it today. She pulled it from her bag and returned to bed. Folded her pillow in half and shoved it beneath her head. Opened the book to its last chapter. At least her nose seemed in better shape. It only hurt when she touched it, which she did often. She heard the practical voice, the one in her brain, remind her that her lot in life wasn't fair, and she was not the true sinner in this household.

Upon reaching the book's final page, Loretta closed her eyes and fell asleep. The dark of night filled each corner of the room when she awoke. She found the flashlight stashed by the side of her bed and reread the *Count of Monte Cristo*'s last line.

"All human wisdom is contained in these two words—*Wait and hope*." Exactly what Loretta planned to do. Waiting was an act of freedom, too, wasn't it? She only need be ready when the moment presented itself. She knew that sometimes choices are thrust upon you without warning. Same as the silent presence of wolves.

On the ride home from school the day Ms. Del kept her after class, the bus had passed free-range brown, black, and spotted cattle, munching, making water stops at small ponds on large stretches of ranchland. The cows plodded to their homestead, head to tail to next head, the eldest leading the herd far from her yellow school bus. Loretta squished her face close to the window and watched the cattle guided by proud Angus and Holstein parents. One of the youngest of calves wandered off, took longer at a watering hole, and then for reasons Loretta didn't understand, made a U-turn and sprinted to rejoin its family.

Brown and black and spotted cows.

The ranchers were seldom nearby. They trusted their herds. No one called out to the calf, alarms were not sounded. The parents led. They never looked back. They didn't check on their young'uns. No reason to. They knew their calves would follow. Their unity was their safety net. They stayed together by choice. *What a blessing*, thought Loretta.

The morning after her three-day layabout ended, Loretta sat up in bed and laughed out loud thinking of last week when Mama had

kicked her in the thigh. "Stop your foolish dreamin'," Mama yelled
and kicked again but Loretta had dodged the other direction.

"You hear me, girl. Keep your head down. There's only one
thing for you to be doin'."

"Only one?" Loretta asked, probably a little smart-mouthed.
"Like what?"

"Whatever your father wants."

But that was not true. Loretta was sure as Dumas. There was
a second and third thing for her to do and a whole lot more. "My
dreams are not foolish," she whispered, "and I can wait."

Loretta's bedroom door was unlocked. That meant she was
expected to appear in the kitchen. She put on her denim skirt and
a black Rolling Stones T-shirt, which William wouldn't like, but
she didn't give a shit. There was no school today, which made her
clothes her call in her opinion.

"Well, look who's rejoined the living." Mama glanced her
direction from the stove. Big skillet of Saturday scramble on the
burner. The sizzle of bacon frying nearby, most of which would
go to Papa. "Eggs today. Set that table, girl."

"Yes, ma'am." Loretta opened a drawer near the sink. Reached
for forks and dull knives, a bunch of cheap paper napkins from the
counter, and made her way along the benches at each side of the
table. Papa's and Mama's chairs at either end.

"Here they come," Mama announced.

Cold wind burst through the door followed by Crystal and
Gayle and the rest of the girls wrapped in sweaters, hands hidden in their armpits. They stomped snow from shoes and boots.
Residents weren't allowed jackets—could make a runaway effort
too easy. Loretta was lucky to have her army fatigue. Had to give
the appearance at school that she was not coat-deprived. Papa
couldn't risk any wrong impressions.

"Loretta!" Tanya was much too happy to see Loretta returned from her sickbed.

"Shush." Mama laid eagle eyes on Tanya, a reprimand for sure. "Get to the table."

"Yes, ma'am," Tanya mumbled. Loretta sent a sweet glance her way. Tanya's eyelids blinked from Mama to Loretta. She gave Loretta an anxious smile.

Loretta watched the single file that broke in two and slid onto the benches. Girls in denim skirts, hair pulled back or braided. Where was Elsie? Papa closed the door behind him, hung his oilskin duster on a hook. Loretta's concern flew from Mama at the stove to the girls seated at the table. Crystal and Gayle were intent on their silverware. Tanya's braid had come undone while her eyes tried to telegraph a message to Loretta that something wasn't right.

"Loretta, come grab these." Mama ladled clumps of eggs onto plates with a loud clack. Bacon smoke lodged above her head. "Now! Before they get cold."

"Yes, ma'am, comin'." Loretta bent right close to Tanya and whispered, "Where is she?"

"Um." Tanya looked afraid to say anything.

"Loretta, get those plates," Papa ordered, taking his seat the farthest distance from the women's work at the stove. "And change that shirt after breakfast or I'll burn it myself."

"Where is Elsie?" Loretta pivoted, hands on her hips, her line of sight direct on her father. Fuck him. He could do anything he wanted to her but not to her best friend. "Tell me!"

"Humph," he grunted and lifted a forkful of drippy eggs to his mouth.

An ugly quiet engulfed the room. The scrape of Mama's metal flipper dredging for the last of the scramble ceased. It wasn't the kind of hush that accompanied the girls' hungry mouths while they chewed their small breakfast rations. This was pure silence. Except nothing about it fell in the category of purity.

Loretta waited. "What have you done?!" she yelled again as she shoved her hair behind her ears, unsure what else to do. She tried not to stamp her feet.

"The girl's fine, Loretta." Papa's stare rose from his plate. Just his eyes. Slow and steady. He set down his fork and held out his empty cup signaling for more coffee. "Don't get yourself involved in none of your business."

"Mama!" She flashed her angriest face to her mother, who was awash in beads of steamy kitchen sweat. Loretta wanted to jump up and down, grab Mama's hand, say *Come on, care! You must care, please care, please care.*

"Listen to your father, Loretta. Elsie is not your business." Mama shuffled to the table, the unplugged percolator in hand. She refilled Papa's cup with burnt Folgers brew.

Loretta watched the stream of coffee, saw it arc and pour, a small gurgle cut into the uneasy silence. More dreadful quiet. She was unsure what to do. Couldn't back away from center stage in the kitchen. Wouldn't be a coward. The residents' heads were bowed, yet they homed in on her—their stares darted quick left and quicker right to see what she or Papa might do next.

"Where is Elsie?" she yelled again.

"She's been cast into Silent Cloud. Best leave her be." Papa raised the metal mug to his lips; his cold eyes bore into hers. Was it a dare? An ultimatum? A *you thinkin' of crossing me?* accusation that floated across the stifling quiet?

Papa waited. But Loretta did not.

She grabbed her faded green army jacket from the hook. Almost took the loaded rifle, too, but thought better—the rifle permeated more than enough of her thoughts. This was not a good time for any weapon to be found in her hands.

"Silent Cloud! How could you?" Loretta spun 'round to glare at William. She hoped he saw the retaliation in her eyes, that he understood no matter his authority over her now, a new day was not too far ahead.

"Because I can." The words drawled from William's mouth, his threat barely veiled.

Loretta slammed the door and ran through melted, defrosting mud. She heard bunnies in the hutches, their teeth rubbing uppers to lowers, their collective sound a buzz, a low purr, like cats but not near as comforting. Snow dribbled off the path. Rivulets of dirt drained south. She didn't care what hell might descend from her father, she had to get to her friend Elsie.

It was a big sky kind of day. The lightest powdery blue drifted far above and well into dissipating mountain clouds. The sun emerged. A gift indeed. Butter-yellow rays draped across the ground. Heart thumping, Loretta was anxious with fear. What would she find?

Nothing bad could happen on such a beautiful Saturday, could it? Not on a morning filled with simmering sweet daylight and pastel skies. Not when freedom was so near her grasp she could feel its palpitations. Not when somehow, in a give thanks and hallelujah sort of way, Loretta felt bathed in the warm possibility of resurrection.

Hallelujah, indeed. Spring had begun its descent on the prairie.

NINE

West of the Rockies

Loretta's heels kicked up a mixture of ice fast on its way to becoming thick mud sure to suck shoes in deep. She burst the bunkhouse door open.

"Elsie, Elsie, you there? Don't worry. It's me."

The room was clean and hushed.

"Elsie!" Loretta's worries moved to her stomach. Her hands shook. Her neck stiffened. "Elsie!"

The cots were made. Army blanket corners tucked under the way Papa demanded. She heard a small cry, a sad "mm-hmm" third cot over, nearest the wall, and saw the crown of her friend's white-blond head of hair slumped against the side of her bed. Elsie was wrapped tight in her sweater, legs folded beneath her on the floor.

"Elsie!" Loretta hurried past one cot, two, then dropped to her knees. Placed a hand on Elsie's arm. She tapped, waited, touched her friend's shoulder. "Elsie, don't worry, I'm here."

"You're not to speak to me. No one is." Elsie at last blinked, eyes so pale the color had washed away with her tears. No marks or bruises. William was cautious, he scared girls with his threats, he patted the pistol holstered to his thigh, waved a belt at them, but he seldom left visible harm on a resident.

Loretta eased deeper to the floor and rested her head against Elsie's shoulder. Elsie's sobs slowed, soft whimpers stronger than fear accompanied her tears of acceptance—slow bedraggled sobs that conceded a truce. Tears that had no choice but to comply for the moment at least.

"He yelled 'Silent Cloud's on her!' in the bunkhouse this morning. Before breakfast," Elsie told Loretta. "Jabbed that finger of his at me. 'All of you listen,' he said, jab jab jabbing, and he ordered no speaking to me today. Not one word."

"Then what?"

"Everybody backed away from me!"

"I'm sorry." Loretta knew that William left the other girls no choice.

"He pointed to the floor. Shouted 'Kneel.'" Elsie's voice was shades above mute, an ashamed whisper. "He called me a whore. Oh, Loretta—"

"What? What else?"

"My head was bowed. His boots all I could see. I wanted to yell but—"

"But?"

"I trembled. At his feet. That's all I could do. Wanted to hit him. Or run. But I trembled. Oh, Lord. Why didn't I do something?"

"Why didn't you? Because it wouldn't have worked. Not yet. Oh, Elsie, I'm sorry. We will go soon. I promise." Loretta bent to one side of Elsie's face, tried to get her friend to look her in the eyes.

"And he ordered them to yell at me. While I kneeled."

"Yell? Yell what?"

"Harlot, tramp, sinner, whore." Elsie's pale translucent eyes were contrite for misdeeds she'd not committed. "I am not a whore."

"No, you're not." Loretta held Elsie's hands tight.

"He said no other talking. Or else they'd be silenced along with the miscreant. Me, a miscreant?"

"You know that's bull."

"And they did it, Loretta. The girls called me names." Elsie lifted her head from the cot. Her whimpers became angry with tears that struggled within a stream of deep breaths.

"They didn't want to. Not at you. They had no choice."

"I know. But still," Elsie cried. "Then they hurried out. Far away from me. To the house. To Mama's breakfast. In a big fast fury to get away from *me*."

"Not from you. Not really."

"Loretta, you need to go. He won't like you being here. He'll do something. Hurt you worse than us. He always does. You shouldn't even speak to me."

"He knew where I was going when I ran out of the house. Nothing, not even me running to the bunkhouse, would interrupt him and his drippy eggs. And you and me not speaking will never happen."

"But what if?"

"Elsie, he's already plotting something for me. I can feel it and I don't care. Tell me what happened last night. Everything."

"Pretty much as you said." Elsie sat up straighter on her heels. "He told me to come to his office except—"

"You didn't go, did you?"

"I told him no way. That I'd rather run to the wolves in the prairie."

"And then?"

"He came close to me. Grabbed my chin. Said 'Be careful,

young woman, or you may be sent to the woods sooner than you expect.'"

"No, no, no. Did he use the word 'banishment'? Anything like that?" Loretta bit her lip, gripped Elsie's hand, and listened.

"Didn't give him the chance. I locked myself in the bathroom. Screamed if I saw his feet through the crack under the door. Laid on the floor watchin' till he gave up. He took off. Said he'd had enough of me. He was back this morning. That's when he put me into Silent Cloud."

Loretta ran fingers through her own messy hair. Tied it back with a cord, pushed shorter strands behind her ears. Got to her feet. Paced a few feet in each direction. Shoved her hands in her pockets. Thought of lighting a cigarette but knew better.

"Elsie, come here." She pulled her friend to the window. "Look outside. Sun! See it. The snow is melting."

"Praise be." Elsie's sadness about flew out the window. She laughed. "Can't believe I'm using my mama's words. But it is praiseworthy."

"It's spring. Almost here, my friend." Loretta dragged Elsie back to the cot. The two dropped cross-legged to the floor. "I graduate in less than two months. Then my birthday. Our D-Day."

"Yes." Elsie reached underneath her cot for her drawing journal, found it and began to sketch. "What's the D for?"

"Nothing so much. In the war, it meant the day. The day of the invasion. For us—"

"What?"

"The day we go. You hear me? We have a plan, right?"

"I sure hope so. My parents. They hear about me being disrespectful to your father, they won't ever allow me back home."

"Don't say that again." Loretta took hold of both Elsie's shoulders. "No respect required where it isn't deserved."

"I know. But I'd do most anything to get outta here."

"Not anything. Promise me that."

"The thing is—" Elsie set her journal aside, scrunched her faint pale face. Her freckles joined forces across her nose. "I'm worse than scared now."

"I know. Me, too. Still, there's always a solution," Loretta said, but she was far from certain this was true. It felt like something Ms. Del would say.

"Is there really? A solution?"

"I think so. You know, today, when I ran over here, I was so damn angry. And worried. But then, you know what?"

"What?" Elsie relaxed, her freckles eased themselves back to their proper places.

"Spring appeared. Like that." Loretta snapped her fingers. "It was a sign."

"You sure?"

"Well, it's almost spring. And we will be gone soon. Trust me. Have to make it past graduation. That's it."

"If you say so, Loretta." Elsie leaned against the cot, reopened her journal, and scrolled the word PROMISE inside a heart.

"I do. Show me what you been drawing."

Elsie flipped a few pages to a sketch of two pronghorns skipping near a broccoli bundle of trees. "They're pretty. I'd swear they're antelope cousins."

"Nope. Some think they're related. But they're not." Loretta pointed to a picture of a peregrine falcon, midair, with a scarf dangling from its beak. "What's that?"

"Oh, something to leave behind. Maybe it marks a favorite spot. Or the falcon may lose it along the way, but that's okay."

"Okay?" Loretta cocked her head to one side and waited. Elsie's take on things had a way of making her think.

"Yeah, cuz a friend will fly by and grab it for her. Like we would. You and me."

"They're the fastest bird, you know? Peregrines. They can dive two hundred and forty miles per hour." Loretta grinned at the possibilities that bounced about while her mind meandered through ideas of moving fast, taking flight, and running far away. "They're my favorites."

"Didn't know that. But makes sense." Elsie smiled. "You and fast bein' kind of related."

The bunkhouse door creaked open. Eerily mute residents single-filed in. Strands of parted brown, blond, red, and maple hair fell half-staff toward the floor, eyes too afraid to seek out Elsie and Loretta. Girls traumatized into the belief that if they dared speak, Silent Cloud or worse would be foisted upon them. Very scuffed Keds were kicked off, boots unlaced and left under the windowsill. Sweaters weren't removed but tightened around each waist until one by one the girls fell into similar cross-legged positions on the floor surrounding Elsie and Loretta.

"Where's Papa?" Loretta raised herself up on her knees to check outside. Her hands shoved deeper inside her army jacket pockets. No sign of him.

"Not sure." Gayle shrugged. "Said there'd be lessons after lunch."

"Heard him say he had an appointment in town," Tanya advised, her stare locked on Loretta's for approval, her hands tucked in her armpits.

"Mama?"

"By her stove. Where else?" Crystal said, a faintly cynical curl of laughter awaiting permission to escape her lips. The young waif pushed curls away from her face.

"Yahoo!" Loretta yelled. "It's okay, Elsie, Silent Cloud is over for now. Everybody, stop looking the way bunnies do on a cold morning."

The girls' heads, same as prairie dogs snug in holes in the ground, popped from their weary mourning. Gayle's shoulders straightened, her skin paler than usual next to her red hair. Tanya pulled maple-brown strands together and began a new braid. Crystal giggled quiet, could be tiny hiccups, until the others joined in.

"You guys," Elsie said in a voice that hesitated until the words stumbled from her mouth. "Remember. Be careful. Don't do anything. Nothing stupid. Not for me."

"But it's not stupid if we do it for you." Gayle was concerned; the weary half-moon shadows beneath her eyes darkened, the girl so thin and evanescent she might well float away.

"He can't banish us all," Loretta told the group, more affirmation than a truth. She bounced from her knees a bit every minute or so, kept sight on the path to the house outside the window, her mind concentrated in thoughts of escape and her desperate wish to solve each girl's plight. She wondered how long she could keep them safe, and what would happen after she was gone? That thought she hid away. How much could she, one seventeen-year-old, do?

"You sure of that?" Elsie asked. Her freckles were again an anxious solid bridge across her nose, her face poised like a scared army recruit trying to portray courage she did not have.

"We're not leaving you, Elsie," Tanya declared.

"Can't banish us all! Can't banish us all!" the residents sang.

"Can't banish me!" Crystal began to clap to the rhythm.

Loretta hoped this would prove to be true. Elsie's face became stoic, maybe resigned. The two of them knew the outcome of cat-and-mouse games was rarely good for the smallest creatures.

"You remember the place?" Loretta elbowed Elsie in her side and waited.

"South. Right at the mangled tree trunk. Run past the rocks. Wait. But then—" Elsie whispered.

"If I'm not there, hit the road. You remember? Get to your aunt's in Denver," Loretta whispered in Elsie's ear. They hadn't shared the details of their plan with anyone, couldn't risk the other girls knowing their route. William was too skilled at forcing information out of residents.

"Stay far to the side of the highway. And don't look back. Get to Denver."

Elsie moaned. Traveling alone was an outcome they both dreaded although they knew it might be their only choice.

"You got it?" Thank God Elsie's aunt was once a runaway and had told Elsie to come any time, no explanation needed.

"I do."

"Can't banish us all," they sang with the others.

"Can't banish us all." The girls clapped with glee. Thin little Crystal laughed, followed by Gayle, Tanya, and the whole group. They fell onto their sides and into each other filled with the gift giggles can be. Laughter offering a shield to the worst of their fears.

"Praise be," Elsie sang. She rested her head on the cot.

The singing quieted. The girls readied themselves for chores. Hair was tied away from faces, wraparound skirts were tightened, feet slipped back into shoes, laces redone.

"She told me I have to do floors," little Crystal moaned. "Me?"

"Yep, you are awful tiny for that mop." Gayle put an arm around the younger girl. "I'll go with ya."

In ones and twos, they began the march up the mud path that led to Mama's house. Before leaving, each turned to Elsie.

"Hey, girl, don't worry."

"If we don't talk doesn't mean we don't care."

"Mama said to tell you to come along, too, Elsie. Said being in trouble don't mean you get out of your duties. She's got stuff for you to do."

Tanya paused, hand on the knob, younger than Loretta by maybe two years but with a maturity to her, a sure knowledge of how life befalls some harder than others. She swung her body outside, then inside, not wanting to leave. "You know what I'd like to tell William?" she asked.

"What?" Elsie straightened her shoulders. Her face was a bit less pale, her watery blue eyes not so frenzied, suddenly stronger.

"To fuck off," Tanya said, her lips a straight line across her tough-girl face.

"Tanya." Elsie reached for the girl's hand. "You don't have to say if you don't want to. But what brought you here to this god-awful home for wayward girls?"

"I told the wrong person to fuck off—with a knife in my hand." Tanya kicked the door to keep it open. Her stare bounced over to Loretta.

"I expect they deserved it." Loretta stepped closer to them both.

"They did."

"The thing is, we know when someone's messing with us. We're strong and nobody likes strong girls."

"That's it," Elsie said, her voice more certain than ever before.

"And I'm stronger now, Loretta. Cuz of you," Tanya added.

"Because of all of us, I expect," Loretta said. "It's something maybe mystical, I'm not sure. But we make each other believe."

"Believe?" Elsie asked.

"Yep, in ourselves. That we'll survive."

"I will." Tanya smiled from the doorway.

"Go, better get with the others." Loretta urged her along. "We'll follow soon enough." She and Elsie watched through the window. Girls in blue denim skirts breezed up the path one leaning into the other. Curly-haired little Crystal whipped around and waved. Their youngest resident somehow as happy as a kid at recess.

"Love them so much," Elsie said, firm on her feet, stoic despite the repercussions of having been ordered into Silent Cloud.

"I know. Me, too." Loretta reached inside her pocket for a folded piece of notebook paper. She uncapped her blue Bic pen. "Wish we could take them all with us."

"Well, for now, we need to get a move on." Elsie went for her shoes. Sat on her cot and pulled on ragged black Keds. "Can't risk any more demerits."

"Like Tanya said, fuck 'em." Loretta clucked her tongue against the roof of her mouth. "Let me use your journal." She spread the lined sheet of paper flat on top of Elsie's sketchbook. Lifted her eyes while she began to write. "He didn't get near you, right? Touch you again? You'd tell me. Promise?"

"I would. Don't worry. Now, tell me whatcha doin'." Elsie popped upright for a quick check outside the window. The world was splendidly calm.

"Makin' a list."

"Of what?"

"Everything that is yet to be."

"What do you mean, Loretta girl?"

"I mean"—Loretta continued to write across the sheet— "every bit of stuff we've promised ourselves."

Elsie pushed a strand of hair behind her ear, straightened her shoulders, sat tall. She lifted her eyes to see the brightness the sun had delivered outside and nodded her head up and down in agreement.

"You know, like freedom." For a second, within the embrace of the peace best friends share, Loretta felt safe, she felt hopeful.

"Freedom is a good thing," Elsie agreed.

Loretta and Elsie's Freedom List
1. Tight blue jeans
2. Twizzlers
3. Makeup
4. Warm coats (with buttons and collars)
5. Books (for L)
6. Drawing paper and colored pencils (for E)
7. A safe ride
8. Boys?
9. College, community college, jobs?
10. Somewhere to live (far away and forever)

TEN

New York City

"The meeting went long," Loretta moaned to Clarke a few days before the conference began. It was late, too late, and she was exhausted. "I'm tired."

"I'm glad you're finally home. You know, Lor, you are the CEO. The boss. The head of everything. You're allowed to take a break." Clarke's smile was more love than concern, although concern was winning. He watched her kick her boots into the hallway corner and hang her blazer in the closet.

"My feet ache," she told him. "I stopped by that new shelter on the way home. Just to check on them."

"No wonder your feet hurt."

Loretta sank into the tan sectional in their open-plan living, dining, and room for shared commiserations. She untied her scarf. Cracked her neck left, right, and left again. "I'm really dragging."

"Well, what happened with the board? You might as well tell me. I know there's something." He gave her his *please tell me because I love you* grin. Clarke was a good example of what being present meant. He was a patient man who rarely showed anger—a constant weathervane who helped Loretta discern her thoughts.

"Did you know that Isabel Allende once had a job translating romance novels?" Loretta watched his face, how what he was thinking appeared in his expression, his lips, and the crinkle in his eyes.

"I did not." Clarke, bottle of white wine in hand, didn't ask, poured, and passed her a glass. A plate of cheese and flatbread was ready. The evening's conversation was only getting started, which meant they might not get to their shows. She'd voted for *Olive Kitteridge*. Clarke was trying to get through the entirety of *Breaking Bad*.

"Thanks. Anyway, Allende was fired."

"Wait, the board fired you?"

"No, no. Nothing like that."

"Okay, so Allende was fired. For what?"

"I read she added dialogue to romance books so that women were not docile but their truly intelligent selves. Amazing, isn't it? And that she changed endings so that Cinderella types became independent. Strong and independent! How cool is that?"

"I'm not sure where we're going here—" Clarke set his glass on the rustic walnut coffee table they'd purchased from a woodworker's studio on a trip through Mystic, Connecticut. They'd left the shop undecided and watched the historic tall ships in the harbor until they turned to each other and said in unison, "That's the one." The way every decision was made. The two of them talked. They pondered. Loretta might throw in a quote; Clarke offered legalese if needed. And they generally agreed.

"Bear with me." Loretta paused to churn together her thoughts. Her mind processed ideas same as math equations. Things fit together for her that others might never contemplate. Her biggest challenge was discerning how to explain her complicated thinking that made so much sense to her but not always to others. "Don't you see? That's what I do. For these incredible women. I'm a means to their stronger endings."

"Sure, I get that." Clarke picked up Loretta's tired feet and began to massage her heels.

Loretta doubted he did. Not completely. She shook her head. Raised her eyes to his and her glance said *Don't try and BS me.*

"I feel a quote coming," he added.

"Right. You know me so well, Clarke." Loretta made a dramatic pause. "So, Allende said that we only have what we give. We only have what we give! It's the most wonderful concept. That's why I have to go to the shelters. Even if my day goes far too long. I have to see the women. Look at them. They remind me why I must do this work."

"I understand. Really." The wrinkle in Clarke's forehead deepened. It was his *I seriously get it* face.

"I am only what I give." Loretta let her head fall back on the couch. The small smile that lived in her eyes moved to her lips. Lips that had become more comfortable with happiness in the twenty-first century. "You, too. You give."

"Me. Nah. Not so much. But you've always been that way, Lor."

"Have I?"

"I believe you have." His cheeks relaxed. His sigh soft, physical but very clear, his honesty appreciated by Loretta.

Where Loretta came from there had only been anger that bled into an unreasonable hatred, no deeper meaning could be found in her parents' eyes, there'd been no moments in which to treasure some special acceptance of who she was. Her only purpose to William had been to support his wicked endeavors. It took her years to understand this. That he'd been the sinner whose manipulations she'd survived.

Days later, with the conference in full swing at Hunter College, Loretta paused in a hallway outside a restroom. She leaned back, a bootheel lodged against the wall, her hand resting on the scarf around her neck. She wished she could smoke a cigarette, a yen she'd avoided for some time, except it never truly disappeared, somehow attached to her need for deep breaths and mindless meditation.

Must be nerves, she told herself. But the yearning for a Marlboro remained. The temptation riddled within her a desire to run free, head to the beach, watch sand sift through her fingers, call Elsie, who'd be waiting to hear everything about this day.

Down the hallway she saw easels holding signs the foundation had ordered. Arrows pointed to meeting rooms, to a gathering area with volunteers to help, a table with coffee, muffins, and water. Everywhere she turned she saw proof that this day had come.

Deep breaths.

Deep breaths.

Loretta knew how hard she'd worked, the donors she'd pretty much begged for funds, the concerns of the board, the vendors and printers she'd haggled with, the guest speakers who were being given meager honorariums.

Deep breaths.

Deep breaths.

Once none of this existed. Except for an idea. A thought. A wish. Her deep breaths slowed. She was sweating. She was nervous. Her hands were shaking. With both excitement and fear. She'd done the heavy lifting. The day was here. But where was William?

Women walked past Loretta in the hallway. Wearing spruced-up jeans and button-down shirts, a few in suits, many in New York City's uniform of black jeans, black sweaters, boots, and jackets. Everyone doing their best with what they had. Some huddled in twos and threes. A few loners tried to appear confident. Each held a Compass conference guide—the cover pictured Elsie's sketch of a peregrine falcon in flight, the sky clear, a bit of fabric fluttering from its beak. Attendees' faces were excited, hesitant, smiling, and hopeful. The foundation's name was on the placards. Everything was just as Loretta had envisioned back with Clarke at the helm of his sailboat.

"I say we go to the Q&A." Loretta heard a few attendees nearby in deep discussion.

"My vote is for this speaker." A woman waved to a friend, made a quick U-turn, and sped to an elevator. "It says she lived in one of those homes."

"Do you think they still exist today?" asked another, agenda in hand. "I'm torn between a talk by a survivor and another by a former runaway who runs a tech firm."

"I know they do," the woman said and whispered more that Loretta couldn't hear. She didn't need to. There were plenty of awful residential programs that still had to be closed down.

"Wait, let's read through the descriptions again." Two women moved by the windows to reconsider.

Those who were alone raised their eyes and tried to hear others around them. Some were unsure where they belonged or what choice would be right for them. Their faces peered at the agenda for inspiration. Small groups followed those who seemed more clued in to what to choose. Everyone wanted to learn. Each had a cloistered dream and sought advice and inspiration.

There were women for whom attendance was purely practical— a job, or career training, social services, or childcare. Others were aspirational. They hoped for the chance to shake one of the speakers' hands. Some had stories of their own. Or wanted to help. It was a game changer to meet a woman who had met adversity and won. Any bit of wisdom that might alter their own lives would be appreciated.

Possibilities were the fuel that Loretta intended to have on offer at the first of what she believed would be many conferences to come. Her announcement today, the new center, the funding, this was her own personal game changer.

A young woman in jeans and a purple sweater walked slower, an unsure gait. Did she hope instructions would leap off the agenda page? Loretta knew the look; she herself had worn the same for years when she was first arrived in New York. Uncertain, at times scared, she had often followed crowds, even took wrong trains because everyone was getting on the 4 when she damn well was sure she should have taken the 6.

During her first semester at Hunter, she'd felt lost in these same hallways. Waiting for an elevator made her nervous. Where should she stand inside? The front or rear? What floor? The laughter of others had ping-ponged into her body. Nervous—she'd been sure people saw her discomfort. To ask "can someone hit seven?" had been an act of bravery on her part.

"Seven, could you hit seven?" her voice barely audible.

"Which one?" some loud student always piped in.

"Seven, man. She said seven," another would throw back.

Loretta didn't have much then. No savings. No family. Few

friends. But she held on to the buttons from her torn white blouse. Her fingers slid into her jacket pocket, held them, and she felt emboldened and stronger. It was that kind of courage she wanted everyone at today's conference to carry home with them, regardless of where that might be.

"Hey." She stepped away from the wall approaching the young woman in the purple sweater. "Can I help?"

"I'm lost. So lost." The woman's purse slipped off her shoulder. A lanyard dangled from her neck. Her conference guide dropped to the floor.

"No, you're not lost, Elaina. It is Elaina, right?" Loretta pointed to the name badge, bent to the floor, and picked up the fallen booklet.

"Yes, that's me." The woman gave a tiny weak smile, much of it in her eyes. Loretta recognized the look, the woman probably not so prone to happiness, same as she herself used to be.

"Don't worry," Loretta said.

"Oh, thanks." The woman sounded worried.

"I'm Loretta."

"I'm afraid I have no idea where I should go." Elaina's delicate hands, nails bitten, pushed away thick curly hair. It fell right back into her face.

"Let's figure it out. Come on. Follow me."

If believing in something could make it so, the day of their first conference was proof positive that when Loretta set her mind to an idea it would take shape, become significant. Many young women in need had found their way to Compass. Almost since that day when Loretta and Clarke sailed near Jones Beach, and she revealed her goals. Once Loretta got vocal about something, it was already a plan. That was how she was. Subdued until she was certain.

What she saw in Elaina, the young woman in the purple sweater, was a misery that she recognized. She knew more than most about the aftermath of inflicted bruises. The painful colors on arms and faces that eventually fade . . . yet they aren't gone, maybe ever. Loretta had seen close-up how bruises fester, how they weaken one's ability to do anything, the way in which they gnaw at a woman's confidence long after they heal. Worse, she believed that bruises cause women to think they are less than others.

It took years to build Loretta's dream, but each time she helped a runaway feel safe, a woman find a job, or a mother with children obtain shelter, she felt closer to the elusive goal she'd set for herself. She hoped it would make up for the guilt she lugged around. Her departure from the ranch had not gone as planned.

Was it possible that today she'd truly leave William behind? Let go of her horrible final day on the ranch? Had her time been served? Enough punishment doled out to her? So many questions still. Who the heck were William and Mama, anyway? Who was she?

When Loretta was eight years old, in the third grade, her yellow school bus stopped in front of the large billboard sign that advertised the Home for Wayward Girls near the road in front of the ranch. It was a spring afternoon. She'd worn a denim jumper with a white blouse and a pink puffy jacket her mother bought from the church secondhand store. A Tuesday. She remembered because that was the day of the week when her teacher brought Nilla wafers for the class.

There were no cookies or sweets inside Mama's house.

"I once knew a girl whose family sent her to this place." Andy, the temporary bus driver, pointed at the big roadside sign when he pulled up to the ranch. His tone of voice didn't sound complimentary. Andy wore a weathered Stetson and his shoulders leaned far forward to release the bus door. He was filling in for Mr. Cody, who was older, sick, and never said much to Loretta.

"Oh," Loretta said.

"Ain't anybody gonna meet ya?"

"Meet me?" Eight-year-old Loretta stopped, glued to the top stair, the doors sliding open. A prairie wind gushed by them. Loretta's hair was short and shoved behind her ears. Mama liked hair to be easy. She carried a tattered book bag her father got at the Army Navy Surplus when he went on business to another town.

"Your ma or somebody comin' for you?"

"No," Loretta told him and hustled off the bus.

"Hey," Andy called to her. "See ya tomorrow."

"Bye." Loretta stood still and inhaled black fumes that trailed down the two-lane highway when the bus curved out of her sight. Loretta took slow steps past the sign she hated. She didn't understand what *wayward* meant, but even at eight years of age, she felt sure having a big billboard advertising what went on within your house couldn't be good.

She stopped at their roadside mailbox.

Some of the ranches Loretta passed on the bus each day had pretty mailboxes. There was one striped red and blue with white stars on the lid that faced the road. Another had happy sunflowers painted across it. William and Mama's was tarnished gray metal. The flag she pulled upward if there was mail to go out was crooked and rusty. The small door whined a mean *cringe!* when she opened it.

Her first after-school chore each day was to check for whatever envelopes had been delivered, circulars from the Walmart, the bill from the utility company, sometimes official mail with bold government crests printed on it that made her father angry. He'd yell that the Washington imperialists should damn well get out of people's business. When William got mad at the government, Loretta hid in her room and hoped he didn't come looking for her.

She reached inside the metal box, grabbed the pile, and flipped through the small local newspaper filled with ads for places in town she'd never been to, a flyer for the print and ship store, and an announcement from the American Legion.

Loretta almost missed a small pink envelope. It was fancy stationery, the paper starched and strong. The postage stamp had a picture of a mother sheep with a baby lamb. It could have been done with pastel-colored pencils. The words *American Wool* in a banner printed across the bottom.

"So pretty," she'd whispered and touched the stamp with soft reverence. Ran her finger across its field of flowers and sheep. Orange blossoms. Patches of green grass in an expanse of bright yellow that faded into the distance. The sky rose above a faraway mountain range—puffy white clouds within light blue dots that grew thicker at the stamp's edge.

It was the prettiest letter Loretta had ever held.

The envelope was addressed in script in the kind of handwriting Loretta had seen in her cursive workbook. The ink darker blue than the sky, darker than navy blue, closest to the Midnight Blue crayon at school. Each letter perfect. She stared at the capital L. It had a fine curlicue that underlined her entire name. She decided she would practice making her L's wisp and curl the same way.

"What are you doing?" William startled her. He'd come from behind. Lost in the curlicued *L*, she'd ignored the crunch of his feet on the gravel ranch road.

"Nothin'," Loretta said. She needed time to read the envelope. L-o-r . . . She had to see the rest of the words. A letter for her?

"Give me that." He grabbed the mail from her hands. Snatched it away. So fast the stiff stationery slipped too quick through her fingers. "Get to the house and help Mama. Now."

"But?"

"I said go."

He used his mean voice and Loretta hurried from his low roar, which could worsen without warning. She didn't hop skip jump along the path that led to the house the way she did when she was alone. She walked fast as she could past that awful sign and turned to glance twice, two times, hoping to see what her father did with the mail, with the letter addressed to her.

How she wanted to touch that stationery one more time. Each day after school, when she opened the mailbox door that squealed its rusted whine, she prayed there'd be another pink envelope with American Wool lambs so pretty she'd keep it forever, the stamp from a distant place she was certain must have happy people who ate Nilla wafers every single day.

Loretta never forgot the pretty pink envelope meant especially for her. If only she'd known to read the postmark, to see where it was from, if only she'd understood to hide it right away, put it in her bag. There were many if onlys in her life. If only she didn't get so anxious. If only William was locked in the jail west of the Rockies.

ELEVEN

New York City

The journalist from the *New York Times* sat on the gray couch in the meeting room; it wasn't soft or comfy but offered enough space for her Mac, her iPhone, her black leather pouch that slumped to the floor beside her perfectly weathered black boots. Her name was Maggie.

"I told my editor," she said to Loretta, "that you're a hero in the world of runaways. The women I met out west revere you."

"You know, I revere them. All survivors. Every woman and man who got away, who made it, who found a better life for themselves despite what they went through."

"At the end of the day, it's about you. Your organization. A nonprofit. Important, but how is yours different? Or significant?"

"I work on those questions every single day," Loretta told her.

"I know. I'm one of your biggest fans now. Your programs address the whole person—their past, their path to the future. You're amazing."

Loretta sat on the couch's twin, on the opposite side of a white laminate coffee table. She held a latte. An Americano for the writer. Annie, looking millennial boho chic wearing jeans, a smocked blouse, and a blazer, leaned in the doorway.

"News flash." Annie brushed her long tawny hair away from her face—Loretta said it reminded her of an owl's wings. "Good news." She paused to be sure it was okay to speak in front of the reporter.

"It's fine. We're sharing everything today." Loretta nodded at the journalist.

"Tanya made it," Annie announced in her most restrained voice. The swaying metal fringe of her medallion earrings gave away her happy relief.

"Fantastic." Loretta rested her head on the couch and released a grateful breath. Tanya from her days on the ranch. One of the many checkmarks on the list that clicked in her head like a register receipt. She'd vowed to find as many girls from the Home for Wayward Girls as possible. "She's okay? The Lombardy is acceptable?" Check, check.

"Ha! She's delighted. Never seen a bed that big. Said the hotel is heaven."

"That's great. Asking for anything?"

"Nothing we can't handle. We'll take good care of her. Some of the staff are taking her to dinner tonight."

"Tanya?" Maggie asked. "The Tanya I met out west?"

"Yes, thank you for getting her connected to us. We brought her here for the conference. I haven't even talked with her yet, but I will."

"Lor, do you want me to get you anything?" Annie asked from the doorway. Her gaze was lodged on Loretta—her mentor. She was one of the few people allowed to use Loretta's nickname. Kind of an honor. Annie's mission was to ensure that no one, not a reporter, nor any guest, dared be a nuisance. Which was made more difficult because Loretta never turned anyone away.

"We're good, Annie. Don't worry. Let me know when I should head to the auditorium, okay?" Loretta's hand went to her scarf. She took a moment to check another of her mental to-do lists: messages from Clarke, try to call Elsie for a last-minute hurrah, thank the team, say hello to Tanya in person, rehearse her speech one more time (although she knew she'd end up ad-libbing the way she always did).

"You got it. Plenty of time yet." Annie touched the mole to the left of her lips. She paused. She'd explained to Loretta that it was a habit she'd had for years—not to hide the mole but to keep the memory of her own mother close. These days, it was how she ensured Loretta had time to think. The two of them were so in sync that they knew each other's signals. Loretta's hand on the scarf around her neck meant she was either deep in thought or needed a meeting to end. A slight tilt of Loretta's head let Annie know she was okay. If Loretta shook her head, Annie was to find a reason to stay in the room for an extra minute.

"Plenty of time? But never enough." Loretta gave Annie the grimacing eye stare that they both understood. Loretta usually asked at the end of each day where the hours had gone.

"I know. Anyway, text if you want anything. Or need anything at all." Annie looked like she might laugh out loud. She and Loretta had many late-night talks in their office about the difference between wants and needs.

"I will." Loretta tilted her head and saluted with her cell. Both were indications she had things under control. She was ready to continue with the journalist who sat before her.

"So, you've waited some time for this day?"

Loretta and Maggie had talked by phone. Several times but not in person. Loretta wasn't surprised by the woman's purposely messy brown hair (how do people do that with such perfection? she wondered) or her slick pantsuit (was it black or aubergine? Loretta wasn't sure). Her large leather bag clearly camped out on the floor for the day.

"I have. But I think planned for is a better word than waited."

"This okay? I'll take some notes, too." Maggie pointed to her iPhone on the table between them and clicked an app to record their conversation.

"Yes, no problem."

"Great."

"Everything about today is pretty great." Loretta unbuttoned her blazer and lowered her eyes to the well-worn corduroy fabric. She was nervous even when she was in control. She was aware of the significance of this moment: the destination she'd finally neared; her worst fears not shed but morphed into strengths. Sharing her past with anyone, especially a reporter, although she needed the press, seemed inconsequential to the rest of this day. The ground beneath her feet was finally solid. But there were still hurdles to pass.

"Loretta, you've accomplished a lot in this city. Done so much. Why take on more and why today?"

"It's complicated. Then again, it's not." Loretta set her cup on the table and checked her phone. No message from Clarke. She fiddled with one of the buttons stored inside her pocket. "I guess it's an inevitability. Maybe a need."

"How so?"

"There's a poet I've read. Amy Lowell. Do you know of her?"

"A little."

"She was from near Boston. Lowell was unique. At least, I think she was." Loretta's eyelids were at half-mast assessing the writer. "Lowell said that when the words came to her, she set aside whatever she was doing and wrote the arriving poem. *The arriving poem.* Those were her words. That's how I feel about responsibility. It's not a choice. The French say *devoir*, something that must be acted upon. Responsibility is placed before us. It arrives. We should not consider it a choice. It is our duty."

"Your personal devoir?"

"Something like that."

"This, today? Your first conference. The new center?" Maggie slipped off her own jacket. She wore a silk blouse that had pretty turquoise buttons, which for some reason made Loretta like her better.

"Yes, today. But the announcement is more a culmination for me. Of many efforts. Mine. My team's. You know, we must do things while we can. Amy Lowell died young, 1925. I think she was barely fifty-one. A year later she was awarded the Pulitzer."

"I read that."

"For a poem that arrived for her and so she wrote it." Waves of hair fell to Loretta's shoulders. She raised her head. Sipped her latte and took a bit of time to enjoy a deep breath.

"And this moment?" Maggie waited.

"It has arrived."

Two years before, Loretta had received a certified letter. She was on her way to work. In a hurry—an important meeting was scheduled. Giorgio sat at the lobby counter and reached for an envelope off to the side.

"Ms. Loretta. For you." He smoothed his gold-buttoned coat and raced to hold the door for her. "This came yesterday. Didn't they call you? You need to sign you got it."

Loretta saw green post office paper remains glued to the envelope in his hand. There'd been a message that she'd ignored. Something addressed to her. But she'd been in a hurry.

"Oh, they did call. I forgot. Thank you," she said and winked. Giorgio winked back. He held out a black gel pen.

"I have the lottery tickets." He clasped a hand to his heart.

"Maybe today is the day." She smiled at the kind man, wrote *Lor* quickly on the green card the mailman would need to collect. It was the simple signature she'd used for years. She dropped the envelope into her battered satchel and forgot about it.

Or had she? Did she really not think of it again?

Loretta's satchel was a treasure chest, a safe-deposit box, a go bag. She'd bought it around the time she began her concrete plan to open the foundation. Found it at the thrift store on Seventy-Second Street not far from her subway station. She'd had a list of things she felt she'd need to make her idea a reality. A small team of zealots. Board members who would trust her decisions. Clarke assured her that she didn't have to worry about when she'd been a teen, a minor. What had happened wasn't intentional. He kept an eye out on all things legal for them.

She found an office in her old neighborhood near Union Square. It came with a good-size conference table. She hired a couple savvy tech people to work on what she considered her *aha* game changer, a national database to help families and friends searching for lost relatives. Luckily, she found techies who were more into saving runaways and people living on the streets than designing emojis and making big bucks. That she did not have.

But there were other items, as critical, and possibly more important. She considered these things her personal accoutrements, the determinate items that would be the talismans for her future. Same way she read her Leo horoscope to get advice on what challenges to expect (this morning's had said "Be calm, you'll shine today"), the list contained items that would help when she most needed to have faith in herself.

It had begun years before with a few buttons. The ones she carried to this day.

For her foundation to grow and prosper, she bought new western boots because she was certain she'd spend many hours on her feet (and she wanted to be shit-kicking strong). She had tons of hooks installed inside their bedroom on which to hang scarves of many colors. Not that Loretta was embarrassed by the crooked scar that trailed down her neck.

"I choose not to share it with everyone," she explained to Annie at work.

"I get that," her assistant agreed.

Wearing scarves reminded Loretta of the pain that had been inflicted on her . . . and which served to strengthen her resolve. She bought two pairs of 501 Levi's that were exactly the same. They were her favorites. With her corduroy blazer and then her favorite perfume restocked, her uniform was set. Only her blouses changed day to day. One day rust, or green, navy, cobalt, or powder blue among her favorites. Maybe last, but somewhere in the list of must do's, was therapy.

"Up to you," Clarke told her.

"How can they possibly understand?"

"They can."

"You think I should?"

"Don't you?"

On the same day she started visiting her therapist, Loretta stuck the certified letter into one of her satchel's compartments. It was left unopened. From a town west of the Rockies that Loretta wanted no part of. Loretta didn't think of the certified letter again until another came in the mail a few months later.

TWELVE

West of the Rockies

On Loretta's final afternoon at school, classes were dismissed early to make way for the midday graduation ceremony. The gymnasium was outfitted in blue and gold streamers and balloons. A satin banner pulled out of storage each year hung over the stage declaring, "Congratulations Graduates!" Sweet Mrs. Ore from the office worked with Joel, the janitor with sagging shoulders and deep wise wrinkles, on the room's final touches.

"More to the front, no, no, in the center, let's try to the left." Her arm flew this way and then the other.

"Yes, ma'am," Joel mumbled, happy to move whatever Mrs. Ore wanted, every inch needed. He loved the kids.

Folding chairs were in neat rows in front of and behind the half-court line. Parents had been sent "a limited number of tickets" to make it seem they'd not get a seat otherwise. There'd be plenty of empties. William and Mama would not be in attendance.

At two o'clock, the hand waving and cheering began despite the request to hold applause until the end. Smiling graduates in blue gowns single-filed to the dais the way they'd rehearsed. Loretta's parents hadn't paid for any extras. She wore her plain denim skirt and a clean blouse to the ceremony. But at check-in, Mrs. Ore handed her one of the shiny gowns.

"It's a loaner." She winked, her black hair styled for the occasion, her Easter dress worn special. "Sorry, but you'll have to return it to me later, okay?"

"Sure thing. Thanks!" Loretta figured Ms. Del and Mrs. Ore were in cahoots and she didn't mind. Despite her efforts to appear unaffected by the moment, Loretta found herself excited, nervous, and a bit perplexed by the goings-on.

"Here, take this." Mrs. Ore caught her eye. Seemed she understood Loretta's confusion. She handed her a bobby pin. "For the cap. Tassel to the right. Flip it to the left after you get your diploma!"

When her name was called, Loretta ascended the three stairs that had been rolled near the small wooden stage. She was not well known in town, despite her father's notoriety, but heard a small round of polite applause. Head lowered, she made it to the podium not bothering to make any grand gesture or bow the way more boisterous kids did. The principal placed the crisp diploma in her hand. Some of the graduates were given theirs in blue leatherlike covers their parents paid for, but Loretta didn't care.

This was the moment she'd awaited.

The life-changing second that she'd hold close to her heart because it could not be taken from her. In her shaking hands was the document that confirmed she had graduated. Wherever Loretta went from this day forward, credibility would travel with her. No matter what, she would go to college. That was what graduation offered her, and she didn't give a damn about William or the ranch or how the hell long it might take to get wherever she was going.

"Did it," she tried to yell when she walked across the stage. Her voice was muted, but her fist shot into the air.

"Yay!" she heard someone in the gymnasium yell.

"Go, Loretta!" another called out.

She didn't know who it was, but the cheers were close to a hug. Loretta's grin so large it couldn't be bridled. Hers a smile in which the seeds of pride would someday grow. She'd survived. She'd graduated despite the many, many despites that had sought to block her path.

Ms. Del hovered a few feet from the principal. The delight on her face made up for the lack of Loretta's family sitting in the rows of folding chairs. Ms. Del nodded to her and within that slight simple motion was the promise of a future certain, something Loretta could not yet define but knew awaited her. Ms. Del shook Loretta's hand and held it a moment longer, Loretta was sure, than she did for others, placed her palm on Loretta's back, and pointed her to the few stairs that returned her to the chairs on the gym floor.

"Almost time," Loretta whispered minutes later and threw her cap into the air along with the others. "Next stop, eighteenth birthday in August."

She stood by unsure what to do. Loretta envied students who wore class rings, girls with lacquered long curly hair, and boys who reeked of Aqua Velva menthol aftershave. She watched teens swept into the arms of family. Girlfriends squealed in groups. Fathers thrilled daughters with bouquets of flowers, turquoise bracelets, a few rhinestone tiaras for Lord knows what. Sons received big clasped handshakes and brand-new cowboy hats of real beaver, bullhide, or lightweight straw for summer with twisted colorful leather hatbands. A tall young man showed off a handsewn gun holster with thigh buckles. Loretta thought it inappropriate. She longed to be somewhere, anywhere, far from bullets and the weapons that housed them.

No one raced to hug her. Family wasn't congregated in the rear waiting their chance to give her praise and gifts. A couple students in a hurry to their families paused nearby.

"Congratulations," a girl from science class called to her.

"You, too," Loretta yelled back.

A young man shook her hand, which made her smile at him, although it was a challenging effort on her part. She didn't know these folks.

"Yahoo! See you at the next rodeo," he said and ran off. Loretta knew this was unlikely.

She spun around the room and declared, in her way, that this would be her final scene in the small town she'd never call her own. She wasn't truly from this place—although she wouldn't forget the school or the ranch. Maybe someday she could do something to help girls like herself. But for the time being, Loretta was as sure as the pronghorns that skipped across her prairie that soon she'd be gone.

"Don't give up on your dreams," she heard the math teacher tell Beau Jenkins, one of the more intelligent boys. "Even an associate degree is a good place to start."

"I'll try." Beau shook the math teacher's hand.

Trying, achieving dreams, a high bar in these parts. Ranchers' sons had to ride the land on horses and in mud-splattered pickups. Keep the cattle in check. Baling season was underway, boys putting up hay before summer storms arrived. Too much rain at the end of growing season was not a good thing. Some kind of chemical reaction and wet bales quick become barn fires. These boys would be working the land first thing tomorrow.

Daughters, too, had preordained futures. A few would be out on horses herding cattle, wearing long oil slickers and western hats of their own. Many were more skilled than the boys. In families not blessed with males, girls were the stand-ins. Others would toil in their mamas' kitchens till the right man came asking—a fate not far off—and a true godsend when ranching families could join forces.

Loretta had no plans to stay.

"Loretta!" She heard Ms. Del's teacher-in-charge voice and saw her wave from across the gymnasium. Loretta almost cried but wouldn't give in to it. Wasn't sure why she felt a rise of melancholy in her throat. This was a good day. It was important. She wanted to jump up and down, to cheer for herself, to tell everybody she'd be headed to better plains very soon. Instead, her feet hesitated in the middle of a gym full of folks she'd never see again.

The blue school banner above the open door thirty feet away beckoned to her.

It was time to go. Except . . .

"I found you!" Ms. Del hurried from the free throw line. She raised both her arms and asked, "Hug for your teacher?"

Loretta stumbled into the woman's embrace. Almost caught herself midstep. This was it. Her last day at high school. She held on to Ms. Del longer than she might have intended. A stream of locked-inside tears slid down her cheeks like snow melting on the school bus windows. Loretta wasn't sure if she was more sad or fearful. She was afraid of the many whatevers that awaited her. The diploma in her nervous fingers threatened to fall to the floor. She sniffled, unsure what to do. Hoped she hadn't stained Ms. Del's powder-blue cardigan.

"I'm sorry." Loretta leaned back. She lingered within the scent of her teacher's violet cologne. She could smell pink lotion on Ms. Del's hands.

"Sorry? No, never be sorry for good tears."

"Good tears? How about scared tears?" she asked the teacher who'd had her brown bangs trimmed perfect and wore a new shade of tangerine lipstick for this special day.

"Both." Ms. Del reached inside the purse lodged in the crook of her arm and handed her a tissue from a small pack decorated with ladybugs. "You're gonna be something, Ms. Loretta. I'm as sure of that as I was when I met you a few years ago. I always knew."

"How'd you know?" Loretta couldn't help but ask. She crossed her arms. Plain frightened. Her future was closing in on her. Plans raced through her mind that dared her to accomplish them. She swayed in place, almost dizzy, desperate from the deepest part of her soul to preserve the moment, the state of grace that came from standing face-to-face with the sole good person who had tried to give her safe haven.

"Come on," Ms. Del said, "I'll drive you home. Tell you on the way."

"You don't have to. I'm okay to walk."

"Not on your graduation day. I'm taking you. Got a stop to make."

Loretta had never been in Ms. Del's car before, a Volkswagen Rabbit convertible, but she liked it. Shiny, hot tamale red, a small two-door with its top down. Loretta had only ever ridden in her father's ancient pickup on the seat covered with Bull's brown rottweiler hair and on yellow school buses. She'd never driven. Didn't have a driver's license. To ever put her hands on a steering wheel was a far cry from her reality. A red car seemed a luxury, a convertible almost unheard of in these parts.

"Buckle up!" Ms. Del pointed to the seat belt and Loretta pulled it across her waist same way her teacher did. Something else she'd not done before.

"Nice color." Loretta's stare bounced left-right-left. The cassette player caught her eye. A red and yellow macramé dream catcher hung from the rearview mirror. Ms. Del pushed the knob on the radio. Rick Springfield was singing about wanting Jessie's girl.

"It's an old song. I love it." Ms. Del smiled.

"Where we goin'?" Loretta asked. Wind zipped through her wavy hair. She felt free. If they didn't stop, kept driving, that would be fine by her. Ms. Del sped down the local road.

"You'll see. Now, go ahead," Ms. Del yelled over Joan Jett, who began to sing of loving rock 'n' roll. A song Loretta decided she'd cherish forever.

"Go ahead?"

"Throw your arms in the air. I would but I can't. I'm driving."

Loretta didn't move.

"Me?"

"Who else?"

Loretta glanced around and took a cautious look behind. Doubted he'd be there but couldn't help but check her father's truck wasn't about to run them down. It was an anxiety she'd had through every school grade, and it would be her companion for years to come.

"Yay!" Loretta raised her hands. Then, as if she did it every day, her shoulders bobbed side to side, her palms waved to the sky, and she hummed that she, too, loved rock 'n' roll.

"Yes, yay!" Ms. Del's head bounced with the music. "You deserve it. And I lied. Two stops." Loretta watched her teacher, realized she wasn't that much older than her, maybe a decade or so. She wondered how it was possible she hadn't thought about that before.

A half mile up the road, they pulled into the local Dairy Queen.

"Come on." Ms. Del grabbed her purse from the back seat. "Let's go wild."

In line, Loretta stared at pictures of sundaes and cones. She hadn't ever been to a Dairy Queen.

"Whatever you please." Ms. Del stopped when they reached the window.

"Hey there, folks. Congratulations, I bet you're one of today's graduates." A happy woman winked at them. Her name tag said Tricia. "What can I get cha?"

"You're right, Tricia. This is Loretta. She got her diploma!" Ms. Del jumped in.

"Can I tell you something, Loretta?" Tricia asked.

"Yes." Loretta bit her lip.

"Don't let anyone stop you from your dreams. You got that?"

"I think so." Loretta wondered how the woman had read her mind.

"And pick whatever you want. It's on me."

"Well?" Ms. Del searched Loretta's eyes for an answer.

The world went still. Loretta worried she might again burst into tears. The menu board was filled with stuff she didn't know. Dipped cones, pineapple marshmallow sundaes, freezes and Dilly bars, none of which she'd ever had. In that moment, Loretta realized how ill-prepared she was for what lay ahead. She'd never ordered an ice cream at Dairy Queen, nor been to a restaurant, in a car, or worn a seat belt before this day.

"I don't know," she mumbled. More locked-away tears clouded her amber eyes. She forced her lips shut, the way she'd trained herself for years, focused on tightening her jaw, her best effort not to cry. "I have no idea."

"We'll have two vanilla cones. Dipped," Ms. Del said.

"I got this." Tricia waved away the teacher's money and motioned for them to go to the picnic tables. "I'll bring 'em to ya."

Minutes later, Ms. Del and Loretta sat with ice cream cones in hand. Loretta couldn't believe the glorious taste of cold soft serve and became invested in not losing a drop. Pieces of the hardened chocolate melted in her mouth.

"This is amazing," she said. "I've never had anything this good."

"You're what's good." The teacher shook her head. Loretta watched her teacher's lips smush together. Not hard like Loretta's did—it was how her teacher showed she was thinking before she said something. Same when she was in the classroom and a student gave an obtuse answer. The teacher's eyes darted over Loretta's head and far across the prairie toward the mountains in the distance.

"What's wrong?" Loretta stopped slurping to ask. "You okay?"

"Of course. I'm fine. It's you I worry about."

"Oh, please don't. I'll be all right. I'm sure of it." Loretta wasn't sure, not quite, yet these were her troubles to solve, to live with, and no one else's. Ms. Del had already done more for her than anyone else.

"You did what I said? With my number?"

"Burned into my memory. Call collect. I'll remember. Thank you." Loretta's voice was very quiet, her stare on the ground. She chanted the number and finished with -3026.

"Remember that I meant it." Ms. Del's eyes jumped about, and her head bobbed until her gaze could lock on Loretta's. "Call me. For anything. Really."

"I will." Loretta bit her lip. She saw little kid feet in sneakers run by her. Followed by shrieks of laughter from a child who chased from behind.

"You know"—Ms. Del's mouth crunched the edge of her cone—"when I came to this town, I never planned to stay."

"From where?" Loretta suddenly wondered about the stuff

she didn't know, had never asked her teacher, and that she might not have the chance to learn.

"Back east. I've told you that, haven't I? Well, maybe not. From Maryland. My father was a teacher."

"What happened?" Loretta asked. "I mean, you're still here." Loretta waved her free hand at the road, the prairie, the mountains.

"I came for a summer teaching job. Ten years ago. Wanted an experience far from home. I needed something different." Ms. Del handed her a napkin. "Around your mouth," she said, pointing.

"Oh, gosh." Loretta wiped her lips.

"You got it." They laughed.

"Anyway, the school made an offer. I liked the prairie lands. My father never understood how I could leave the East Coast, the Atlantic, crab cakes." She raised her eyebrows and grinned. "But the outdoors got me. I hike, you know?"

"I didn't." Loretta felt the return of the tears that had been shoved back into the closet behind her eyes. For a moment, she regretted her intention to run from this town, that she might never see her teacher again. Sitting at the picnic table near families felt good, kids racing in circles with ice cream mustaches, mothers holding babies. The Dairy Queen speakers blasted Toby Keith singing about wanting to be a cowboy. She watched Ms. Del's face. Wished the teacher had been her aunt or cousin and that she'd spent many summer days talking with her like this.

"So I stayed. Figured there had to be a reason."

"Was there?"

"I believe so." Ms. Del reached for Loretta's hand and pulled her to her feet. "Come on, one more stop."

They drove a few miles from town. On the radio, Faith Hill sang about a wild girl. The car hurried past ranches with herds of cattle huddled close to one another, sides to sides, best friend steers. Loretta marveled at how cows could have so much prairie to wander but they stayed clustered together. Again, one young calf had wandered off. Out of nowhere a guy on a horse rode in, no commotion, but next thing the calf sauntered back to its family. Like it had been taking a break. Such caring between ranchers and their animals. Loretta was befuddled by why she suddenly felt sad about leaving.

The sun traveled close to due west. Loretta needed to be back at the house soon, but she didn't want to mention it. The thought of saying anything, of asking Ms. Del to turn the car a different direction, felt like opening the door to the misfortunate reality that was her life.

Instead, she again locked her lips one to the other, contemplated nothing, and gave thanks she had a teacher who cared, who gave a shit about her, who could be many other places on this fine sunny late afternoon but chose to be with her.

"Glorious, isn't it?" Ms. Del smiled, raised an arm, and waved her hand at the roadside ranchlands. Her bracelet jingled and Loretta watched the charms swing this way, then that. A big green John Deere loaded with bales of hay honked a hello. Low mountains far off near the horizon appeared within reach, although they weren't, not close, not hardly.

"I guess so," Loretta said. Her feelings mixed. Glorious to be with her teacher, to have wanderlust stir in her soul, to see an open road. But freedom wasn't hers. At least, not yet.

"Wait," Ms. Del whispered with a chuckle nestled within her voice.

The car made a quick left down a dirt road with wide-open rusted gates. Didn't seem they'd been closed in a long time. No signs warning off trespassers. On either side of the car, the prairie offered early summer blossoms—exclamation marks of color that rustled in the breeze.

"Wow," Loretta whispered.

"Bluebells. Some bloom yellow here. That's unique. In another month, this will be a carpet of Monet watercolors."

Loretta grabbed the windshield frame. Lifted herself up from her seat for a second. She wanted to be on the land—to run her fingers through the leafy green stems and flowers. Her hair rustled with the wind and it struck her that this was it, this was the moment she'd needed, the very second on the clock when she felt 100 percent certain of both the present and the future.

"You happy?" Ms. Del asked.

"More than." Loretta was sure of this. She was close to delirious because she was going to get out of this town, away from her father, the Home, and take this near staggering feeling of flowers rustling in the breezes with her. She was as sure as Joan Jett loving rock 'n' roll.

Ms. Del parked near a small sand-colored adobe not visible from the road. Prairie grass mingled with dust outside. The arched doorway could have been in one of the books Loretta had read about mythological warriors like her favorite, Boadicea. Who knew what waited within? It was hard not to jump out of the car and race inside.

"Come on." Ms. Del undid her seat belt. "Follow me."

The adobe was unlocked.

"What is this place?" Loretta asked.

"A chapel. Been around a long time. Door's always open. I've never seen anyone out here." The teacher led her into a small room with a dirt floor. A wrought-iron stand of red glass votive candles stood against ragged walls. A lone cross and kneeler rested by square window shutters open to the far-off mountains.

"Whose is it?" she asked.

"Some kind of land grant," Ms. Del said. "I think there's a plan for restoration. In the future. It's historic. But for now, I needed to show you."

"Why?" The question popped out of Loretta's mouth.

"I'm not sure," Ms. Del said. "I guess I wanted you to know there are safe places nestled out of sight. Some empty. Others where people try to help. You'll find yours, Loretta."

"I sure hope so. By the way, I wondered . . ." Loretta paused.

"What?"

"The *A* on your bracelet? What's it stand for?" Loretta asked, afraid she might not get another chance.

"Oh, that." Ms. Del brushed her bangs to one side. They walked to the car, took a last deep stare at the prairie flowers about to bloom in stellar blues and yellows. "My mother gave it to me. When I was unsure if I should stay here."

"Uh-huh." Loretta waited. She knew Ms. Del well enough to know that in a few seconds there'd be more to the story.

"She quoted Amelia Earhart when she gave it to me. Can you imagine?" The teacher shook her wrist. The charms clinked against one another. The smell of her pink hand lotion drifted in the air.

"And?" Of course, Loretta could imagine. Although this piece of information about her teacher's mother was the more awesome revelation—she now knew where her teacher got her quoting skills from.

"The *A* was to remind me that Amelia, brave soul she was, said that the most difficult thing is the decision to act, that the rest is merely tenacity."

"What does that mean?" Loretta swirled 'round, basking in

the late-day orange and yellow sun that streaked across the big sky she still considered her own.

"Well, the charm has to do with making the decision to act." The teacher lifted the A from her bracelet. "My mom always said decisions matter. Like the one I made to come here. And I think Amelia Earhart meant that once you make a clear decision and put it in motion, then you'll get where you're going if you stick to your plan."

"Like a flight plan?"

"Yes, Loretta. Exactly like that."

Loretta's father greeted her return from graduation with words that were a warning.

"Kind of late, aren't you?"

"Went longer than I thought," Loretta said, eyes to the kitchen floor. Dinner dishes already put away. No food saved for her. She didn't mention she'd been with Ms. Del. Couldn't risk implicating her teacher. She knew better.

William grabbed his slicker from the hook by the door, settled his thick arms into the sleeves, shook his big shoulders, could have been a dog shaking off rainwater.

"Pride goes before destruction," he declared. Proverbs from the wannabe preacher. Those words of his—the manner in which he bird-dropped messages. He opened the door but first tipped his black western hat her direction. The act in and of itself was ominous. His stare darted across the kitchen and dared her to respond.

"But patience is better than pride." She quoted Ecclesiastes in her own quiet but *don't fuck with me* voice. She had read the Bible, too.

"Careful there, girl," Mama warned from her chair by the

potbellied stove, the few words she would offer. The rancher's wife who had no authority or power.

"Right." Loretta hurried upstairs to her room. She wanted to add, "Win the battle or perish, that is what I, a woman, will do." It wasn't from the Bible but a quote from the Celtic warrior, a woman with hair that blazed like a sunset on fire.

THIRTEEN
New York City

"You said no one ever visited you at home?" Maggie asked and shifted on the couch. The way she moved, straightened her blouse, and leaned forward, she created a hesitant pause that allowed them the chance to breathe, time to get more comfortable with each other.

Not that Loretta was put at ease. Being scrutinized about events in the past elicited a physical response from her. She raised a hand to the scarf that covered her scarred neck. As if it were a fresh cut, the old wound began to itch; it could still be scabbed although it wasn't. Her scar beneath the silk material was ever present.

"You mean the ranch? No. Never." Loretta hadn't used the word *home* regarding William and Mama's house maybe ever. She believed that the constants of the equation that added up to home were both *care of* and *longing for*. She'd had neither.

"Did you find it odd that you didn't have any relatives?" Maggie's eyebrows raised. Her lips pursed. It was hard to tell if her stare was as sincere as it seemed or she was simply well practiced at being patient. "Didn't the phone ring? Did you answer it? Christmas cards? Mail?"

"No. I didn't know to think it odd. Phone calls, mail? Nope." She had longed for mail. There had been the pink letter that she didn't get to read, that she held for too quick a second.

"So no long-lost relatives ever showed up?"

"You know, it wasn't that there were and then there weren't. Relatives, I mean. There were two people. William and Mama. And residents who came for a spell, and then they were gone." Loretta used to think the girls were new sisters, friends, until the realization set in that they would be allowed to leave, and she'd be left behind. "It was a state of being. Hard to explain. It's not that questions aren't allowed when you lived the way I did. They don't exist."

"They don't?"

"Isolation; it's not something a child, or I at least, ever considered. It just was. It reinforces itself. You don't know the questions to ask. Or you know better than to open your mouth." Loretta's hand drifted back to her lap, but then she again reached to her scarf, to memories of when she was that girl on the ranch.

"Did you ever? Try to ask, I mean?"

"Think about your own childhood," Loretta said in a kind voice. "Did you ask questions when you were a girl about why you lived however you lived? Probably not, right?"

"Okay, I get that," Maggie agreed. "I lived here. City schools. What some would call pretty normal. I guess I'm trying to understand where your strength came from. Your story is really something. It can help others, you know? Did you know it wasn't okay—the way you lived?"

"Here's the thing." Loretta paused. She had serious beliefs about how people like William created worlds that entrap young people. "You have to have a concept of what normal is to understand what you're missing. That your life isn't what others have. People like William make you believe in their sort of normal. But then I started to know. I have to tell you, I'm not sure which was worse. Not knowing or realizing how very trapped I was."

Loretta was perplexed by how her childhood had given her strength. Were dire circumstances a requirement to become strong? Is it a win-or-lose proposition? She thought of women on the streets. The people Compass served. Helen from Baton Rouge who drank. Eva from St. Louis whose facial wounds were not pretty. Women who hadn't become stronger. Those who were battered and left on sidewalks, under bridges, and in subway stairwells.

"Excuse me." Annie pushed open the squeaky meeting room door. It needed WD-40. Annie was a welcome interruption. Loretta arched against the couch. Cracked her neck side to side. Closed her eyes for a second.

"Hi there." Loretta sat up, shifted to her softer voice, her not-business tone. For someone so often on a dais or in negotiations for funding, she was comforted by the presence of her team—the people with whom she could relax. They knew her. She knew them.

"Hey, how's everything?" Annie waved her phone in the air. "Any messages?"

"Oh, wait, let me check." Loretta grabbed her mobile and motioned to the journalist. "Sorry."

"Sure, of course." Maggie reached for her own.

"No, nothing." Loretta stared at the blank screen. Bit her lip, calculating hours passed and time zones in her head. "How's the conference going? Almost lunchtime?" Her stomach made a nervous lurch with each footstep she heard pass the doorway. Loretta had secret mantras she recited when anxiety threatened to overcome her. But today she expected to pack her worries into storage for good. This day was to be different.

"It's amazing out there." Annie pointed down the hall. "As you planned."

"As *we* planned." Loretta stuck her phone next to her thigh. Screen right side up. Reminded herself to stay calm. Today would be an incredible event for young women and the many female elders gathered in the large hall. Organizations at tables in the foyer offered assistance. Volunteer professionals were available with employment advice, psychological counseling, and resources. Women doing for women. No more total reliance on others. Women learning to accept help, to take accountability, and to believe that doing for themselves was a good thing.

"You have an hour or so. I can bring salad in. Sandwiches?"

"Water. Fizzy would be super. I can't eat." Loretta turned to Maggie. "But you go ahead. Are you hungry?" she asked.

"No, I'm fine. But, yes, sparkling or flat. Doesn't matter. I'd love some."

Loretta tilted her head. Annie saluted with her cell.

"Got it, Lor."

"I appreciate you."

"I know you do." Annie's eyes paused, zoomed to Loretta's, a virtual hug. "I'll have that water in a flash."

"Give me one second—" Loretta jumped up and hurried into the hallway behind Annie.

"What's up?" Annie was waiting.

"I'm nervous. I'm a wreck." Loretta leaned against the hallway wall. She took a few deep breaths.

"I can intercede. Take Maggie to meet other people. You're doing so much today."

"No, I'm okay. I just needed a minute."

"Me, too." Annie offered what Loretta called her smile of

commiseration—they both had one. It was a grin that accepted that they could only do so much.

"All right. I've got this."

Loretta took another breath. Closed her eyes for a second before she marched herself back into the meeting room.

"Sorry, sorry. Where were we?" She returned to the couch.

"You were talking about isolation?" Maggie pushed her phone app to record and set it again on the coffee table.

"It's hard to explain."

"Try me."

"I think—" Loretta wondered what it was exactly she wanted to say. She was careful when she spoke to reporters or people in the public forum. "Well, you'll find I think about ideas, constructs a lot. It's a thing for me."

"Tell me more."

"Isolating women, especially in some states in this country, is very acceptable. It's a box. A compartment."

"In what way?"

"Once a construct is touted often enough, we can be fooled to believe it has value. It's used for so-called wayward girls or miscreant teens. For anyone someone with power wants to control."

"So what do we do?"

"The constructs need to be dismantled. Sooner rather than later."

There had been a student in Loretta's class with Ms. Del. His name was Terrance. He'd been quiet, slight, far from a strong ranch-hand sort. He used lots of big words. Pretty words. One day he didn't show up for class. Loretta never saw him again. Today, she could think of three possibilities. She hoped it was the third.

"And your work helps, doesn't it?" Maggie pushed her hair

away from her face as she moved forward to the edge of the couch. Her eyes paid close attention.

"We're a Band-Aid. That's all. We do what we can. The women I've met on the streets . . ." Loretta shook her head. She had to be sure what she said was understood. "I guess survival is like winning the lottery."

"To what do you attribute your survival?" Maggie touched one of the pretty turquoise buttons on her blouse and let Loretta breathe a bit longer.

"Well, for one thing, I learned to read maps early. How to use a compass. Lucky for me. It's important. I hope kids do that today."

"Maps and a compass? That's your magic trick?" The writer cocked an eyebrow and waited for more.

"Absolutely. That's why we have our name." Loretta reached for her corduroy jacket. Her burgundy nails glimmered. She felt inside a pocket. Found her own treasures. A few buttons. The metal compass she'd stolen from the Guns & Ammo when she was a teen. "A compass. It's such a wow. The arrow always points north. It's a godsend."

"Today's kids. God forbid the GPS goes out."

"Well, that is a dilemma." Loretta laughed. She thought of long, tall Drew whom she'd hitchhiked with for a time. His slow, cool words. His I'm-in-awe reaction to her compass. "I'd say that my true lot in life might never have unfolded if I hadn't been able to read a map."

The door squeaked again. Annie slipped in with LaCroix. "It's lemon. Hope that's okay." She set two glasses with the college's purple-and-gold emblem on the table.

"Great," both women said and smiled at the synergy of their responses. They listened to the fizzy gasp when Annie opened the bottle.

Loretta's childhood hadn't been normal. So far from it that even being asked to try and recall her past tied her stomach in a big double knot, burrowed her shoulders tight into her chest, and tears formed before she had the chance to remember a single moment. Sometimes she took long walks in the park, by herself—imagined herself stretched out on her and Clarke's living room floor, arms above her head, stretching, stretching away her tension and her pain. Other times, she lay on their couch, pulled her knees to her chest, and tried to focus on HBO or Showtime, on any movie that might wash away her thoughts. But that didn't work.

When she was in elementary school, she hadn't had any friends. None.

"I had no one," she told Clarke.

"Didn't anyone sit by you on the bus? Or at lunch?"

"No. And today I've got to ask *why is that?*" She stared at him but knew he couldn't answer for her. "How the hell could I have been so alone?"

"I don't know." Clarke sat down next to her. He held her hand. Nothing more. Just sat and waited in quiet.

"I think it was like seventh grade when I began with the maps."

"The Rand McNallys?"

"No. Not real maps. I think I created maps in my head. What a kid's life was supposed to look like."

"What do you mean?"

"One time, I was outside the school's front door. I have no idea why. A mother drove up in a Ford Explorer. I remember that. I'd never seen one before. All I knew was trucks. She jumped out of the car and ran past me with a paper bag in her hand."

"Okay—"

"She laughed, in a nice way, and said 'Jim Junior forgot his lunch' and then she flew inside."

"Okay—"

"That's it. My big important memory. But I knew then that my map wasn't anything like that kid's. No mom ever parked in front of school to run inside with anything for me."

"Right."

"There's a bunch of kinds of maps," Loretta announced. "Maps that lead girls God knows where."

It took counseling and long discussions and eruptions of anger (and screaming and meltdowns) for Loretta to learn to separate those years on the ranch from who she'd become in New York. She was successful, she had achievements, she overcame her childhood, yet William's voice had simply migrated to a space within the ranch girl's head she brought with her.

You some kind of whore? Those words the hardest to hide from.

She learned in the city that she was one of many with pasts like her own. Especially those on streets, hidden, forgotten, and abused who lived among *the others* who are, in fact, *the many.*

"You know," she'd told Annie during a late-night discussion before the conference, "if the many formed a line, it would stretch across the country and loop all the way back to Lady Liberty herself."

"So we're going to cut in line? Or stop it altogether?" Annie had her leather journal open. She took meticulous notes during their after-work talks accompanied by a cup of tea or a scotch on the rocks, depending on how challenging the day had been. Annie was strong, organized, and reminded Loretta of girls on the ranch who'd been hell-bent on escape. Once Annie told her how, after her mother died, it wasn't that her father didn't care, he just vacated the premises. Went and found a new wife. Got busy with new wife stuff. Annie said she took off and rarely looked back.

"We're going to change the game." Loretta rubbed her temples. In the midst of a late evening yawn, her eyes were excited. "We're going to surprise everyone. You know, I've had unexpected good fortune in my life. Some experiences that I don't yet fully understand. But others that changed everything. Everything. Sure, I worry, get kind of crazy anxious."

"I know." Annie nodded. She had found yoga and her own kind of calm.

"But I'm working on it."

A blurred hodgepodge of pictures from the past sifted through Loretta's mind at some point every day or so. It was not unlike how walking down a set of stairs is mostly easy or rote. Except not always. A month ago, Loretta caught herself midstep before a fall might have occurred in a subway stairwell. She'd hurried out startled. Deep breaths ensued. Big gulp inhales. She stopped by a Starbucks, leaned against the wall, her satchel dropped to the sidewalk.

"I'm okay," she had whispered, the words more a cough, her lungs trying but her breathing so fast she fell over in pain.

"Ma'am . . ." A young woman on a Domino's delivery bike hurried to her. "Do you need help?"

"I don't know." Loretta, hand to her heart, recalled the instructions from her therapist. *Breathe. Go over your list. Breathe.*

"My bag, oh my God, where's my bag?"

"Right here, don't worry." The lady in a royal blue shirt with a red collar embroidered with the name GEORGIA reached to the ground and held up Loretta's satchel midair.

Loretta's breaths shifted from gulps to a more measured

pace. She began to recite, "Got my satchel. Check. Got my phone. Check." She smiled at Georgia.

"Anxiety, huh? I get it."

"Yes, how'd you know?"

"You aren't the only one. You carry Xanax?"

"I do. But I try breathing first. Thank you, Georgia. Nice name." Loretta nodded at the embroidery.

"Time for me to split. You take it easier on yourself, okay?" The woman slapped the insulated pack of pizzas on her bike before she took off zipping in and out of cars on the street.

"Got my satchel. Check. Got my phone. Check. I'm safe. I'm good," Loretta listed again. No bones broken, she was grateful a rush of strangers hadn't been needed to call 911.

"Elsie"—she had called her best friend while hurrying away—"it's happening more. The panic."

"You okay, Loretta girl?"

"I don't know." She repeated what she'd said to the Domino's lady.

"Talk to your therapist. Be honest. Tell her. Try not to be so damn strong."

"Not?" Loretta halted in front of Le Pain Quotidien and considered canceling her appointment at an office up ahead. Shrimp salad with mango and avocado beckoned.

"Being strong isn't helping you, my friend. Cut yourself some slack."

"Hmm. Slack would be a blessing. I'll try. Thanks, my wise best friend."

"Praise be," Elsie said. They laughed at words only they ever shared. Loretta could imagine the freckles across her friend's nose, her hair so light that gray was going to be an easy transition.

"No laughter ever?" her concerned therapist asked. Perhaps she hoped a hidden recollection would emerge. Any good experience Loretta might discover.

"Not when I was a child," Loretta repeated. "Occasionally with the girls in the bunkhouse. But never with William and Mama."

"That's such a sad existence."

"Not being loved was sadder."

"Maybe something will come to you." The therapist left the question hanging.

Only more blurred pictures layered themselves within Loretta's days and the images scared her. Their lack of color. The memories she didn't have. No photos of birthday cakes with candles. Never a pretty hair ribbon. Her father hadn't ever lifted her off the ground or swung her into the sky. She couldn't remember any laughter in the house with William and Mama, not on the big sky ranch that had been her childhood prison.

Loretta's phone flashed. A message box popped onto the screen from Clarke. If her volume weren't muted, she'd have heard the slow-slow quick-quick-quick elongated chirp of a falcon. The yearning squawk such a lament, a worried parent on surveillance duty or hunting for gulls and bats to capture midair. Good parents— not like hers.

Call read Clarke's text. He was a great trial lawyer, but sure wasn't big on words in his messages.

"Excuse me." She again held up her palm to Maggie, who gave a slow nod, the two of them now in sync with each other. They'd established trust. Loretta stood and with no privacy available, she fled to the hallway.

"Loretta?" Clarke answered almost before it rang.

"Yes, tell me." She squeezed the phone closer to her ear as if that confirmed the urgency of the conversation. Heel against the wall, head down, her hair curtaining her from conference attendees.

"I'm still waiting," he said.

"But?"

"Breathe, Lor."

"I am."

"They gave him three days. He was supposed to turn himself in by yesterday. Except he didn't."

"And?"

"They are sending deputies to the ranch right this minute. To pick him up. It's early there, remember? I asked the sheriff. He promised to call the moment they have him."

"I have to know he's in custody."

"You will. I'll have an update soon. Promise." Clarke became silent. Loretta, too. Neither hung up, a way of being with each other that made them the couple they were. They could easily have been across from each other at a table in their favorite diner. Their shared pause was as good as holding hands.

Her therapist had asked about any good cheer in the household. Had her school pictures been taped to the refrigerator, were there Christmas rituals, did her report cards merit any rewards? The answer was no. Within Loretta's miserable existence, her happiest moments were when she was banished to a log beyond the prairie. Banishment an ironic gift. Sent to where she could read a book in the wild, be with nature near rocks and dried bush in the prairie with mountains beyond. Once a run-in with a wolf. She'd jumped up and down. It sauntered off. Scared her much more than she scared it.

Still, Loretta was tenacious when given a task. The therapist asked her to try to remember any less than awful moments on the ranch. Somehow this was supposed to help her. Except she had no fairy-tale gossamers in which to wrap her story. But, then again, maybe there had been, when Loretta concentrated deeply, and her brain hardened and ached with the many coulda's and shoulda's—

The months before her escape had been painful. Brutal. There had been little winces of time when face-to-face with the father who thought he owned her, or when locked inside her bedroom, she curled into herself with fear. Held her green army blanket to her mouth to muffle her staggered breaths—certain her gasps would warrant more punishment.

More.

Loretta came to believe that it is in the more, the much more, and the more so that one finds their personal truth and perhaps absolution. Similar to how happiness is only possible when there's been sadness. It took days and months and more to carpet over her traumas, which were vacuumed and resuscitated again and again.

There had been a day one summer between elementary school and high school. Some residents had gone home, and the ranch was empty. William was angry every morning. He complained about the loss of income. He and Mama expected Loretta to do the chores herself—gather eggs from the chickens, clean the coop, feed the bunnies, dig up vegetables, and help Mama with the house. She wore her blue T-shirt and denim skirt.

"What you lookin' at?" William trekked in from the prairie. Rifle slung over his shoulder. He'd gone hunting for a wolf that dared terrorize local ranchers.

"Nothin'," Loretta said, scared. She'd taken a break to stare at the mountains, to dream about whatever was on the other side. However, taking breaks wasn't allowed.

"Stop that." He pointed to her boot. Her toe took nervous stabs at the hardened mud beneath her foot.

"Yes, sir." She froze in place. His presence a cause for concern. He stood too close. It would be like him to lean over, glare, hit her upside the face.

"That's more than mud," he said. Solemn. His eyes on the ground, not on her. "It's layers of earth. Slabs settled on top of slabs. Millions of years right there under your sole."

"Yes, sir." She hadn't known what to say.

"Get back to your chores." William jerked his chin in her direction. Turned away. Returned to his usual self and muttered, "Worthless dirt. This ranch a waste."

Suddenly, so many years later, in New York City, Loretta could hear his voice. *That's more than mud.* She, too, was more than that scared girl. She was of that earth. *Slabs settled on top of slabs.* She was of the prairie west of the Rockies. This was her fuel. It was her energy.

Her therapist said, "Find a memory to replace all the others."

The next week at her session, Loretta wept. She'd cried small tears before but on this day it was more. Her own much more. A letting go, a scream, a cry of self-forgiveness. A recognition that she'd never meant to hurt her mother. Never meant to grab the rifle. Except it was there. Waiting in the corner by the door. And she'd had no choice.

FOURTEEN
West of the Rockies

The ranch was quiet, almost too much so, after graduation. Elsie's isolation had ended quickly. Loretta hoped William had truly backed off. Days later, the girls were busy at Mama's house doing chores. Loretta took the chance to roam around the prairie. William was off in town doing whatever it was he did there. Loretta was caught in a whirlwind of emotions, at one moment ready to sprint and the next committed not only to Elsie, and staying until she was eighteen, but to each of the girls in the bunkhouse.

"Hey, Loretta, what are you doing?"

It was little Crystal.

"What are *you* doing?" Loretta asked in return. She stood by the chicken coop smoking one of the few cigarettes she had left in a pack someone had dropped outside the G&A. She felt pretty cool, almost stronger-taller-braver than anyone else with her cigarette in hand, a slow stream of smoke floating into the sky, which she hoped might lead to the answers she needed.

"Mama sent me to bring in eggs. Don't know why me. I'd rather stay here with you."

"Let's take a walk."

"Should we? Is it okay?"

"You know, Crystal, I have no idea what is okay, or what isn't. Truth is, I'm tired of trying to figure that out." Loretta ground her cigarette with her boot and stuck her hands in the pockets of her army fatigue jacket. "Come on, just for a few minutes."

"Yes. I say yes. Let's go."

The two of them took a few steps, Crystal checked twice behind before Loretta said, "No one's watchin' us," and they both laughed not because it was funny but because they could. They walked southwest to where the ranch prairie was framed by the more dense lodgepole pines, rocks, and trails that led into the backcountry.

"This is that place, isn't it?" Crystal asked.

"What place?"

"Where you and Elsie talk about. Where you'll run to." Crystal stood still. She was barely past childhood, only thirteen, with hair that yearned for ribbons and bows, the look on her face a youngster's beg for an answer.

"Yes." Loretta saw no reason to lie. Crystal knowing where they'd run seemed a small concession. "We'll head this way."

"Tanya told me something. Made me kinda nervous."

"What?"

"Said she's going the same direction when she can. That whatever Loretta does is good enough for her."

"Don't worry. I'll talk to her. Give her some advice."

"Where will you go?"

"I'm not sure." Loretta sat herself on a rock. Her feet tapped the ground. "That's the thing about running away."

"What's the thing?"

"It's that you don't know. You can't really be sure. You can try to get someplace, but then find yourself somewhere entirely different. Does that make sense?"

"When my daddy found me and that neighbor boy"—Crystal sat herself on a rock nearby, settled her skirt around her—"I was so scared."

"I bet you were."

"I'm never scared with you, Loretta."

"With me?"

"You know, Loretta, I'd do anything you said. Anything."

"Why? I'm no expert. I'm just like you."

"No, you're not. You're going to get out of here." Crystal kicked her feet when she made this declaration.

"Okay."

"And that's powerful."

"Powerful?" Loretta hoped this was the case, hoped this bright young teen was right.

"It is to me."

"You'll get out, too, Crystal."

"How?"

"Keep your head down. Stay near Mama. I know she can be awful but she's not him. Stay away from William. I been through this before. Your parents will come pick you up soon. Probably before school starts in September. Happens every year. Parents all of a sudden decide they want their girls back. Trust me. Go on. Get those eggs and take them to Mama. You hear me?"

"I always listen to you, Loretta." Crystal smiled like they were saying goodbye, even though it wasn't yet upon them. She ran to the chicken coop. Turned back and yelled, "Always."

"I know." Loretta gave a thumbs-up and smiled, not ready to go.

Alone, Loretta stayed a small while longer and watched big furry clouds lounge past in the sky. She listened to the calls and whistles of birds overhead. The prairie was, as ever, a quiet place. Any excitement was a gift of nature—thunder, a flash of lightning that cracks the sky in two and in its own magical way stops people midstep. Storms cause the sagebrush and the many critters nestled within to become silent; even the whirl of the wind slows as ranchers and their families urge animals into their barns for safekeeping. Sometimes a dog's bark echoes across the land, the birdsong withers, and inside each storm is heard the prairie's sad bugle call.

About to kick the ground, dig a heel in, Loretta stopped. She'd miss the safe resting stones where she had sat and pondered and wondered and found no answers. She had more often than not discovered that peace descended near the lodgepole pines, one of nature's gifts, and that peace might not hold answers, but it allowed for questions. Her questions.

Loretta walked back along the trail that led to Mama's house. The afternoon sun was already dipping. The light of day declaring itself near over. With her hands in her pockets, she trudged up the stairs to the kitchen. Mama was inside waving her towel this way, then that. Gayle stood at the table with forks and knives in hand. Crystal was setting out the dishes. Loretta caught Elsie's eye when her friend glanced up from peeling potatoes. The two of them nodded, a weird but wonderful transfer of friend energy.

"Hey," Tanya said.

"Mama, okay Tanya and I go check the hutches are latched?"

"Why wouldn't they be?" Mama swirled around, her wrinkled face filled with suspicion.

"Some wind's kicking up. Just want to be sure."

"Okay, do it fast. Five minutes. Got it? Five minutes!"

"Sure thing."

Tanya and Loretta hurried out the door, down the few steps, took a left to the rabbits.

"To check the hutches are latched?" Tanya began to laugh.

"I know. Kinda lame, right?"

"Yes!"

"Listen, I wanted to talk with you, Tanya. Alone."

"Okay. What's up?"

"Girl, I see how you memorize the stuff I tell you, about the trails, the wolves."

"I have to. I need to get out of here." Tanya didn't look scared. Loretta hadn't noticed before how brave the girl's maple brown eyes were, that when she stood tall and crossed her arms, as she did just then, she sure seemed strong.

"But I got to warn you. You being only sixteen, going now would be a mistake."

"You sure? Are you sure, Loretta? I know what you're planning. Can't I go with you?"

"Oh, damn, Tanya. Don't I wish?" Loretta swiped at her own eyes, afraid of the small tears that were forming. "We'd get caught so fast. And then it would be even worse for you."

"I guess I know that."

"If you were at least seventeen, then maybe."

"I will be, come winter."

"Promise me, until then at least, try to stay on. It will be better for you. And gosh, Tanya, the other girls, Crystal, Gayle, you being the oldest after me and Elsie, they'll need you."

"So, you are going, aren't you? You and Elsie?"

"Got no choice."

"Then you make *me* a promise."

"Sure, what?" Loretta bobbed her head yes, hoping she could do whatever was asked.

"Promise me you'll run far and—"

"And what?"

"That you'll never forget me."

FIFTEEN

New York City

Maggie clasped her hands in front of her lips. She leaned very far forward from the hard gray couch cushions in the college meeting room, her head gooselike above the small coffee table, her half-moon earrings, perhaps silver scales, swaying to and fro. She appeared to linger within a thought and brushed a strand of hair away from her serious stare. Loretta wondered if she was reconsidering a question.

Loretta, in turn, almost shifted farther back but thought better of it. If she didn't trust now, when would she? She took a second to check her phone even though she'd have seen if a text, *if the one text she desperately awaited*, had been delivered to her screen. She placed the cell by her thigh, ran her hands over the knees of her Levi's, and watched Maggie straighten her blouse before arching inches closer as if to share a critical secret. Except the secrets belonged to Loretta.

"Time for some tougher questions. Is that okay?" Maggie asked. Her silver earrings stopped swinging.

"Yes, of course." Loretta nodded. She'd exercised the muscles that protected her memories, done what Elsie told her—opened up about her panic and anxieties to her therapist, had shadow-boxed with her fears. She was prepared for the awkwardness, for the bloodletting certain to occur when revelations arose from the ashes of her past. Reminded herself that she was the one who wanted her story told, to help others, and to free herself.

She'd known this day would come.

"Exculpatory moments," her husband, the ever-calm lawyer in his breathable Adidas sweats, unnecessary because he never sweat, had counseled her the evening before. They'd sat near their tall windows and stared at the light show offered by the sky-high buildings beyond their co-op.

Exculpatory: tending to clear from a charge of fault or guilt.

"The charges were dropped," he reminded her. "It's clear. Passes a legal hurdle—but for. But for that dog, the incident would not have happened. Might be a bit of a stretch using 'but for.' Except in your case, it works."

"Yes." Loretta agreed in theory. She'd changed from work clothes to her favorite leggings, a soft fleece top, and thick cable-knit socks, which comforted her tired feet. "Exculpatory. But for. Got it."

"It's akin to the idea of grace," Clarke continued. "We are given the chance to be cleansed from unwarranted recrimination over things in the past. Despite how guilty we may feel, false cul-pability is not ours to cradle to the grave."

Cleanse: to rid of impurities, to wash.

"Yet . . . I'll be asked about it. I have to be honest." Loretta had never been 100 percent convinced by Clarke's legal arguments—guilt had a way of doing that. She scratched her neck, ruffled her hair, wondered if maybe she should have it cut short, shook her head back to seriousness—trying as one might to loosen sugar too long stored in a jar.

"The facts. No more. Don't pile on yourself. Don't bring up what-ifs—things that didn't occur. Remember we are all human," Clarke told Loretta, his most valued jury. "And shit happens. *We aren't always to blame. We are allowed to be cleared. Everyone is.*"

"Everyone?" she asked.

"Yes, no matter what you feel. You were seventeen. You were cleared. The first and second certified letter confirmed it." Clarke shook his head at her, still a tiny bit cross about that. "Remember? The letter you ignored."

"Okay, okay. I know that was stupid of me." Loretta hated unexpected mail. She ignored it if she could. Thankfully her lawyer husband had picked up the second letter.

"Right. And don't go giving in to that weakness of yours."

"What weakness?"

"Your unfailing ability to grant others a reprieve but not yourself. You're allowed to be cleared. Even you, Loretta."

Allowed. Allowance: to grant as one's right. Loretta did her best to hold on to these words during the interview although her mind stored anger and anxiety.

"Loretta, I want to be honest with you." Maggie unclasped her fingers.

"Honest?" It was the way the writer had used her name. It felt intimate. Like sitting near to someone in a hospital waiting room and saying things that otherwise would never be shared.

"About my research. I don't usually do this, but I want you to know everything."

"Meaning?"

"I pored over online threads for months. I researched stories on Reddit. I traveled west of the Rockies to meet teens who are in programs today."

"Okay." Loretta leaned forward. She felt her shoulders relax.

"I learned some awful things. I talked to a lot of people. And then just recently. After I let you know about Tanya—"

"Yes?"

"I found Crystal."

Maggie told Loretta about two sisters who'd disappeared together, then about a girl's brother who hanged himself from a barn ceiling beam rather than be sent to a conversion home. She'd met with girls who'd been food deprived—with meals awarded only to those who followed the rules about reciting Bible passages daily, sounding happy on calls to their parents, and never questioning what they were told to do. Other girls said their skin had paled because they had no leafy vegetables to eat, that their lives became so translucent they couldn't discern what was real from their terrors, that they'd been abused physically, many thrust into a deftly created alienation.

The journalist said she'd been told that residents in some programs had been ordered to yell "Sinner, bitch, whore" at girls forced into punitive silence. That girls took sides, they became mean. A teen told her that if rocks had been at hand, the girls would have thrown them.

"Take her, take her," girls yelled at a resident Maggie had interviewed. The girl said she was held down on the floor. She said a male guard did much worse to her. "He took me" was the only explanation she'd offer.

Former residents met with the writer in town cafés and whispered their stories across diner tables to the sophisticated lady from the big city. Maggie said she could tell they were scared by her request to record and hesitated when she took notes.

"Loretta, they were as honest with me as they could be. I think the intimidation from their past was sometimes just too vivid for them to speak too much out loud."

"Thank you for going to them. For listening to them."

"Once I started, I couldn't stop," Maggie continued. "They shared with specificity what could not be theatrics, I'm sure of that. Every ounce of luminosity had disappeared from their skin and souls." She listed more from her interviews. Girls locked in cold wet cellars with mice. Banishments. The torture of silence. One girl's older sister was shot on adjacent ranchland—running away doesn't absolve a girl from a trespasser's punishment.

"And then I got this call. Unexpected. Someone had told her to contact me."

"Her?"

"Yes, her. Crystal." Maggie gave Loretta a weak smile. "A tiny victory, I think. I raced to LaGuardia, only a week ago, and flew out. Met her in a Denny's in a town not far from the ranch. A Denny's, how about that? A waitress named Virginia asked if I was from somewhere else."

"No, that's the place I'm from." Loretta laughed. "It's called somewhere else."

"Right. Anyway, in walked Crystal. A tiny woman. Long curly hair. Massive curls. She told me about the Home for Wayward Girls. About you and Elsie. And, by the way, she said to tell you she's fine now. She married that neighbor boy. I told her I was sure you'd reach out to her soon."

"You found Crystal! This is awesome. I definitely will call her. But what else did she tell you?"

"She talked about the office back of the bunkhouse, too."

"Oh, no."

"She said she was the youngest. That she never thought she'd have to go into that room. That you all were afraid of him."

"Crystal was such an innocent. I never heard this. I only know pieces from after I left. Bits I've put together. Lots I wish I didn't know."

"She said he made her do what sinful women do. Afterward, he locked her in a room with no light."

"I remember the closet."

"Can you tell me about it?" Maggie reached for her water and waited.

Loretta began. When she was very young, her father had pushed her in a closet whenever he accused her of being impertinent. He screamed, "Come here, you blasphemous child," grabbed her arm or her hair—her very being it felt—and shoved every inch of her into the dark.

"Inside," he'd boom, unscrew the ceiling bulb, take it with him, and slam and lock the door. "Pray for your sins."

Sins? She was never certain what her misdeeds had been.

The last time was when she was eleven. He left her there till morning, a long night's penance in the room with no light, stuck on the floor in between his muddied work boots, a mop, a bucket that smelled of Pine-Sol, and a single-shot hunting rifle. If it had been loaded, if it had a cartridge ready to kill some trespasser who dared cross their prairie, well, Lord knows what might have happened. Instead, Loretta sat with her index finger on the trigger till morning. She barely slept. In the darkness, her early planning began.

"Don't mouth off, say nothing, and be ready for your escape," she told her young self. That had been the first night in which she found the hope that would guide her. She knew she'd run away.

Might take years, but for certain she'd be leaving when the day came. Whatever it was she'd done, whatever horrible sins, she would take them with her.

"In the dark, everyone is a sinner," Loretta told Maggie. "Myself included."

"Were you able to put that behind you?"

"I'm still working on it. Sometimes I can. Not always. Kind of a tape recording in my brain. Hard to turn off. I don't know much yet about Tanya. Where did you find her?"

"I met up with her in a Denny's on Eighty-Fourth Street in Omaha. Same coffee, different city. Wow. She went through a lot. Do you want the whole story?"

"I do."

"You ran away?" Maggie had asked tall, strong Tanya. She had tattoos, a full sleeve up her arm. She wore a black T-shirt, black jeans.

"Took a few tries. Getting caught was harsh." She pulled up the arm of her sweater to show round circles, cigarette burns. "There are more of these, but you get the picture."

"He did that?"

"Yes. He got meaner after Loretta took off. Like he had something to prove. Girls got locked in the cellar with the Preble mice a lot more."

"What's Preble mice?"

"Oh, awful critters." Tanya undid her braid. Hair the color of pancake syrup. She banded it into a knot on top her head. "They're these mice with long tails. They jump at least nine feet in the air. Out of nowhere. Tails swoop across your face or arm. Harmless though."

"They don't sound harmless." Maggie physically cringed.

"I had to go. Had to run from that damn ranch. I took off during afternoon chores. Ran down the highway. Avoided the prairie completely. Wasn't sure I could handle a wolf. Thankfully, some guy in a turquoise pickup stopped and gave me a ride. Odd color. I remember it. Anyway, he dropped me near a friend's house. I never went home."

"Did they come after you?"

"Yes, but I hid. Till I could get away. Went to a friend of a friend of a friend's. Pretty much been in Omaha since. I'm in night classes at the college. I know it sounds funny. I'm kinda old for school."

"Doesn't sound funny. What are you studying?"

"Okay, don't laugh."

"I won't."

"I want to be on radio. Some kind of host. Maybe my own show. Don't know. Does that sound completely impossible?"

"For you, Tanya, no. Seems to me, well, it seems you'll do whatever you set your mind to."

"From your mouth—" Tanya laughed. "Or whatever."

"So, anything else you can tell me about the ranch? William and Mama? As awful as they sound?"

"Hmm. Not sure where to begin. I knew it wasn't gonna be okay on my first day when he demanded my clothes. He—"

"William?"

"Yes, I try not to use his name. One day, he ordered me to his office. I knew better. His office meant nothing good. It went downhill from there. And worse."

"Right. I've heard."

"Made me kneel. At his feet. In silence."

"Did he do more? To you?"

"Made me do it to him. Kneeling."

SIXTEEN
West of the Rockies

Not long after her high school graduation, after the drive to Dairy Queen and the visit to the prairie chapel in her teacher's red convertible, and despite a couple calm days, unexpected and not good things began to happen on the ranch. Like the slow drip of a faucet that leads to brown water swirling with grime—Loretta should have, *damn it, damn it,* she should have anticipated the chaotic winds headed her way.

Even more telling, Loretta felt a minuscule glimmer of potential happiness, which in and of itself was something she knew carried risk. Pebbles of anxiety were normal within her stomach. Chills up and down her arms generally weathervaned her father's moods. Any thoughts that her last weeks on the ranch would pass easily should have been considered fair warning to be on guard for potential storms.

One morning, early when dawn's sky above the prairie dissipated to a beauty so clear even the clouds exuded awe, Loretta's head was consumed with possibilities. Ms. Del had shared with her the sanctity of a small adobe chapel, flowers soon to bloom blue and yellow, and a quote from Amelia Earhart about acting on one's decisions. Loretta felt freedom was close.

"Stay at the table." Her father chopped an axe straight into her mood when he made this announcement as soon as breakfast had been cleared. If a man could own a person, it was clear Loretta was his property.

"What?"

"I said sit," outpoured his officious voice, his ownership of the Home affectation. The sly creep of his eyes sidled toward hers. His finger tapped the bound ledger beneath his hand. Everything wiped clean, it was her, him, and Mama.

"Why?" Loretta watched Elsie and the other residents file out the kitchen door. Their sweaters tied not so tight, the weather warmer, she saw their shoulders trudge down the path without her. Crystal rustled around, glanced on purpose to Loretta, ventured a gentle wave her direction. The others skipped ahead, or walked in twos, their heads close to each other. Loretta was desperate to run to them, grab Elsie's hand, and feel the closeness of her friend.

"Be quiet, girl," Mama said. She hung a dish towel over the sink and slunk to her chair by the potbellied stove. "I'll take a rest here, William."

Loretta didn't like any of this, not one bit. She was penned in. Her skirt was suddenly uncomfortable—the waist cinched her skin too tight. Her inside-out STOP FOOLISH SINNERY T-shirt choked her neck. William to her right in his seat of power. Mama across the room. Loretta watched her prison wardens and reminded herself of something her teacher had talked about in class—a sentence a Persian poet in the 1200s had written.

This too shall pass.

The words scampered through her mind. She almost smiled

but figured best not. She needed to wear her serious face to convince her father she was listening. He'd watch to see that she accepted whatever his demands. She bit her tongue, coerced herself to keep almost silent.

"What is it?" she asked. Why stave off whatever hell was about to descend?

"Loretta," her father began. This was unusual. He generally called her "girl" or worse. To use her given name was beneath him. "You've finished with school and it's time for you to make more of a contribution. To the family."

"Huh?" To this family? What the fuck? Loretta barely opened her mouth to utter a reply.

"Mama can't be doin' so much anymore. All these years working for you."

"What'd you mean? For me?"

"Everything here." Her father lifted his head, did a one eighty of the kitchen, and grunted. Could be he was passing on some great inheritance. "We built this for you. And now it's time."

"Time for what?" Loretta ran a hand through her hair, jammed strands behind her ears, bent her face to the table. She wanted to run far. To bolt through the prairie. The voice inside her, the one that kept her close to sane, held her back. *Make it to August. Make it to your birthday.*

"Schooling is over. You have responsibilities, girl." Her father's boss man voice took over. "You're to be down here early every morning. Helping Mama in the kitchen. Learning."

"Learning? What don't I know?" Loretta knew everything about cooking and cleaning and keeping the food stocked for meals.

"What don't you know? I'll tell you what," her father began, the curl of his lips in sync with his mean stare. "You'll be takin' over for Mama. Be in charge of makin' sure residents do their chores. Help with new girls. Keep records for the inspector."

"I don't want—"

"Don't matter what you want. Don't go gettin' any miscreant ideas about running off. You know I can send those transporter folks to get you, I've got an arrangement with them. And, like I said, we done for you all these years. Your payback is due."

"Payback?" Loretta stopped short of slamming her hands on the table but the voice in her head interfered. *Hold on . . . this too shall pass.*

"We kept a log." Papa's big hand opened the green ledger. His long, rough finger flipped page to page. Ran down a column on each. "Yep, got a record of what you owe us. Every dime we've spent."

"What?"

"You've got plenty to settle. Rent on that bedroom upstairs. Meals. Every piece of clothing we done bought you. School fees. Lots of days' work owed. Interest due, too."

"You didn't think you'd be goin' anywhere, did you, daughter?" The slick undertow of Mama's voice drifted from her corner by the stove. "You be needed here. By my side unless you out helping your father on the Walmart runs." The corners of Mama's lips bent upward, a mean attempt at a smile. More a leer.

"Right. You can start a list right now."

"Now?" Loretta's heart was bouncing, her throat parched, trapped, but her eyes were on alert. Except for one thing. Had she heard right? She'd be going to Walmart?

"You get everything out of the larder. Clean those shelves good. List what we've got. What we need from the Walmart. You and me's got work to do, daughter." Mama sat forward in her chair, her chubby fingers massaging her feet. All Loretta heard was Walmart.

The next day was the first of her trips with William to Walmart. They parked in a spot outside the blue-and-white entrance. Loretta's eyes opened wide. William slammed his door shut, told her to get a move on, and rushed her through the aisles for what they needed. Still, Loretta couldn't help but pause, stare at what she saw in a store that was so big, truly majestic, and filled with more stuff than she'd ever thought existed.

"You went to Walmart?" Elsie asked when they were out digging for vegetables after she returned.

"Oh, Elsie, the garden of Eden for sure. Aisles and aisles I wanted to explore. Wasn't no G&A store. Closer to Shangri-la! Everybody in those snazzy blue vests."

"Did you go to the juniors? See their jeans?"

"Nope, William raced us through so fast. We hit the food aisle, then feed for the critters, and munitions. He loaded boxes of ammo into the cart. What the hell for, I don't know. You'd think there's a revolution coming. But Lord, that store. Everything neat and organized, sparkling from the big shining lights in the ceiling, signs everywhere, this on sale, that on special. Specials! God, I wanted one of those. Any special at all! We passed quick by a whole row of plastic trash cans. Pink, white, yellow. So many colors. Can you believe it? Well, you know, you been there. It sure is something."

Loretta took many deep breaths that afternoon, folded her mother's laundry, and washed the kitchen windows with a mixture of vinegar and water. When William led the girls into the house for lessons, Loretta knew it was her only chance to trek across the prairie.

"Hey, where you going?" Elsie said in a low voice as the girls single-filed past her.

"Taking a break. But soon. Us," Loretta whispered. She knew that Elsie understood her meaning. They were both counting the days until August.

Sunshine dipped in and out of big cottony cumulous clouds. Overheated one second, she was cold the next. A couple months shy of eighteen, Loretta considered her options, which weren't many. If she took off now, she'd be a runaway under the laws of the state. Caught by any sheriff, they'd haul her ass right back to William and Mama. Or more awful, she'd be sent to one of her father's associates' establishments. He'd threatened this before.

"You have it good here, girl." He'd jabbed his finger her way earlier, concluding his declarations at the kitchen table. "We treat residents better than most. You best trust me on that."

Trust him? The idea was as lame as a fox in a wolf's grip expecting mercy.

Thing was, Loretta didn't have many people to get help from. Her teacher and Elsie. She had no other friends, no relatives, nobody had ever come calling, no grandparents mentioned. Seemed not a single person cared—if they were even aware of her existence. Other than Ms. Del, no counselor at school had asked what was next. There weren't even forms to fill out. Once you graduated from high school in prairie country, further records weren't required. A quick *Here's your diploma, good luck. File closed. Go work on your father's ranch.*

Loretta passed the mangled tree trunk where she and Elsie had promised to meet if either were to run first. She wove her way through a stretch of tall pines that could withstand the state's winds and winters—their sap the greenest scent in the prairie. She hiked between small rocks then larger boulders, behind bushes, headed to a narrow creek that ran until the summer dry spell would turn it to a mess of cracked ruddy earth. It was still nature's nap time—spring becoming summer. The warmer temperature swarmed around her like sheets pulled off the clothesline on a sunny day. No critters approached; snakes not yet roused for the season; wolves busy remodeling last year's den for a new litter. If she left now, she'd be a little safer from the wolves. Later in the summer, they'd be everywhere.

Stooping to the ground, she slid down a small grade above the creek, landing close enough to settle her hands in the cold runoff that traveled from the snows of the Laramie peaks glued close to the edge of the Rockies. Loretta's fingers flicked the clear water; she saw her reflection and plopped into a sitting position on the ground.

"What the fuck now?" she uttered.

Loretta raised her eyes to the white clouds. The big sky was aquamarine, a reliable cohort, and she imagined that its particular blue mirrored oceans she'd never seen. She did love the quiet land and the ballet of pronghorns outside her bedroom window. If William hadn't such a hold on her, if freedom were possible here, she mightn't have to flee. Her heart beat fast. Her arms tightened 'round her chest.

Loretta wanted to fly. She wanted to soar with joy like characters in the novels she read. Without any fears. Few quotes came to mind. This too shall pass? When? And how? What had she done but be born? How could her missteps merit what had been imposed on her life?

The controlled tears that she kept packed away rolled down her cheeks and caught the collar of her faded green camouflage jacket. She didn't care.

"Why the fuck me?"

Loretta hugged her knees. She reached for one of the white

buttons in her pocket. Stared through the button's holes toward the sun. She was jealous of the falcons, envious of the residents who would eventually get to return to their homes, and more than anything she wasn't certain she'd have the ability to fulfill her promises to Elsie. She'd again seen William watch her friend, she knew the lecherous eye he had, the way his furrowed brow calculated each of his next steps. No good could come of that.

"I got nothin'," she muttered. "Nothin'. A couple buttons. Some books. A knife, a compass. A few bucks I've hid away."

Loretta dragged a hand across her wet face. She rocked. Forward. Hesitated near the water's edge—then rocked back, unable to stop her tears. The caravan of plump white clouds in the perfect big blue sky floated east without her.

"Why me?" she yelled.

The air was silent. No sounds but the ripple of the creek.

Days faded each into another. Without the allure of the school bus coming, nor classes with Ms. Del, the routine that began each morning took precedence over Loretta's plans for escape. Dawn was early in these parts. Sunrise about five thirty, quick out of bed she headed to the kitchen and tied an ancient yellow checked apron around her denim skirt.

"That's your uniform now," Mama had announced. "Be grateful."

"Grateful, right."

Loretta was far from it. Not in the least. Especially not for a ratty old apron. Loretta pulled bowls from the cabinet for oatmeal, spread pieces of bread on a baking sheet to make toast in the oven. On a small notepad, she kept a list of food needed for her Tuesday trips with William to Walmart; the only change in her life was that once a week she got to see the world beyond the Home.

"Get those girls assigned their chores," Mama told her while the residents ate breakfast. "Stop your chattin' with them. They're not your friends. You're in charge of them. Make sure they know it. The bathroom here and in the bunkhouse better be Clorox clean today."

"Uh-huh," Loretta said. Wanted to say *yeah, sure, whatever.* They didn't even use Clorox. Like everything they had, it was Walmart's Great Value blue-and-white jugs of ammonia.

As little Crystal listened to Mama, her whole face frowned. Elsie raised her eyebrows. Loretta nodded to them both. Her signal she'd get over to the bunkhouse that night if she could. The girls missed her. She and Elsie had plans to discuss. Except she was exhausted after dinner. Mama kept her busy. William didn't stop checking on her either.

"How's the daughter working out?" he'd asked Mama right in front of Loretta and patted the gun on his thigh. The prison warden making sure Loretta saw his definite advantage.

"She's learnin'."

"She best learn fast," William said. "New crop coming in September. Girls she needs to be ready for."

"Doin' our best here, William," Mama told him and gave Loretta a face. Was it a sneer or another warning? Loretta wasn't sure. One wrong move and what might happen?

Loretta wiped her hands on the yellow apron and walked to the cabinets. She knew what needed to be done.

Lunch the next day was bologna in between two pieces of white bread. Walmart's fake Oscar Mayer version called Bar S, pork and beef sandwich meat made from the slaughter industry's leftovers—organs, trimmings, and end pieces ground and mashed into something that could be sliced. A glass of milk for each girl.

Loretta had snuck a red bag of Great Value chips into the groceries and poured some onto each plate. She quartered Honeycrisp apples grown nearby, a welcome treat.

"We've got work outside," Loretta announced to the residents after the chips were gone, the dishes washed and put away. Their eyes raised. No nods needed. There was nothing they wanted more than to be with their leader in the warm afternoon sunlight. Summer had arrived. With it came an unjustified jubilation, a sense that anything was possible. Still, Loretta held to her plan. She wouldn't do something stupid before her birthday. She counted the days.

Loretta led the way. Tiny Crystal followed in a too-big denim skirt. She held her waistband with one hand. Elsie brought up the rear.

"Don't lose your grip," said a laughing Tanya. "You skinny runt."

"Am not." Crystal whipped her head around to Gayle, who was busy tying her red hair back with a piece of string.

"I'd give you a hair tie if I had one," Crystal said.

"I'm sorry I called you a runt," Tanya said.

"I know." Crystal skipped ahead. She, the youngest resident, who missed her mother and fluffy dog, was unable to stay angry at anyone. Loretta said it wasn't in her character to do so.

"Come here a second." Loretta reached for the girl. "Let me make your wraparound tighter." She pulled the denim ties into a double knot. "Don't worry," she whispered in Crystal's ear. "You'll show them all someday."

They stopped near the hutches. Loretta spun on her heel and watched the girls fall into place around her. Sweet Gayle. Tougher Tanya. Loretta's eyes veered off toward the mountains. Little Crystal bounced from one foot to the other like something exciting was about to happen.

"Can we hold them? Please, Loretta." Crystal jumped closer.

"Sure, everybody, go for it." Loretta backed away. She kept watch on the kitchen door in case her father appeared.

"Hey—" Elsie took one sidestep then another over to her.

"Shh. Here comes William."

"But we'll talk tonight, right?" Elsie kept her head lowered. Loretta had told her to be cautious, that their lips could be read, that words can travel on a breeze.

"Hope so. I'll try." Loretta crossed her arms. "But don't worry, my friend. Six more weeks. Then we're pronghorns."

"Yep." Elsie lifted her stare to her friend. Her smile brought light to her pale eyes. "Hitting the road."

"You got it. Count us gone."

A few days later, William called Loretta to come to the edge of the prairie. She was with the girls scrounging for radishes and onions in the vegetable beds. She hesitated, flicked dirt off her skirt, wiped sweat from her forehead. Tanya and Elsie jumped up beside her. Everyone turned upon hearing William's voice.

"Now," he yelled. So tall. An anvil of a man. His stance even at this distance crushed any rambling thoughts of rebellion.

"What?" Loretta took slow deliberate steps away from the residents. "Stay here," she whispered, waved them to back away, and headed the thirty feet to where he stood.

"Take this." He grabbed her hand. Slapped his pistol into her palm and crushed her hand around the wood grip.

"No!" She tried to shove it back to him. Loretta had been forced to use his gun before, when he tried to make her take target practice on the prairie dogs that popped from their dugout holes in the land, but she'd wanted no part of it.

Pistols are cold. They're heavy.

The weight in a hand truly a warning.

"There." He pointed to one of their rottweilers. Not Bull but another of the guard dogs that weren't household pets. She didn't know if it had a name. The dog lay bleeding on the ground. One leg bent the wrong way. Its eyes were half closed. The animal had been in a tussle with a fox.

Loretta watched the dog's chest pump. Its open mouth gasped for breaths. One paw pushed from the ground. Poor thing unable to stand although it tried.

"In its head," William said.

"I can't do that." Loretta's voice was shaky despite her effort to sound strong.

"You will. It's what must be done."

"Why?"

"Do it. Lord! Bull's brother. Pity the poor thing." William's cold eyes quaked, his lids drooped for a moment. Might be the saddest she'd ever seen her father.

Loretta didn't want to shoot. Not the dog. Not anything. Not ever. The rottweiler's stare was dim. He took a last glance at her, and Loretta was certain the animal was begging for a reprieve.

"Now," her father said, his authoritarian no-choice voice taking charge. His moment of pity so short-lived. William reached to her hand, shoved it against the side of the rottweiler's head, and pulled her finger on the trigger so hard Loretta would carry the bruise for weeks.

Blood trailed south like tears from the animal's face to the ground. The dog's mouth stuck open, its pointed teeth on display. No more breaths. No movement. Chest stilled. Bits of flesh and skin, a piece of ear, littered the ground.

"Stupid son of a bitch," William said. He replaced the pistol in the holster on his thigh.

"It didn't do anything—"

"Clean that mess up." He pointed to the dead dog. Kicked the sliver of ear into some crusted dirt.

"How do you know?" She wanted to be sure it was dead.

"Ain't your job to know. Dog lost the fight. Now, get the girls to dig the creature a place in the ground." William turned on his heel and left her there. Alone. Her head bent to the ground.

This was her new life. It was easy to see months, years into the future, how prayers become but petitions to the Lord requesting quiet and a chair by the stove. Even new seasons on the prairie would offer nothing more than withered promises. Life wouldn't change here unless—or until—she refused to stay.

SEVENTEEN

New York City

Loretta and the journalist sat in silence for a while. Loretta felt small palpitations, a bit of sweat on her neck. She was shocked— even by things she'd suspected but kept hidden like a file she knew she'd have to address someday.

"Now Tanya's here. Today. At our conference," Loretta said, her voice quiet.

"I think she's pretty incredible."

"You know, Maggie, they all were." Loretta reached for her glass of water thinking that if this were about a regular school these stories would be filled with laughs and smiles. "Every girl who came to the ranch had this special spirit. An inner strength. Like they knew what William preached was a crock. And—"

"What?"

"They also knew they were better than him and Mama. I knew it. Every one of us knew we were, I don't know, we were the good people. We were not what he said. The girls weren't whatever the fuck, oh, sorry, whatever their parents thought. We just needed the chance to break free."

"And you did. You broke free, Loretta."

"I know. Did anyone tell you about Silent Cloud?" Loretta hated to bring it up, but it was important.

"Yes. First I did some research. Found out about wilderness therapies where young men are left in the woods for weeks at a time. Also, the conversion therapies. Plenty of homes for girls. Then I got to talking with the waitress at that Denny's. She remembered William and the other owners. Guys named P. George the Third, Big Joe. That they had meetings like rotary club only different. She told me what she heard. She said one time they talked about punishing girls with silence. Like they thought themselves pretty damn clever. She was great. Said she never felt right about serving them their Denny's specials again."

The journalist checked her phone. Both women frowned, not at each other, but at the wickedness of the men who ruled the lives of so many teens.

"Can I segue for a second?" Maggie asked. "Tell you something personal?"

"Please. I'd love a break from the memories that are flying around my head."

"Gosh, this is odd. I rarely do this. But I have to tell you. When I got back to New York, I became a nervous wreck about my kids. Had to check on them constantly. Total anxiety. I even filled a prescription for Xanax."

"I can totally understand." Loretta didn't tell Maggie she had her own bottle tucked in her satchel if needed.

"One afternoon we were sitting in our kitchen. We've got this great window but only in the kitchen, go figure, with a view of the East River. And I started lecturing them about how they should not let anyone ever hit or touch them."

"That's not a bad thing to do."

"I may have gone on a bit too long. My third grader asked for Twizzlers from our snack drawer."

"Well, Twizzlers rock. Anything else?"

"Here's the thing. My fifth grader just said thanks. Like that. Thanks, Mom."

"That's good, right?"

"It is. But there's a reason I wanted to tell you about them. It was so you'd know this story, your story, the women I met, and those I didn't, well, it all matters. And it's part of me now. I'm a journalist. I'm not supposed to take sides. But I have." She gave Loretta a tiny but kind smile and asked, "Was it as bad for you as I've heard? As I've been told?"

"Yes." Loretta nodded. She, too, smiled but then set her most steadfast stare a distance beyond. It was how she'd protected herself for so long, a bit like deep breaths, her own defense system so she didn't fall apart, cry, stumble again in the subway, drop to her knees in pain and dismantle the tough exterior she'd worked diligently to build.

"And you got out."

"I did. After so much that wasn't pretty, wasn't ever fun, it was painful."

"You mean the beatings? The ones you've told me about?"

"There's more. He had a belt kept in the kitchen. In a drawer. He'd threaten residents with it. Warn them about punishment for their demerits. Me? All he had to do was hold it in his hand. I'd shake with fear. It was like that until the day I fled." Loretta's lips locked together, but then she hesitated, sighed, and accepted that the time for honesty was upon her. The moment of devoir. Her story needed to be told.

"Can you tell me?" Maggie sat very still. She didn't move. It was clear she'd be patient until Loretta was ready. "I heard there was a gun involved? Before you left?" She asked the tough question she'd probably held in abeyance long as she could.

"No, not a gun."

"But I thought—"

"It was a rifle. William kept it by the kitchen door." Loretta lifted the glass of water to her lips. Her eyes stared over the rim to the woman across the table. "Have you ever been so afraid of someone, or for someone, that you'd have killed for them?"

"No, I haven't. But I can imagine. For my kids." Maggie was again quiet, then she asked, "Have you?"

"Yes," Loretta told her. "I would have done anything."

"What happened?"

If a clock were ticking, it would have been heard. Silence swept the room. Hard truths take time to be revealed.

"One second," Loretta said. She checked her phone. No texts. No distractions to pull her away from this hour of judgment, her personal courtroom hearing, the reporter from the *Times* her judge, the many people who would read this piece her jury who would then postulate as to her motives; some would side with her, some against. Loretta expected recriminations. Accolades? Would there be accolades? Would the verdict side with her? Or not?

Verdict: the finding or answer of a jury given to the court concerning a matter submitted for their judgment.

EIGHTEEN
West of the Rockies

With few weeks left to go, Loretta was biding her time, doing her best to stay on her father's good side. Not that he had one—Loretta had spent years maneuvering the difference between her silent acceptance and his manipulation. William might think whatever he wanted, that which served his contrived conniving, but Loretta didn't care if he was happy, only that he believed he was in control. She opened her eyes on a Tuesday morning. The sun on its ascent outside her window. She threw on her blue jean skirt and T-shirt.

Downstairs, she hurried to help Mama. First things first. Filled the percolator with water, six scoops from the Folgers can; she inhaled the scent of coffee. With the percolator plugged in, Loretta reached for the cardboard canister of Great Value oatmeal. Getting through breakfast was her easiest time; there was something about people just woke up that usually made for calm—boiling points not yet simmered, anger somehow suspended so early in the day. She turned from the stove. Watched Elsie and the others file to their benches at the table.

"Hey." She placed a bowl in front of her friend and leaned in close.

"Hey, you," Elsie whispered, her head lowered.

"Get a move on, Loretta," William said and took his seat at the end of the table. "Need to go early. I have things to do when we get back."

"Yes, sir." Loretta gave a quick small smile to the girls, winked at little Crystal who was sucking on the edge of her collar.

"Go upstairs and get yourself ready for town," Mama told her. "Elsie, you come over here and pass out this toast."

Loretta hung her apron on the hook by the woodstove. Stopped for a second to take in the scene. Girls either side of the table. She was no longer allowed to sit among them.

"That foolishness is over," William had declared and reminded her. "They're not your friends. You're in charge of them's chores. Also, you're to log their demerits here on. Got that?"

"Yes, sir," Loretta agreed but no way in hell would she do that. Make chits by their names for not cleaning a baseboard or, worse, for a frown. No facial expressions were the rule at the Home for Wayward Girls.

Before she took the stairs, Loretta watched Elsie assume breakfast duty. Her ragged Keds made hurried steps to help Mama with toast. William was earnest in his chewing. He held out his empty tin cup for more coffee. A silent command. Mama, fast as her slippered feet could, shuffled to him percolator in hand. Tanya looked to Loretta. A barely noticeable greeting passed between the two of them.

Loretta and the older girls had talked about plans, about life, a couple days before. They were alone at the vegetable beds. Crouched to their knees, checking on the progress of the parsnips. Not that they cared.

"My teacher showed me a chapel west of here. Not far. Set back a ways from the road," Loretta told them. "Safe places. I bet there's others."

"Other whats?" Tanya asked.

"Safe places. Spots to hide in. They're out there. I'm sure of it."

"Me, too," Elsie agreed. Her pale blue-gray eyes on Loretta's. The feeling that passed between them strong as the distant mountains.

"You're gonna run soon, aren't ya?" Gayle asked, except it wasn't so much a question. Merely a fact they each understood.

"I think so," Loretta whispered.

"You know when?" Tanya's face was frightened.

"Nah." Loretta had already shared more than she intended. Except there was a bond between her and these girls. Maybe had to do with their similar strengths, Loretta wasn't sure. It was a recognition of their will to get the hell off the ranch and far from this town. Or pretty much die trying. A possibility that did not frighten Loretta near as much as being a permanent resident would.

"I hope we'll get to say goodbye," Tanya said.

"You know what Boadicea said?" Loretta asked them.

"What?" The girls huddled closer to her.

"Only one choice for women. Conquer or die."

"So you'll conquer, right?" Gayle pulled her hands from the dirt. Her pale face was getting too sunburned. Loretta rocked back on her heels. She hoped she was as brave as her quotes made her sound.

"I'll try my best."

"Loretta?" Tanya squinted into the sun. "Here's the thing."

"What is it?"

"You owe it to us. To us residents. Me, the others."

"What do you mean?"

"Well, I don't mean owe. Except I do. Because it's really important you get out. Then the rest of us can hope—"

"Hope?"

"Yep. Because you gettin' out. That will let us dream. About where you've gone to. And then, damn it, we can dream we'll get there, too."

Inside William's truck, Loretta sat by the window. Bull between her and him. The rottweiler upright, mouth open, drippy wet tongue hanging out. Bull's deep breaths kept pace with the tires on the road. The smell of dog everywhere. Loretta opened the window. Wished she was in Ms. Del's red convertible with Joan Jett singing about loving rock 'n' roll, or that she was at last on the highway out of town and heading most anywhere that heralded freedom.

"We'll get diesel on the way back. First, Herb's office."

"Herb?"

"Herb Muldoon." William slapped an envelope he'd set on the dash. "Bought me a plot in the cemetery. So you know."

"Uh-huh." Loretta wondered what that meant for Mama.

"Then a quick stop at the Walmart. You got the list?" William asked from the driver's seat. Didn't turn his head or look at her. She might well be invisible. He had what he wanted. A servant to do his chores.

"Yes."

"Stay here. Don't move." William slammed the truck door and ran inside an office. The sign on the window advertised LEGAL SERVICES, INSURANCE, LLCS, WILLS, BURIAL PLOTS.

"Where would I go?" Loretta whispered and turned her eyes to the passenger window. Across the street three boys in cowboy hats walked together. One burst into laughter. A woman holding the hand of a toddler pushed a baby in a stroller with her other. The boys tipped their hats when she passed by.

"That's done." William plopped back in the truck. The groan of the engine started—*chuck chuck chuck*—and he shifted into gear. "Good. I'm gonna drop ya." He stopped the truck at Walmart near its blue-and-white grand entrance. "You get what is needed. Nothin' more, hear me?"

"Uh, uh, sure."

"Then see Don, at the service desk. Tell him it's to go on our bill."

"Don. At the desk? Since when?" She'd never done this before. William always came inside with her, told her no wandering allowed. If he left her side, he waited up front and met her at the cashier. Didn't trust her with cash money. She'd never roamed the aisles, too afraid he was watching her.

"Don't question me, girl. Do it. Meet me outside here. I'll be back."

"Back when?" Loretta was stunned. She wondered if this was some kind of test. What the fuck was going on?

"Shut your mouth and go do it. I'll be back when I'm back. You better be here waiting for me."

"Okay."

Bull turned his head. The mean old dog panted at her.

Alone, with her hands on the grocery cart, Loretta stopped a few feet within the Walmart doors. She was on her own! In Walmart! So much pure unadulterated stuff. Every bit of it in the prettiest yellow, red, blue packages that she'd been hurried past before.

With William, she'd had to scurry through the aisles.

"Just here for the basics," he said, always a few steps ahead. Loretta was expected to keep up. "Eyes forward, you hear me," he ordered.

But today, she stopped. To her left, a section of clothes for juniors. Duran Duran, The Police, and Madonna T-shirts on mannequins. Blue jeans. Underwear the likes of which she'd never had time to peruse. To her right, displays of chips and cookies next to a full aisle of shampoos. She hadn't used anything but a square white bar of soap for washing and that included her hair.

On this day, Loretta had two choices. At least two. One was to scurry about, take in everything, and then fill the cart with the items on her list for the ranch. The other choice was to run. Except that was much too easy. A trap. William had to be outside in the truck, his eyes on runaway alert, waiting for her, for his prey. She knew better. She'd fill the cart. See Don at the service desk, whoever that was. Then wait outside. But for now, Walmart was all hers.

"Can I help you?"

"What?"

A young woman in a royal blue vest stood in front of Loretta. Shoulder-length hair, brown eyes with golden spots that sparkled a smile Loretta's direction. She wore tight jeans and makeup, and Loretta woulda bet she probably had a boyfriend. Her blue badge said RUTH next to a yellow happy face.

"Need some help?" Ruth asked again, not impatient, glad to assist.

"Um . . ." Loretta was unsure. "Uh."

"I can show you"—Ruth pointed to the list in Loretta's hand—"or tell you the aisle."

"Okay, I think I want . . ." Loretta took a deep guzzle of air and her gaze lifted the same way she paused when peregrines were overhead cawing for her to follow. "I want Twizzlers."

"Oh, that's easy. My favorite, too." Ruth led the way. "Come on, follow me."

In the candy aisle, a feast she'd never before encountered, Loretta stopped before a large bag of red licorice, the likes of which she'd had at school on rare occasions.

"Anything else I can do?" Ruth asked. Her smile easy, simple, could well be she had reason to grin every single day.

"I'm good." Loretta almost reached out to touch the young woman, to take her hand, to hug the close-to-a-mirror image of the girl she wished she'd had the chance to be. "But thank you so much."

"For Twizzlers." Ruth laughed. "Probably the easiest ask I'll get all day."

"Really?"

"It's summer. You should see campers when we run out of bear repellent." Ruth's eyes laughed harder than her lips. With her hands in the pockets of her blue vest, she pranced down the aisle, a sureness in her step that Loretta watched with envy.

"Thank you," Loretta said again. Her own hands held tight to the cart. She stared at the shelves of Twizzlers, Red Ropes, Sour Straws, and more.

She felt the essence of what might have been, what could have occurred in the years now so far in the rearview mirror it was near impossible to consider. Some kind of plausible semblance of whom she might have become. Would Loretta have been a blue-jeaned music-loving boy-crazed girl, not so wild, who worked at the Walmart, wore pretty blue eye shadow, and smiled so big it was hard to miss her optimism?

She touched a family pack of Twizzlers and thought to put it in her cart. It was number two on the Freedom List. Rations for her journey with Elsie.

But she slid it back into its spot.

Today was not yet the day. Not that day.

She began to push her cart down the aisle, afraid, always afraid, what if she was seen, perhaps he was nearby. Loretta couldn't run, of that she was sure. He was watching one way or another, that was certain.

"You want those?" Ruth sauntered back, a quiet approach.

"I can't." Loretta turned to see the sort of sweet smile she wished was on her own face.

"You go do your shopping." Ruth grabbed a pack, one farther down from the top. "They're fresher." She laughed. "I'll get these for you. My gift. Go on, now. I'll find you."

"I—"

"It's okay. I want to." Ruth hurried the other direction, a bag of red licorice in her hand, a quick pivot so her eyes could again sparkle at Loretta's.

Loretta offered a small half smile of gratitude to Ruth.

She heard something and realized the unusual sound was her own soft laughter.

The day for tight blue jeans and makeup was near. Close as a silent breeze. Loretta was expert at the art of biding time. The weeks to go couldn't stop her nor pass quickly enough. With her licorice hidden deep in a bag, and after her stop to see Don at the front counter, Loretta found William, waiting at the curb. She'd expected as much.

NINETEEN

New York City

"Before the rifle. There's so much other stuff. I mean—"

"Start anywhere," Maggie said.

"I think there's two kinds of beatings on women," Loretta began. "At least two. Not only women. Physical is one. It may even be the easier to endure."

"How so?"

"After a while, bruises and cuts heal. It's an odd gift because our bodies recover, not always, but mostly they do. When you're bruised, deeply—I certainly was—that map fades."

"What map?"

"I used to sit in school. Back then." Loretta lowered her shoulders toward the coffee table. Her hand went to the scarf around her neck. She lessened the distance between herself and the reporter. "I'd stare at my arms or legs. I'd recount for myself that a particular bruise was from the day he ripped my blouse, or that one's from the branch he swung into my legs, and that is the peeling burned skin from the day he slammed the hot percolator onto my wrist."

"I can't imagine," Maggie said. She waited while Loretta lifted her head and stared far beyond the walls of the meeting room.

"You're lucky," Loretta whispered.

"I know."

"The bruises were a pattern that I alone could see." Loretta paused to remember. "How they became blue-purple, almost black. The outer edges blur, you know. Sort of like an eclipse of the sun, spreading . . . spreading from the darkness, mustard yellow, garish, sometimes green. Or both colors at once. Ugly. On my arms. My legs. I watched them for days. I couldn't stop checking how they would fade. Kind of."

"Kind of?"

"Bruises don't disappear quickly. Not fast. And it takes a long time to stop checking that map. Sometimes I had to search for them. Had to. I'd wonder where one had gone. Even had to remind myself that my body was able to heal. Hardest were the ones that would surprise me in the mirror."

"How's that happen?"

"I'd go brush my teeth. Comb my hair. I'd forget that his hand had cracked me on my nose. Or how he used the limb of a tree to drag its burls, those knobs in the wood, you know, to whack me. The nail that cut into my neck. Didn't leave a clean scar. Ragged."

"Sounds painful."

"That kind of healing takes a god-awful bunch longer. When the scars startle you in the mirror." Loretta closed her eyes for a heartbeat. She wasn't a person who cried in public, these painful memories a recitation she'd kept in her memory for days-months-years in the hope they'd be replaced by how far she'd come.

"And the other kind of beating?"

"The other kind? Well, those begin with words, the absolutely powerful words that these psychopaths sling at us. Horrible words.

Whore, sinner, bitch, Jezebel, worthless, slut, and there's more. Worse words. Once he called me a damn mule. Don't know why that hurt so bad. Mules are pretty decent animals. The thing is..." Loretta held her hands in front of herself, palms outward, stopping everything in the room for a very long second.

"Yes?"

"The thing is the words don't ever fade. Not truly. Don't even have to look far to find them. They live underneath our skin." Loretta swallowed. "These words are palpable. Always. Ugly words that torment us, even in front of our own mirrors." Again, she lodged her lips together tight for a moment. "People like me, and the women who are here today, we can look good. Put on nice clothes. Seem okay. Like we're doing well, I mean. But we're not. We're not well and we're far from okay."

"You don't wear any rings. I noticed. Is there a reason?" Maggie's silver earrings dangled east to west.

"Oh that." Loretta stared at her fingers. "I don't like identifications of any sort. Anything that might be taken to define me. I am me. No one else. A person. Responsible for myself. For how I live in this world."

"Except those nails. Nice."

"Well"—a laugh escaped Loretta's tight lips—"small pleasures, right?"

"I get it. So, today, your work, your announcement? What would you say it's most about?" Maggie looked at her notepad and waited some more.

"It's about letting go of the bruises, and the ugly words, and the people who have scarred us. Becoming our true selves." Loretta raised her eyebrows in a question mark. "You understand? Once, maybe a year ago, some of the women, the clients we help, and me, too, we wrote every ugly word we could remember onto scraps of paper. Then we lit them on fire." Loretta waved a hand in front of her face. Her dark nail polish shushed the smoke of the past into the far distance.

"Did that work?" Maggie held her pen midair. The recorder was going but she continued to jot notes.

"No. But it helped. That's what we do at Compass. We help us be whole. Each of us. On our own."

"Did it help you?"

"A bit."

"But?"

"I left girls behind at the ranch. I struggle with that." Loretta's neck itched. "I'm still trying to find them all." She stretched her legs under the table. Thought about Gayle, who she'd yet to find, and the many unique girls she'd befriended over the years on the ranch. Their nights in the bunkhouse. Tears they buried beneath laughter. Friendship a salve. Holding each other's hands. Young girls do that.

She lamented why the hand-holding of women ends.

Hands need to be held forever.

Maggie peered left to right across her notes. Took a breath. Flipped over to a blank page in her pad of paper. She seemed about to take a next step.

TWENTY
West of the Rockies

None of it came to pass the way Loretta had intended. Not the plan she'd planned for. Nor in the dead of night when Loretta would have squirreled herself and Elsie away without fanfare or notice. William was everywhere. His eyes watched her more than ever before. Since that day at Walmart, he appeared at odd moments, lurked outside when she was with the girls, and then on this day, a chilly day for summer, when sunshine over the prairie was more a smirk than a smile, Loretta's hopeful anticipation waned within the murky gray skies.

Why was William's belt in a tight roll left on the counter?

Loretta wore her denim skirt and one of the tees she'd grabbed from the church free box. Felt a chill and threw her army jacket on while she sat at the kitchen table to work on the list William had demanded she put together. Still, the belt again caught her eye, made her quiver. He brought it out when he threatened those who had demerits. Why today?

"If I'm to crawl around in dust, I'm wearing this," she'd told him, meaning her T-shirt.

"You change that before lunch." William had scowled in her direction.

The smell of burnt toast mingled with the odor of green Pine-Sol used to wash the floors. Loretta had inventoried cans of beets, peas, and beans, bags of rice, canisters of oatmeal. Next, she would head to the attic's boxes of ammo, noting the caliber, whether each box was full.

"Don't miss countin' how many rounds of .30–30 for the Winchester," William declared, meaning his most treasured rifle; he believed using its name added a sort of dignity. He jabbed his finger at her face before he raced off to town. "List the number of army blankets, canteens, the rations and tarps stored up there, too."

"Yes, sir." Loretta forced the words from her lips, his jabbing finger still close enough to make her wary. Lord knows what he had in mind to do with the survival crap he hoarded—she had no intention of being around when it happened. Nor did she envision dining on dehydrated beef jerky, apples, and potato slices in her lifetime. Not if she could help it.

"I won't be gone long. Get your work done," he said, except there was an anger to his words. He grabbed the belt from the counter. His black western hat. The screen door banged behind him. She heard the groan of the truck starting and then the skid of its quick departure.

She could hear Mama outside giving orders.

"I said dig deeper," Mama told the residents who worked the ground with metal spades. They were to turn the soil in the vegetable bed that was depleted of radishes and onions. "You call that clean? You aiming for demerits?" she yelled at those working in the chicken coop.

There was that word. *Demerits.* Loretta sat still. She was in no hurry to get to the attic. Loretta stared from one end of the ·

kitchen to William's chair. The belt meant only one thing. He'd be announcing demerits and meting out punishments. Sometimes he just held it in his hand and a girl would cry; last year he hurt a girl with many demerits, welts that became infected. She ended up in the hospital. Loretta thought he'd stop after that.

He had whipped Loretta with it, too. Last time in seventh grade maybe. She hadn't come straight from the school bus. Ran down a path that looped behind the house near the prairie where she liked to watch the pronghorns run.

"What you doing out here, girl?"

"Nothin'." She had circled 'round to face him. Scared. Dropped her backpack.

"That how you treat your things!" William pushed her the other direction. Sent her flying to the ground. "Get inside."

Moments later, his big hand grabbed the kitchen drawer so hard it might have hurled across the room. He pulled out the belt. Made Mama hold her.

Her own mother bent her over the table. Her own mother held her firm.

"Be quiet," Mama hushed into her ear. "Don't make it worse."

"Should belt you for each year of your life. When I say come straight home, I mean it."

"William, that's enough," Mama said after four harsh strappings.

"Don't you tell me what's enough," William yelled at Mama. "Sinners all of you."

Loretta caught William's eyes. His cold glare. He threw the belt to the floor and marched outside.

"Just do what he says." Mama handed her the backpack. Waved her up the stairs. "Go. Go now. Before he does worse."

On that day, seventh-grade Loretta's mother had both held her down and come to her rescue. Was that which imprisoned Mama far worse than Loretta's confinement? Loretta hadn't been able to run, not back then, but now she was. She believed in the possibility. She would be free. No doubts allowed. This gave her a faith that she suspected her mother had never been blessed to receive.

Loretta stopped work on the lists for William. She listened to Mama and the girls outside.

"Crystal, go get another bottle of ammonia."

"Yes, Mama," Crystal called over, or sang, her voice a cascading trellis of little girl giggles.

Loretta didn't have to see to know that skinny Crystal was running to the storage shack beyond the hutches. That girl belonged somewhere much sweeter than this here home for wayward girls.

"Stop those whispers, you two," Loretta heard Mama caution a couple residents. "Or you'll be doing chicken shit duty in your bare feet. You hear me?"

"Yes, Mama. Yes, yes." The girls knew better than to risk such awful punishment. Only thing worse than the feel of chicken shit squish beneath your toes was the prospect of trying to clean it off after.

There descended a sudden quiet. Caused Loretta to put down her pencil. She lifted her hand to her neck. Ran a finger over the crusted scar. Its trail had settled without fanfare—in much the same way that each passing day since graduation insinuated itself into the next. The scant smell of onions and bacon already a daily festering within her own beads of sweat.

She was two weeks from her eighteenth birthday.

The silence outside outlasted any reasonability. Loretta rose from her seat at the table and hurried to the kitchen door. The rifle leaned nearby. She watched the high-speed skid of William's truck arriving on the gravel drive. He leaped out and slammed its door. His harsh steps to the vegetable beds were crass, intentional. The belt from the drawer in his hand.

The metal spades ceased digging. Whispering girls closed their mouths.

"Got it, Mama." Crystal came running with the bottle of ammonia.

Everyone stopped their chores. To watch William. The grand master. His arrival a thud that halted life.

"You girls get to your knees. All of you now," he declared.

Little Crystal raised her eyes to Mama. The others uncertain, too. Mama's hand on Crystal's shoulder urged her to the ground. Tanya, Gayle, Elsie followed suit. Blue-skirted waifs dropped to the hard-crusted dirt. Mother Mary come to me statuettes on the prairie. A silent truce that would not last.

"I've got the list here of your demerits. Time to settle up. You hear me?" he announced. The wannabe minister's command. The belt in his hand.

Loretta reached for the Winchester 94. Caught a long-traveled mountain wind whistling through the stillness. Her hand slid over the stock, the wooden forend beneath the barrel, the trigger but a breath away.

The rifle had 7+1 rounds. Loaded by William. Always was. The +1 in its chamber. Locked and loaded. At the ready for what was imminent. Because you never know, do you? Except there wasn't any doubt when something had become imminent. Clear as the looming—that which must occur. When what once lay below the horizon is raised to true prominence, there is no choice. It looms.

On her last day at the Home for Wayward Girls, the rifle was shot. Loretta pulled the trigger. She'd aimed for Bull, but everything went wild crazy horrible. The dog growled, reared, and lunged.

The single bullet a straight dead-on shot not meant for Mama in her awful stained apron. A mangy towel draped over her shoulder.

"Loretta. Don't be stupid," Mama called to her a half minute before. Or a half second? A warning? A plea?

On that wild crazy god-awful final day at the Home, a place that bore no resemblance to safe shelter where affection brews and love grows, Loretta didn't intend to shoot the rifle. She meant to scare William. Stop his torrent of demerits. His threats. The curl of the leather belt in his hand. His damn boots that lodged before the knees of her sisters, her girls, residents in blue denim skirts and STOP FOOLISH SINNERY tees.

She flung herself out of the house and cautioned her father.

"Stop, stop, by God, stop." Her voice was calmed by the rifle in her hands. Oh Lord, it is not power but solace proffered by a loaded weapon. "Stop. Stop! No more."

He didn't stop. His feet plowed through the dry soil, dust flew, he grabbed Elsie by her hair. Grabbed her best friend. By her palest of ponytails and dragged her to her feet.

"No!" Loretta's voice louder, almost a scream.

"Get back in the house, girl," William yelled. "Or I'll burn her damn book." He waved Elsie's sketches in the air. "I found it in the bunkhouse. I told her no drawing!"

"But—"

"I told her it would be the belt. The girl has left me no choice!"

"Let her go!" For Loretta had no choice either. She couldn't stop, wouldn't, she'd come too far. The couple weeks before her on this prairie raced through her blurred vision and she hurried, the rifle's weight heavy, yet she knew that which folks locked and loaded know. The ability to act lay in her hands, within her sight— the decision was hers.

"Watch out," Crystal screamed. "It's Bull!" Crystal whose

scream became a tear-infested poor little child cry. Tiny Crystal, who prayed to go home to her hair ribbons and fluffy dog and the father who had whipped her for swimming naked in a creek with the boy from next ranch over, screamed again, "It's Bull!"

The mean dog with teeth that were daggers.

Whose growl was a crescendo of fierceness.

William motioned with his hand—a signal Bull understood.

"Let Elsie go!" Loretta yelled. She tried. So hard. "Give her back the sketchbook!"

Except, in her haste, in her hurry, she aimed the rifle.

Forgetting Bull didn't know a rifle for what it was.

The dog lunged.

She pulled the trigger.

Pop. Then *whoosh!*

The far too simple-frightening-horrible rifle sound so quick it was impossible to gauge the killingness contained within one single bullet.

Pop. Then *whoosh!*

"Run!" Elsie bent at the waist bound by William's hands. "Go, Loretta girl," her voice a plea, an instruction, a best friend's urging.

"Run!" Crystal jumped up and down. Tears drenched her stop sinnery tee.

But Loretta didn't run. She lowered the rifle. Set it on the ground. Watched blood gush from Mama's thigh. Mama teetered. Mama fell. The towel slumped off her shoulder. Mama waved her arm. How one bats away a gnat. Her eyes caught Loretta's.

"Go," Mama muttered. Not quite audible but easy enough to read. Her mother muttered or did she yell? "Go," the single word from her mother's lips.

"Go."

Loretta watched the girls' frantic waves for her to run, run,

run. She stumbled to choose a direction. Her eyes took a last con-cerned turn to Elsie, whose ponytail had come undone, who was caught within the stranglehold of William's arms.

"You get back here now!" William yelled. "I've got your friend!"

"Go, Loretta girl!" Elsie yelled. Elsie the absolver. Elsie the girl who forgave Loretta any debt to friendship. "Go, Loretta girl!"

"I'll get you, girl, you know I will." Loretta caught William's words, but her gaze remained on Mama, who had muttered, "Go."

Loretta ran.

Through the prairie, and rocks that offer shelter to snakes, on alert for wolves, past the mangled tree trunk where she and Elsie had promised to meet if ever it came to this instance of both dread and gosh yes hope. Breathing hard, crying with fear and trepida-tion, she raced on. She was too intelligent to stay. Street smarts, it is called in the city. Prairie wise, west of the mountains. William would come after her; he'd hold some piece of clothing, probably her underwear, to Bull's snout, order the dog to find her. Loretta had no options. She had to break her promise to Elsie, the girl who'd been delivered by transporters so that Loretta would have a best friend. She had no choice.

Loretta ran to the chapel. It would be her rescue. The chapel was safe. Her teacher had told her so.

The next morning, after a fractious night's sleep on the chapel's hard dirt floor, Loretta pulled her knees close to her chest. She'd been startled awake more than a couple times—precious glimmers of moonlight tried to offer her assurance but failed. Images too re-cent to be called memories reminded her from what she'd run and blurred the act she had committed. At some point in the near dark, she caught a lone hobo spider that dared crawl across her wrist.

"Get your own ride," she said, about to flick the two-inch-long mustard-brown creature off her arm. Her voice, or its vibration, was an alarm that sent eight translucent legs on a quick scurry along her fingers.

She shook it away and watched the spider, far more crustacean than arachnid, dart across the ground. To a corner? Maybe a secret tunnel into the prairie?

In the early light, Loretta stared 'round the adobe. She checked the floor. No sign of the hobo. A few tiny insects crept single file up the far side wall. The wrought-iron stand of red votive candles in its place. The kneeler near the small window that offered a southernly view. She wasn't ready to drop to her knees. No pleading prayers that might beg forgiveness came to her mind.

Loretta raised her eyes to the ceiling.

"Mama, I hope you're okay." Her plea beseeching but for the shake of her head. A doubt, an unclear recollection. She'd seen Mama fall to the ground. That mournful face of hers wailing. Her arms flailing. The shock that seemed more conjoined to disbelief than pain. The crumpled words she mouthed to Loretta. Not quite audible but easy enough for a daughter to understand.

"Go!" That single word the closest thing to a kiss she'd ever received from her mother's lips.

Loretta set her head on her knees. Her skin was a mess of shaking and trembles and cold then hot sweats. She took very deep breaths. She didn't want to relive any more of yesterday. But what about Elsie? Was she okay? Bits of the horror lodged in her mind. Pieces stuck to the sides of her throat like a rough cough that wouldn't, couldn't be expulsed. The shouts and screams of caustic crows on rewind in her head.

"I never meant—" she cried.

Suddenly, Loretta heard a car roll across the gravel outside the chapel.

She figured she'd find the sheriff there, lights flashing, his pistol drawn. One lone door led from the chapel. No other way out. She stepped to the window by the kneeler. Took a good hard stare at the freedom that would not be hers beyond the open shutters.

"Well, I tried," she said. "This was my big getaway chance."

Loretta twisted about, took slow, tepid steps, one foot forward, the other trickling behind, so similar to nights when she hesitated between the bunkhouse and Mama's cabin. If she'd just waited, she'd have been eighteen, she could have run free, never to be returned to William and Mama. Now, she was ready to be arrested. Hands in her pockets, her fingers played with the ridges of the buttons she'd rescued from the floor of the kitchen. She'd always known her plan might fail. But this? Her long sought-after freedom was one night on the dirt floor of a chapel? Today she was sure she'd be sent to jail because, truthfully, what more could possibly befall her?

But she was wrong. So very wrong. Outside a red VW Rabbit was parked feet away. The red convertible that she knew along with the teacher, her teacher, someone who believed in her.

"Look who I found wandering down the road." Ms. Del sprang from the car. Elsie jumped out the passenger door and ran to Loretta.

"Elsie!" Loretta screamed.

"Loretta girl!" Elsie threw her arms around her best friend.

"Elsie, I'm so sorry—"

"Stop it. Not your fault. You had no choice."

"But how did you?" Loretta asked and convulsed and shook and shook some more.

"William was busy with Mama. Commotion everywhere. The ambulance came. He sent us to the bunkhouse. Yelled we better stay put. Not me. I had no choice. He even dropped my journal. I grabbed it and took off. And ran. To the mangled tree. Where we planned. You know? I fell asleep there. No wolves!"

"Elsie, it's you. I can't believe it's you!" Loretta's hands didn't know what to do. She grabbed her best friend, hugged her, hung on, too afraid to let go.

"This morning, I remembered what you'd said about the chapel off the highway. You said there are safe places. I knew if you weren't at our meeting place, you'd have to be here. So I started walking."

"And I saw her. On the side of the road. In that skirt. Easy enough to figure it out." Ms. Del stood to the side. Arms crossed. In khakis and a crisp blouse. Loretta had never seen her teacher so casual.

"I'm shocked." Loretta's eyes jumped from Elsie to Ms. Del, to the ground, the sky, and back to her friend.

"Here, drink." The teacher handed Loretta a bottle of water. "And jump in the car. We don't have much time."

"What about Mama? I don't know what to do. Should I turn myself in? I'm scared, Ms. Del." Loretta gazed back to the chapel door, hated that this had happened, her plans for escape had been step by step, solid, in the dead of night. Not like this, not this horror.

"I heard everything from a friend at the sheriff's office. A good thing about small towns—everyone knows most everything! He knew I'd care about two missing teenagers. Told me the whole mess," Ms. Del announced. "Your mother is doing okay. She's at the medical center. He said the doctor stitched her up. Loretta, you have to go. Now."

"But—"

"You can deal with this. Except not from a jail cell here. No buts. They're out searching for you both now. There's no time to waste."

"I can't move." Loretta quivered. Her body tilted forward and away. Her hands slapped her thighs. "I have nothing. Nothing. What's the point?"

Ms. Del hurried to her student. Face to her face. Her arms tried to still Loretta.

"You're the point. You. I wouldn't be doing this otherwise."

"But I shot my mother," Loretta cried. "Who does that? How can I run?" She crumpled, her knees gave way. She crouched to the ground. Searched the sky for the morning star, for a sign. Wiped her eyes with the sleeve of her jacket. "I don't know what to do."

"Yes, you do." Ms. Del pulled her to her feet. "You're going to live your life. You'll make us proud. I know it. Remember the Persian poet?"

"This too shall pass?" Loretta let out a deep breath.

"Yes, and it will."

"And Mama's okay? You're sure?"

"I am. If she wasn't, I'd have brought the sheriff along with me. Now, come on." Ms. Del dragged her to the VW. Opened the passenger door. Flipped the seat forward. Elsie leapfrogged into the rear.

"You sit next to your teacher," Elsie said.

"Thanks."

"If I see a car coming our direction, any car, I'll tell you both to duck. Okay?" Ms. Del scanned the road and sped away. Both girls nodded.

A breeze lingered within the sea of blue and yellow bluebells outside the car window. Loretta gave a small wave goodbye.

"I'll take you far enough outside of town. Then hopefully you'll get a ride past the state line." Ms. Del explained that if she took them across it that would break the law bigger than she may already have. She wished she could do more. "I'm only agreeing to this hitchhiking under duress."

"You don't have to do this." Loretta was worried.

"Yes, I do," Ms. Del said. Her charms jangled against the

steering wheel. "I need to know you are on your way. And that you will call me. Collect. Right?"

"We will."

Thus, their journey began. Two best friends who hugged Ms. Del when they exited her little red VW not far from the state line.

"Quickly, go to the other side of the car and change." She handed them each a pair of jeans. "You're an easy catch in those denim skirts."

"Really? You brought us jeans?" Loretta was dumbfounded. "They're Guess!"

"I did. I have a niece who stays with me. About your size. She left some stuff. Long story. Anyway, bring me back the skirts. Don't leave them here." Ms. Del pulled a lever in her car and popped open the trunk.

"Jeans! I can't believe this. Thank you, Ms. Del. So much." Elsie returned first, her skirt in hand, sketchbook in the other. "Loretta, jeans were on our list!"

"Hurry, Loretta." Ms. Del reached for the skirts from both girls. Threw them into the trunk. She turned and handed them fifty dollars and two brown bag lunches.

"Wow." Elsie and Loretta stared at the money in disbelief.

"Now, go! It's getting hot. Be sure to drink lots of water. Elsie, I'll call your aunt. I've got the code word you gave me." There were tears in her eyes. "You have this, Loretta. Remember the maps you've studied."

"Yes, ma'am." Loretta and Elsie stood side by side, lunch bags in their hands.

"You'll call me tonight? Let me know you get to Elsie's aunt's house. No excuses."

"We will. We will." The girls took slow steps along the shoulder. Nine steps on, Loretta did a 180 and jogged back to her teacher, who stood by her car watching their getaway.

"I—" Loretta wanted to say something meaningful. She caught sight of the charm on her teacher's bracelet. The decision had been made. Loretta had to go forward now.

"I know," Ms. Del said.

"You do?"

"Yes. You and Elsie will make it. You'll be fine."

"You sure?" Loretta stared at the toes of her boots afraid to leave but more afraid to stay. She leaned forward. "One more hug?"

"Yes, please!"

Everything was still. A break in the craziness. Before her next beginning.

"You know what Eleanor Roosevelt said?" Ms. Del stepped back and glanced from Loretta to Elsie not far away.

"No, tell me." Loretta kept her eyes on Ms. Del.

"She said . . ." Ms. Del paused as teachers do. "Well, something like you have to look fear in its face. You must do the thing you think you cannot do."

"Thank you." Loretta, tears and sniffles, and plenty convoluted, tried to smile. "You think I can?" Loretta knew that she didn't really have a choice, but she needed to hear confirmation from her teacher, from this lone person in her life who stood apart from the ranch. The only outsider who'd understood her insides.

"Don't worry, take this." The teacher handed her a small pack of ladybug tissues, reached to tuck a strand of hair behind Loretta's ear, kneaded Loretta's shoulders with her fingers, and turned her east. "Get going. You're close to halfway there."

TWENTY-ONE

West of the Rockies

Just shy of Loretta's eighteenth birthday, she and Elsie were runaways under the laws of the state. Three legal outcomes were allowed if caught. A parent shows up and takes you home. The runaway opts to go back of their own accord. Or a nonvoluntary return occurs when the parent demands it. Nonvoluntary. By parental demand. Handcuffed and returned. The most dicey of options. Unless the teen claimed there was abuse. Which would boil down to *father said, daughter lied.* Loretta knew who'd win that argument.

Loretta was determined. She was stronger than Elsie, braver and more able to ward off lecherous jerks. Also, by fluke, she had her army jacket on when she ran. Knife, compass, matches, and assorted pocketed treasures within. Even half a Twizzler (unfortunately the remaining pack was hidden beneath T-shirts in her dresser at the ranch). The red pocketknife in her grip was good— she felt as prepared as Celtic queen Boadicea with torque and spear.

"First stop," she told Elsie, "is our most important stop."

"I know." Elsie retied her ponytail. "Can we really make it? Seems far." Elsie's eyes kept nervously ticking backward, to the west, to the prairie town they'd narrowly escaped. Her face displayed uncertainty, perhaps a yearning to return. Loretta was sure her friend was wondering if the two of them hadn't realized how good a life they'd left behind.

"It's not far. And we will make it." Loretta's defiant gaze traveled east beyond a local peak that preceded the Rockies, which would appear soon enough. "I haven't found the right quote yet but . . ."

"About what?"

"About goin' the distance."

For years Loretta's dreams of escape hadn't included having a friend with her. She'd envisioned a brave if lonesome journey, the risk being only to herself. The commitment to take Elsie to Denver was a late addition. The shortest route east would have been a straight line—the rule about the distance between any two points passed through her mind. This first stop would lead to other turns, spur-of-the-moment impulses, and some out-of-the-way travels.

But on this glorious day, the decision made, Loretta found she no longer cared where they headed other than that she travel many, many miles from William and Mama and the Home for Wayward Girls. Her original plan had been to head out by fall, before the blinding winds and snow of winter set in. Leaving today was an almighty risk. Local authorities were on the lookout. Ms. Del left them ninety minutes outside of town. The girls waved from the interchange.

"Be careful," the teacher called from her window. They watched the red VW Rabbit disappear. The teacher held tissues to her face. They didn't know till later that Ms. Del circled back to watch and write down the license number of whoever picked them up. They were alone but not uncared for. Not long after, Ms. Del called Elsie's aunt. Gave the code word "sketches" and everything was set. The aunt would not leave her phone until she heard from the girls.

"We're on our way!" Loretta pulled Elsie by the hand down the highway ramp.

"I guess we are." Elsie stepped backward, then forward, finally gave in to the amazingness of what was happening and ran alongside her friend.

"We're wearing jeans!" Loretta screamed, and despite the not knowing, the unsure wherewithal to proceed, and the limited means with which to flee, she felt buoyant and incredulous, and that survival was near. "We are unstoppable!"

"We better be." Elsie tried to agree.

Loretta began to sing a song about not letting anything stop them now. Perfect for their road trip. "Elsie, it's like a hundred miles to the state line. We can do this."

"How do you know that?"

"See the USA!"

"What?"

"A map. Mrs. Barry saved it for me." Loretta remembered the day. Standing at the librarian's desk. Mrs. Barry had told her *when you're ready, your journey will await you.* Had the librarian known what was on the horizon or maybe, same way Loretta felt then, was Mrs. Barry gifted with insight? Loretta stared at the sky, the cars that rushed past, and she smiled.

The day was getting warmer. Loretta took off her jacket. They stood with their thumbs out. Nobody stopped.

"We're gonna make it." Loretta held tight to Elsie's hand.

"I'm not so sure," Elsie said. Her body twitched, she had goose bumps from a chill that wasn't weather. She gasped or hiccupped trying to breathe. Soon tears streamed to her chin. Loretta stretched her hands to Elsie's shoulders and waited until Elsie raised her frightened eyes. "I'm scared."

"I know. But tell me anyway."

"Tell you what?"

"Whatever you're thinking. Spill it."

"Well, truth is if you'd left without me, I'd be lost. I couldn't do this on my own."

"I'm not so sure of that."

"You're my best friend, Loretta girl."

"That's not gonna change no matter what."

"I hope not." Elsie pulled on the wrist of her sweater and wiped it across her chin, her eyes clouded with fear that rambled left to right across her pale face, unsure where to settle.

"I'm not going anywhere. Not now. Today is our day. And I won't leave you again. Not until you're safe. Until we're ready. I promise. I'm so sorry."

"It wasn't your fault," Elsie whispered. She lowered her head. Loretta remembered how William's arms had vised her friend so tightly. That he'd been whispering something in Elsie's ear. How Elsie had screamed for Loretta to go.

"Still, I'm truly sorry," Loretta said.

"I believe you."

"You know what Harriet Beecher Stowe said?"

Elsie shook her head. She didn't. She knew that Loretta talked like the famous woman was a member of her group of friends.

"She said that the past, the present, and the future are really one." Loretta paused and took a deep breath of her own. "And they are today."

"You're saying our lives start now?"

"Something like that. I think she meant all that's important is this very instant. This iota of time. It's everything and more. Elsie, if we hadn't run? We'd still be there. Trying to escape. Me owned by them. You, Lord knows what he had in that depraved mind of his. But this. This today. This moment of now. You and me going for our destiny. This is right."

"I get that."

"It's ours. No one can take today from us."

Loretta watched Elsie's resting face appear, the freckles across her nose relaxed, her fears maybe a little less frightened. They were two seventeen-year-olds who stared at the highway before them and the big sky overhead and hoped for incredible things they were not yet able to define.

"You sure are confident." Elsie wiped her eyes again and offered a small half smile that would cling to her face for many years to come. Always half a smile and half a question mark.

"Got no choice," Loretta told her and jumped in the air at the sound of a horn.

A jalopy of a maroon pickup chugged over, and a kind man named Al told them to hop in. He let Loretta change the station until she found Whitney Houston on the radio.

"How will I know?" they sang along.

Except Loretta did know. She was certain of everything she needed to comprehend at that moment. Getting Elsie to her aunt's served a greater purpose. The act uplifted Loretta's soul. Dumas wrote that a good deed is never lost, and on this morning, Loretta experienced the kind of excitement that sometimes buzzed inside her head when she'd believed something great was about to happen even though it rarely had in her life. The midday light descended through the scratched windshield of the old pickup and the battered thump of the truck's tires on the highway offered the sound of the independence they sought.

"Freedom found," she whispered to Elsie not two hours later and pointed to the WELCOME TO COLORADO sign.

"Praise be." Elsie clapped her hands together. "Much better than the sign we left behind."

Al said, "Beautiful country."

Elsie and Loretta laughed with jubilance. Alone as she would soon be, Loretta knew that her past, the true history she would choose to carry with her, had begun mere hours before.

"It's incredible," Loretta agreed.

"You girls sure you'll be okay?" Al bent close to the passenger door of the truck, shouldering concern when Loretta and Elsie jumped out at the exit.

"Don't worry, Al." Loretta poked her head through the window. "Elsie's aunt told her to go to the Conoco. There it is! We're gonna call her. She's not far. You saved us, sir. Plain saved us. Can't thank you enough."

"No thanks needed. Got daughters of my own." Al hesitated. "Here. Let me give you some change. For the phone." The big, kind man whose hands were larger than his pockets began to dig. "I wish I could do more. Or wait with you to be sure your aunt arrives. But my wife is expecting me."

"We got this. Thank you, sir!" Elsie yelled but she reached for the quarters in his hand anyway, saw the warmth in his eyes, and felt safer. They began the hike up the exit ramp.

"We're free!" Loretta yelled. She threw her arms in the air. Same as when Al had picked them up on the side of the highway in the midmorning sunshine.

Honest to God, Loretta and Elsie were indeed free. They were happy. Ahead, the red-and-white Conoco sign welcomed them to their new lives.

They couldn't wait.

"We made it." Loretta nudged her elbow into Elsie's side. The both of them laughed and stumbled, drunk with giggles, their lack of sure-footedness belying the determination that guided them to the 7-Eleven at the rear of the gas station lot.

"Slurpies?" Elsie pointed at a sign on the store window. She leaned far forward, her ponytail flopping about. "My stomach is aching for that." She raised her head to the sky.

"Huh? What's a Slurpie?"

"I have no idea. But it looks incredible."

"I agree." Loretta stared with awe at a poster of the red-frosted drink.

"I want one. I want everything!" Elsie laughed some more.

The girls stopped still beneath the midday sky. There were scarcely any powder-blue streaks disrupting the delicate cloud patterns that showcased the gateway to the Rockies.

"Listen, Loretta girl."

"To what?"

"Cars. Wind. That sound." She pointed to a man who tossed an empty Coke can into the trash bin. "People. It's people. And we're part of them."

"Very true."

"We've made it. Right?" Elsie dropped onto the ground off to the side of an air pump.

"Right." Loretta sat as well. Two teen girl-women sitting cross-legged on the parking lot staring at nothing. Digesting life around them. Civilization. And wearing jeans! Seconds ticked away, quiet time in a slow river of motion, as the welcome feeling of freedom settled into their skin with tingles of excitement.

"Hey." A man in a beige truck slowed down on his way past them. "You girls all right there?"

"Better than," Loretta yelled with a smile on her face, pushing her hair behind her shoulders. "We are blessed."

"Well, get your blessed bodies off the parking lot before someone hits you," he called out and drove to the exit. "Safety first!"

"Thank you!" the girls yelled after him. Seemed everyone was watching over them. They scooched farther away from the pump.

Loretta reached for Elsie's hand, her serious face poised to speak.

"You got something to add?" Elsie asked.

"No net ensnares me: I am a free human being."

"Let me try and guess." Elsie stuck her face in her hands, squinted her eyes, and pushed strands of hair away from her face. "Is it Eleanor?"

"Nope." Loretta raised her hands to the sky and waved at the clouds. "But that's a good try. It's my old friend Charlotte."

"You had a friend named Charlotte?"

"Well, you know what I mean. A great writer."

"I'm going to read books." Elsie swiped bits of gravel off her jeans. Pulled her sweater tighter around her waist.

"Yes, you are!" Loretta jumped to her feet, grabbed Elsie's hand, and they ran through the 7-Eleven's open door. "Slurpies, it is."

"To freedom," Elsie announced moments later and clinked her paper cup to Loretta's. Soon Elsie's mouth was encircled in blue, and Loretta's in strawberry red.

"Your aunt's on her way?" Loretta's eyes lowered to her boots, a hand in the pocket of her army jacket. One of the few times she let Elsie see her nervous and unsure. "Maybe I should go on my own now."

"No. Please don't. Please. Don't worry. Please. Remember, my aunt ran away years ago. She told me she'd help if I ever needed her. I'm sure she will."

"I remember. But still, I'm only staying awhile. Till I know you are set."

"I understand." It was Elsie's turn to stare at the ground. Loretta knew Elsie couldn't bear being without her best friend, the one person who'd guarded her, protected her since her first day on the ranch.

"Sure could use a shower." Loretta made a face. "I probably smell like dirt and sweat."

"You do."

"Well, thanks, girlfriend."

"Ha! Any time."

"Your aunt won't call William and Mama? You sure, Elsie?"

"I'm pretty sure. If there's one thing I know . . ."

"What? What is it?"

"She'd never send us back there."

Honk! Honk!

Loretta and Elsie watched a dented two-tone tan-and-brown Ford Bronco race into the 7-Eleven's lot. Driver's-side window open. A hand waved to them.

"Elsie? Is that my Elsie?" a woman yelled.

"Aunt Tammy!"

"And this must be Loretta? Your friend? Ms. Del's wonderful student? Word is Loretta is the bravest young woman I've not yet met." Elsie's aunt jumped out of the truck, leaving the door open, and ran to the two of them. Threw her arms around their thin girl bodies like they were returning war heroes.

"Yes, I'm Loretta, ma'am."

"Welcome, welcome." Aunt Tammy took a step back. Stood

before them in Levi's tucked into well-worn leather western boots, a carved turquoise belt buckle, vibrant pink lipstick, bright red nails, and a checkered scarf knotted around her neck. Her long pale hair mirrored Elsie's. "If you girls aren't a sight!"

"Aunt Tammy, is it okay we're here?"

"Better than, my niece. It's about time!"

"You sure, ma'am?" Loretta took one step forward. She was ready to get back on the highway, stick out a thumb, and hurry off if she was causing trouble.

"Sure? Of course. And Loretta, I'm not a ma'am. Call me Aunt Tammy. Come on, you incredible women. We're going home. I've got a tri-tip ready to roast, red potatoes to be mashed, and three-bean salad in the fridge. My Lord, I'm glad to see you."

Aunt Tammy jumped into her truck. Elsie and Loretta slid in through the passenger door. Rosanne Cash sang "Runaway Train" on the radio. Aunt Tammy's bright red nails kept pace with the song on the steering wheel. Elsie and Loretta swayed left to right to left.

Everybody smiled.

Freedom does that to girls.

Elsie's aunt owned a small frame house on Lincoln Street in Globeville, a mostly industrial area triangulated within what locals called the Mousetrap, where I-70 and I-25 intersect, near freight train tracks and the South Platte River.

"It's really North Denver," Aunt Tammy told them.

"Then why's it called Globeville?" Loretta asked when they drove in. She'd never seen houses so close to each other that people could probably see in their neighbors' windows. One had a lime-green door and she thought that was fantastic.

"Not sure. Maybe because of the immigrants who came here

to work in the smelting plants years ago. A bit out of the way still. It was the cheapest thing I could find. Lucky for me. It's all mine now."

The house was tan and brown and battered like the old Ford Bronco, the front walkway anchored by two oaks with trunks wider than big burly men. Friendly overhanging branches full of green leaves arched over the front door eager to touch the cheeks of visitors.

"Wait." Loretta stopped walking when she heard a siren. "Could that be—?"

"Don't worry." Aunt Tammy grabbed both their hands. "There's a hospital not too far from here. You're safe with me. You okay?"

"Sure." Loretta swallowed hard. "I think so."

"Come on in. It's not the Ritz. Could be called the *far end* of the line." Aunt Tammy's laughter was loud, it poured from her, it was contagious, and both girls burst into giggles. "Nothing much beyond here, but if you look to the left of the house and squint hard, you might catch sight of the edge of the Rockies. I like the view."

"I think I saw them," Elsie said. Aunt Tammy held the door wide open.

"Nice."

They passed through a front room filled with lumpy, lived-in, sat-on furniture. Loretta pointed to a metal rack of record albums on the wood floor next to the stereo and television. There was nothing in common with the horsehair red couch back on the ranch that scratched legs and smelled like a parlor too long kept closed off from fresh air.

"I'm old school. Stickin' with my favorites," Aunt Tammy told them. Bonnie Raitt's *Luck of the Draw* was front of the stack. "No cassettes allowed on my property."

"Wow." Loretta lingered a few steps behind. She stopped before a painting of three women riding horseback at a rodeo.

"Friends of mine." Aunt Tammy paused near the archway to the kitchen.

"Really?"

"Stay around till next April and I'll take you to see them."

"Wish I could," Loretta said. Her resolve wavered. Thoughts flew about—like peregrines high above the prairie back at the ranch. She considered if she might stay with Aunt Tammy in this little house that was everything the ranch had never been. She wanted to flop on the couch, turn on the television, and watch whatever came on. But staying in Globeville or North Denver, whichever it was, wasn't part of her plan.

The three of them sat at Aunt Tammy's dinette set, the table covered with a blue-flowered vinyl cloth. Wooden kitchen cabinets were painted robin's-egg blue. A red teakettle was set on an ancient stove that Aunt Tammy lit with matches. Her good old dog named Elmer, a golden retriever with spots, nudged his way between Elsie and Loretta to sit at their feet (might be half Dalmatian, Aunt Tammy declared, and more addictive laughter bobbled out of her mouth).

"So what's on your list?" Aunt Tammy, real serious, asked.

"List?" Elsie whispered, her hands on the table, her eyes on the window over the sink. She had seen the few goats her aunt kept in the backyard and two llamas to the rear in a tiny fenced-in area. She told Loretta she wanted to sketch them and was anxious to sit outside.

"Why you whisperin'?" Loretta shook her head at Elsie.

"Oh my God," Elsie said in a slightly louder voice. "I can't help it."

"When I made my own getaway"—Aunt Tammy checked the ceiling, then smacked her hands on the table, which startled them both—"I had a list. Things I had to do. My wish list because—"

"Because what?" Loretta asked. She'd kept her jacket on in case she needed to head for the road fast. It was hard not to trust Aunt Tammy, she was sincerely nice, but Loretta had cautioned herself for a long time not to take chances.

"Because . . ." Aunt Tammy pulled a pack of cigarettes from the pearl-snapped pocket of her plaid shirt and offered one to each of them, which they declined. "Well, truth is I was always fearful. I wanted to do everything possible *because* you never know. Right? What if I got hauled back?"

"But you didn't? Get hauled back?" Elsie's eyes opened wide. Fear rooted within them. Her freckles frozen across her nose. She knew that being returned to her hometown would mean hell to pay.

"No, I didn't. And you won't either."

"Are you sure?" Loretta asked.

"Okay, girls, here's the deal." Aunt Tammy reached across the table. Held on to one of Elsie's hands and one of Loretta's. "I won't let them catch you. We're keeping you secure till your birthdays and then some. Both of you. I promise. Agreed?"

The girls nodded.

"But what if?" Loretta stuck one foot over her other forgetting that Elmer was there. The dog whimpered. She reached down to pat his head. She had read about sweet dogs. Pets that don't bare their teeth. That don't exist to threaten.

"You know"—Aunt Tammy's face took a serious note, her eyes squinted into straight lines—"you're gonna live with fear for the time being. Like an acquaintance you'd rather had disappeared. Fear doesn't quickly hightail away. But you've done right. You made it here and thank the Lord, you're on your own now. And there's folks who will help."

"You think so?" Elsie's finger traced a white flower drawn in the tablecloth.

"I know so. How about me for one? I think I qualify to be someone who wants to help."

"Thank you, Aunt Tammy." Loretta bowed her head, a bit embarrassed by the tears that had collected in her eyes.

"It's all good! You two ready for some real food? Then we'll go shopping."

"Shopping?" both girls asked.

"I'm pretty sure Elsie needs a new drawing pad. And I suspect you ladies would like some different T-shirts. More current era! Deodorant, too. Stuff like that. Charlie perfume—you ever tried it? You'll love it."

Elsie and Loretta exchanged a look that said *Oh, we do smell of sweat and dirt.*

"Maybe some makeup, too," Aunt Tammy added.

"Makeup?" Both girls screamed. "That's on our list!"

TWENTY-TWO

East of the Rockies

Elsie and Loretta settled in at Aunt Tammy's. They shared a twin-bedded room with walls that displayed framed photos of women riding and roping steers, doing all manner of things men had done for years. There was a certificate from the Women's Professional Rodeo Association with Aunt Tammy's name written in fancy script.

"Wanna go for a walk?" Aunt Tammy leaned in and asked every day.

"Sure," Elsie and Loretta agreed each afternoon.

They strolled along the sidewalks, past small houses, kids playing out front, teens who zipped by on skateboards, moms holding babies.

"That lime-green door gets me every time," Loretta said.

"Wait, wait." Elsie held up a hand. "There's a red one up ahead. It's my favorite."

During the second week, very late one afternoon, Loretta was reading Aunt Tammy's anthology of women cowgirls that detailed Annie Oakley to Dale Evans to current times. She had a pillow smushed behind her head, could hear country music from the living room, and had maybe never before felt so safe and comfortable.

"Hey, how're you doin', you okay?" Aunt Tammy stood in the bedroom doorway.

"Great. I like your book. Thanks for letting me borrow it."

"No thanks needed. Up for a walk?" Aunt Tammy had her boots on, which meant she was ready to head out.

"Sure, should I go get Elsie?"

"Nah, she's out back with Larry. Making him pose for her." Larry was a llama named after one of Tammy's exes. "I told her we'd be back soon." Loretta followed Aunt Tammy through the front door. They turned left and walked toward the freight train yards. A good spot for standing. The rusted crank of braking trains, screeches, could well be violins warming up.

"You remember what I said about fear?" Aunt Tammy stared above the locomotive beyond them. Farther away. Her words not so much a question but something else.

"That we live with it? Like someone you'd rather had disappeared. Doesn't go away fast?"

"Yep. That's it. And that's why there's something I need to tell you, Loretta." Aunt Tammy bent her knees and crouched down, her eyes on the metal wheels of Union Pacific and Minnesota Southern freight cars that churned by. "It's not good but I think you can deal with it."

"What is it?" Loretta stooped next to Aunt Tammy. Felt tears at the ready. Didn't even know what the news was but sure as she could pinpoint old bruises on her arms and legs, anxieties began to simmer within her chest, her fingers twitched, and her neck began to itch.

"I called Elsie's mom. I'm sorry. But I needed to let my sister know her daughter was safe. I didn't have a choice."

"Okay." Loretta did understand but couldn't help that daggers attacked the insides of her stomach. "Any chance, like, did she know how my mother is?"

"Yes. That's the good part. Your mama's fine. She's home. From what I heard she's gonna be one hundred percent."

"So what's the other part?"

"Two things. First, I know you're plain afraid. Every time you hear mention of folks back there, or have a dream that's more gray than pretty—?"

"I have those," Loretta whispered, her eyes locked on the tiny flashes of golden light within the complicated iron train wheels.

"That fear's gonna race through you. But you'll learn to tame it. I promise you that."

"And? Seems you've got somethin' more to tell me."

"My sister called me a little while ago. Said your father is sending someone. I don't know how that happened." Aunt Tammy shook her head, retucked her jeans into her boots. "My sister, well, she's got no willpower. Must've told Elsie's dad. You know?"

"I do." Loretta bounced to full standing. She remembered the card William took from those goons who brought Elsie. "He'll send transporters. I know it. I need to go."

"There's a Greyhound later tonight. I can take you."

"No. That's too easy for William. He'll have them at the station. Or they'll pull me off at one of the stops."

"Loretta, we'll drive you to the highway if that's what you want. I'm really, really sorry, girl. I hope you believe me."

"The ride would help. And I do believe you, Aunt Tammy. You already did so much for me. Please promise me you'll tell them I've been gone a few days. Or that I did take the bus. Make it harder for them to find me."

"No problem. Leave that to me. If anybody can steer them off track, I can."

"What about Elsie? Will she be safe?"

"Sure. My sister may be weak, but she listens to me. They decided to leave Elsie in my care. I said it was time to let her go."

"Okay. I gotta tell Elsie. I'll get my stuff." Loretta knew Elsie was prepared for this. They both were. They'd known they'd soon separate but had thought they'd have more time.

"You need anything?" Aunt Tammy asked.

"I've got makeup now. Jeans. A backpack. Charlie perfume. Even more Twizzlers. Think I'm set. Except—"

"What?"

"I can't thank you enough."

"Nah, I owe you." Aunt Tammy let her arm fall across Loretta's shoulders. "Helping you, well, it's a way of repaying those who did for me."

They hurried back to the brown-and-tan comfy house. When they arrived at the burly oak trees, Loretta's tears deluged down her cheeks. She turned and hugged Aunt Tammy. She would have liked to stay. Seen that rodeo. Finished reading the book about real cowgirls.

A siren careened within the wind. Loretta jumped. Her body began to shake.

"Don't worry. That's not coming here."

"Okay, but I better get a move on."

Going it alone had always been her plan.

"No, don't do nothin' or say nothin'," Aunt Tammy told someone on the phone in her kitchen as evening neared. Loretta and Elsie sat nearby. Elsie's finger traced flowers in the tablecloth.

"What's happening?" Loretta asked when the phone was hung up.

"Friend of mine been listening to CB radio for us. Somehow she gets the sheriff's stuff. We gotta go. Now. They got the cops involved and they're coming." Aunt Tammy didn't laugh. Grabbed her fringed jacket. "Don't forget that backpack we loaded up for you. Hurry."

"All set." Loretta threw the bag over her shoulders, reached for Elsie's hand, and they raced to the Ford Bronco. They heard sirens—closer this time.

"I'm gonna take you out of Globeville. To a highway entrance farther to the south. 'Fraid they mighta sent a deputy to wait by the Conoco." Aunt Tammy hit the gas. The Bronco sped off. No one turned on the radio, silence a needed ingredient for their fast getaway. "A friend of my CB friend is gonna meet us there. Take you farther past Denver."

"What? You shouldn't—"

"Don't worry. Lots of runaway girls are grown women now. Rodeo girls stick together. Take the assist." Aunt Tammy hung a quick right. Her shiny red nails tapped the steering wheel more impatient than following any rhythm.

Elsie patted Loretta's arm. She shook her head and half smiled.

"Take it," she agreed with her aunt.

"You two quick now. Hug time." Aunt Tammy handed Loretta a roll of cash at the on-ramp to the interstate. "This is from me and my ladies. Don't forget what we've talked about. Call me collect any time. Got the number?"

"I do. And thank you, thank your ladies!"

"Loretta girl." Elsie grabbed Loretta's hand at the top of the highway entrance. Aunt Tammy stood ten feet back. The Bronco's headlights spotlighted them both. "When will I—"

"We don't know. But here's the thing. We are together always. Distance, well, it's temporary. Okay?"

"Okay." Elsie hugged her best friend. Loretta hugged back and hoped it wasn't for the last time.

"And friendship has no expiration date."

"Said who?" Elsie asked before the short honk of a Jeep jolted them back to reality.

"A great teacher." Loretta offered a tiny smile, more in her eyes than her lips, and jumped into the rugged vehicle.

"We're off"—a lady in a gingham shirt and jeans shifted the Jeep into gear—"and nice to meet you, Loretta. I hear you're quite a young woman."

"I don't know."

"Trust me. I know smart and lucky when I see it."

"Thanks. I sure hope so."

Loretta didn't dare take her luck for granted. Couldn't help but think *thank you, God, thank you, God* for Aunt Tammy, the rodeo ladies, and for her best friend. Hoping for the best had never been Loretta's strong suit, but it sure seemed life was daring her to believe.

An hour later, Loretta was on her own. Some college kids stopped and she got her first ride. By the next dawn, she was one of the tribe of hitchhikers trying to get somewhere, anywhere, only requirement was that it be as far away as possible.

At pit stops, Loretta planted herself to the right of the entrance ramp, thumb out to cars that passed. The temperatures not far from the foot of the mountains were moderate; moist ground seeped into the soles of her lace-up boots leaving her both chilled and wary. Her clothing needed a protracted shelf life, her budget was spare. What would she do when real cold set in?

Honk! A souped-up royal blue Firebird flew by. The driver waved but didn't stop.

"Oh jeez," she said to no one.

"You okay?" A long, tall guy lumbered over. Shaggy hair spilled from under his black knit cap embroidered with angular gold letters that spelled out DEF LEPPARD. His shoulders curled toward the ground. He hurried in the manner tall guys have; the way they spring sideways from one shoe to the other while in a slow-sprint forward. He hustled down the ramp as if a conversation with her was an important mission. At least, that's how it felt to Loretta.

"Me? I'm all right. I guess." Loretta did a bit of a to-and-fro side-step herself, straightened her coveted one pair of jeans, slapped her palms together, crossed her arms, uncrossed her arms, and shoved her hands into the pockets of her army jacket.

"You're cold. Admit it." He spoke in the language of the brigade of young folks on interstates and at roadside cafés. None of them knew one another, yet they were immediate friends of a sort. They wore well-fatigued army jackets, knit caps, scarves no matter the season. They couldn't afford to lose any piece of their limited wardrobes.

"Not so cold. It's early."

"You look cold."

"Hmm." More, she was tired.

It had been slow going after Denver. A few rides. A night alone. She hid whenever she saw a sheriff or highway patrol car. She'd declined a couple offers from drivers who made her nervous. A teen headed south gave her a ragged crocheted hat that Loretta pulled over her ears. She knew that by noon, the sun would warm away any chills—then she'd feel overheated and sweaty. Her hair needed to be washed; her scalp was dry and itchy. She'd learned quick to be careful, a young woman from Idaho told her not to show any weakness or they'll get you.

"They who?" Loretta had asked.

The woman said there were folks who stop and say they are on a mission to help poor girls fleeing bad families. "Those people are plain worthless. They're bounty hunters after runaway teens. People who'll sell you back before you get any taste of freedom. Remember evil doesn't reside on a dead-end street. It's everywhere."

Loretta wouldn't ever forget that.

"Hey, where'd you go? I'm Drew." The hand of the long, tall guy waved at her. He both bent forward and stepped back at the same instant. Might be how he assured fellow hitchhikers to feel safe, a move that indicated *don't worry, I'm not a menace, I understand personal space.*

"I'm Loretta," she said and shook his hand. She, who was neither tall nor short, reached inside her pockets. Found the buttons stored in one, her red pocketknife in the other just in case.

"Where you headed?" Drew rubbed his fingers along his stubbled chin, his eyes cast away from hers, at the ground, then to the top of the ramp, watching for a van or a pickup that might hold promise. A county cop would not be a welcome sight.

"East of here." She didn't have a cardboard sign. The metal compass in her pocket ensured she knew which direction to take. Short-term destination didn't matter to her. She needed rides that eventually would lead to the coast farthest from William.

"East is kinda big, don't cha think? Care to narrow it down?"

"East of everything." Loretta raised her eyes to the early morning clouds. "Far from here and east of everything," she repeated.

"I understand."

Loretta was still learning the nuances of hitchhiking life. Who gets the next ride? Is there an order to things on the road? She was smelly and gritty, her collar was scented with used tobacco smoke, her mouth tasted of cheap coffee and the Coke she'd had at a road stop. Her breath carried last night's dinner—a hot dog from the rotisserie in the front of a gas station. She shouldn't have squeezed on the mustard that now lodged in her stomach. No matter how crappy she'd thought the food on the ranch, there was worse stuff than Mama's egg scramble and burnt bacon.

"We could see who comes along. Wanna try together? For a bit?" Drew bounced a step away, again scoped out the top of the ramp, in the manner that long, tall guys do in the early morning, willing a spigot of kind drivers to descend.

"Hmm." Loretta let her uncertainty float between them. She didn't want to be a fool. Trust some guy because he was tall and acted like he'd written the rules of the road.

"Up to you," he added.

She wasn't sure, her fingers tight around her shiny red pocketknife. The question was, would she ever be certain? She hesitated. Remembered a Bible verse on replay in her head the last few days. When she'd first heard the words preached, they hadn't taken hold. But since fleeing the ranch, sermons collided with memories in her head—of Mama's heavy-lidded eyes, William who ripped the blouse off her chest, the night of no stars, and the scar that crusted into her neck.

Loretta had escaped. This was true. But would she ever forget?

She'd run from William with the pistol on his thigh, and from Mama whose face had become a ghastly mask of horror. From Bull the rottweiler and his hungry growl. And from the utter madness that ensued, Crystal's screams, the residents shaking with fear, their arms outstretched to her, their halted steps that backed away, did they move away and not toward her? Had they been afraid of her? Of Loretta with the rifle in her hands?

"Return to your stronghold, O prisoners of hope," the minister once cautioned.

She was sure he meant that prisoners of hope needed to return to the church. To his church. To William's church. But there would be no such return for her. She was prisoner of a different sort of hope.

A new morning was upon her.

Loretta had survived, and her fate was up to the goodness of strangers. It was time for her to find a new faith, to have faith in others. Such a small idea, yet it was the stronghold she needed. It would lead her far to the east where liberty waited with open arms.

"Well?" Drew asked.

"Yes, let's do it." She hoped she wasn't making a grave error.

No cars stopped for them. Muscular Ford Tahoes and loud diesel F150 trucks raced by, the entrance ramp heavily scented with oil fumes. Like early morning schoolchildren, an onslaught of additional hitchhikers arrived. Loretta and Drew settled onto the damp ground nearby. Ripped pieces of cardboard extended from the much-too-tanned hands of the young wanderers. ALBUQUERQUE in black marker on one. Another declared WEST!!! A guy with a guitar strapped to his back held a many times unfolded sign with ~~LAS VEGAS, SALT LAKE, DENVER~~ and then barely legible scrawl that pleaded: KANSAS PLEASE!

"Hey, come on." Drew nudged Loretta. "Let's go for coffee."

"But?" Loretta felt her eyes lodge into a cynical question mark and the crease deepen at the bridge of her nose. "What about?"

"I've got an idea." The long, tall guy began sidestepping up the ramp. He turned around and said, "Trust me. It's just coffee."

Trust me. Such uncomplicated words.

Loretta followed. She could count on one hand the number of people she'd ever had the chance to trust. So far, since this journey began, three. Maybe Drew would make that four.

"Don't go." The guy with the guitar waved to her.

"Not headed to Kansas," she called back, shrugged, and offered her less cynical smile.

She hurried after Drew. Walking, moving her legs, and shoving her hands deeper into her pockets felt really, really good. Not being alone, for even a little bit of time, was like the promise of new clothes, of maybe shopping at a Target one day, or when her teacher had told her she'd done well on a paper. It was like holding a brand-new tiny bunny, which made her feel that there was unconditional love that didn't hurt.

Next to each other, Loretta and Drew loped down the road that right-angled off the top of the ramp. Loped, because that's how Drew walked. Loretta fell into his rhythm. Each step a bit to the side then forward.

"See, I'm not so bad," he said. Lowered his eyes, which were way above hers. Another of those tall guy skills. "You're not in a hurry, are ya?"

"Guess not," she said. Her own head unsure where to look. Up at him or to the tar beneath her feet.

"Come on then. East of everything will wait."

"Okay, you're probably right."

Hurrying, getting fast onto the highway, took a back seat. She wondered how that was. That she'd had a timetable ticking inside her brain, a voice that kept saying *move, move, move,* and in an instant that very same voice asked, *Why the hurry, why, why, why?* She had no good answers. The experience so different that Loretta was elated and scared and smiling. Which felt better than all right, something so entirely new that she wanted to sit on a log and contemplate the feeling deeply. Except there were no logs nearby.

"You okay?"

"I am," Loretta told Drew.

"You look kinda like . . . I don't know. Got something on your mind?"

"Nah," she said. "I did. But I figured it out."

"Care to share?" he asked, which she'd come to learn was a favorite question of his.

"Not really." She burst out laughing. "It's just. Like. About choice. Choices. Having them. It's cool, you know."

"I do. Look." He grinned and pointed. "Mickey D's or that diner. Your choice."

"There." She pointed to the golden arches. Something else new to her. In a world where it was said a new McDonald's opened somewhere every five hours, Loretta had never entered one before. She couldn't wait.

It wasn't that Loretta would necessarily recommend hitchhiking. But sometimes, one has no choice. Seventeen-year-old Loretta made her first new friend on the road. Someone who knew nothing about her, who had never seen her in a wraparound skirt or lost in the aisles at Walmart.

"I'm talkin' destiny," Loretta told Drew. It was nighttime. They huddled by an on-ramp, thumbs out. Exasperated when no rides appeared, they gave up and hiked along the nearby service road.

"Not sure that's a concept." Drew dropped to a sitting position on the ground. He wore his Def Leppard cap, shoulders hunched forward, such a large tortoise that his chin rested on his knees.

"Destiny is not a concept," she argued. "It's a reality, I think." This was their second day together on the road. She'd grown comfortable with Drew. When they first met, she kept one hand in her pocket gripping her red pocketknife. Then she began to trust him.

"So, your father, the awful William, you think him beating the shit out of you was some kind of destiny? I'd like to think not. And what about this mother of yours?"

Drew was older and wiser. At least twenty, he had seniority in the hierarchy of road warriors. He used words in a certain manner. She thought that he would have been happier living in an Emily Brontë novel than in the '90s and told him so.

"You know what Brontë said in *Wuthering Heights*?" she asked, keen to shift the discussion away from anything to do with Mama.

"Can't say that I do."

"There you go again."

"Again what?" Drew stretched far back from his knees. A human teeter-totter.

"The way you talk. It's unusual."

"Hmm. So, what'd this great writer of the nineteenth century have to say?"

"Oh, right." Loretta squeezed her army jacket tighter around herself, pleased to be having such a conversation. And the fact that he knew when the book was written confirmed her thoughts that he was more well-studied than he purported to be. "She said that this lady in the book burned too bright for the world. Some people take that differently. But I think Brontë was saying the woman was a star, a force, someone better than the rest of us simple humans."

"Simple? I take you to mean what?"

"Like the way you asked that. You're a bright star, Drew. You make me think. Same way Brontë books do."

"I hope that's good." Drew raised his hands high above his head and yawned.

"It is."

"What does that have to do with destiny?" he asked.

"I believe, or at least I want to believe, that even welts and the meanest words can ultimately glisten. They can shine a light on the path. On where we're headed, where we'll get to. They must. Elsewise, how could so many of us survive?"

"Okay, I get it. The worst of times can lead you somewhere you're meant to be. Right?"

"Yes, something like that. Do you really understand?" Loretta twisted to see his face.

"Only in principle. Not sure. But I'll give it my sincere consideration."

Loretta lowered her forehead to her knees and grinned bigtime. She almost began to cry, not sad with misery, but joyoushallelujah-jubilated tears. This conversation was awesome—she decided dialogue might well be an inalienable right. It was wonderfully baffling that people could disagree, and yet fistfights did not break out. In fact, arguments were a good thing. It mesmerized her that she might have one opinion and someone else another and they remained friends on this road of experience.

No one lashed out. No one hit anyone. If anything, young hitchhikers she met pondered their differences, laughed so loud she understood the meaning of the word *guffaw*, and sometimes they cried in commiseration with each other.

It was simple plain talking.

She lifted her head and stared at Drew. He'd lowered himself to the ground. One arm over his eyes. Asleep. Loretta took out her matches. Lit a cigarette. She realized she'd never before felt the deep breaths freedom allows, hadn't ever paused a moment, not even a second, without the river of fear that tingled within her veins.

The wings and slate-gray tail of a falcon could well have been close. Loretta lifted her gaze to the night. Her eyes shifted across the sky, and she felt a presence. It might have been the knowledge that somehow her life before, everything that was in her past, was also the bounty that ensured her future would be better.

"Yep," she whispered and took a drag of her Marlboro. "Must be that."

Loretta exhaled and watched the smoke drift away. She raised her palm into the sky. Churchgoers did similar in the small town she'd escaped—raised their hands to the Lord. She ground out the last of the glowing tobacco, lay back to the earth, threw one arm over her eyes and the other felt 'round for the loose buttons and red pocketknife in her jacket, because, well, again, you never know.

Still, she smiled. And slept.

Loretta was scared, but certain she'd done the right thing. It was within the company of Drew and other hitchhikers that she discovered her footing and her voice. Sitting on the ground near a highway on-ramp, they sang happy birthday to her. A fellow hitchhiker gave her a bracelet made of colored string. Drew presented her with a pack of Dentyne. She was happy and within this brigade of boy-men and girl-women, thumbs extended, hurrying to destinations south, west, and east, praying for rides to some special place they believed must await them . . . she learned that each one was running from someone or some act for which they hoped they'd be forgiven.

A special place. Must. Must. Must await them.

The hitchhikers she'd joined dreamt of destinations the way others hoped for riches. Had the road brigade only known the foundation they laid before Loretta's feet, the invaluable lessons with which they helped prepare her for the big city!

They were the guarantee she'd been given.

They were her survival warranty.

Exactly what she needed to continue her journey.

TWENTY-THREE

East of Everything

"Nice car," she told Andy, the driver of a snazzy Ford Torino, a guy from Upstate New York (one of numerous terms she'd learn to meld into her vernacular over time). He blew cigarette smoke out the driver's-side window with very cool-guy abandon.

"It's a two-door. That's a plus," he said. "A muscle car. Collector's item. Pace car at the Indy."

"Nice color."

"Ivy gold. Took Amtrak to Philly special to pick it up. Myself."

"Hmm. Philly." Loretta wanted to tell him that what he'd said was obvious—that he was after all by himself. So was she. She didn't care about cars. Or pickup trucks. Not now. Maybe never again after jumping in and out of fourteen of them since Ms. Del dropped her close to the state line. A huge metropolis awaited her. She stared through the bridge's wires and beams to the river on her right. A patchwork of brighter and brighter late-day sunlight streamed across dark waters far as she could see and illuminated tall skyscrapers in the great beyond. She heard loud thumping noises beneath the car—the bridge bouncing in place.

"You're crossin' the Hudson." Andy pointed to the river. An extralong brown cigarette hung from his mouth. "This is a suspension bridge. The bouncing? That's what we're on, the bridge is suspended by cables attached to the towers above. Get it? Like a road that's suspended! Two levels and almost a mile long. Bet you didn't know that."

"I didn't. Truly did not." Loretta leaned her head out her window to try and see the tall arc de triomphe tower they passed beneath.

"I took the top level so you could get a view of your new home."

"That's New York!"

"None other. And you're entering on the George Washington Bridge."

Loretta waved her palm at the city outside the windshield. She'd thought it was New York but needed to be sure. There wouldn't be a welcome committee waiting for her. Still, she was ready.

"The Big Apple, kid," Andy continued. "The City. You've made it. Bumper to bumper. Traffic at a standstill. Of course." The Ford Torino stopped then rolled forward a few feet at a time.

"I've made it." She sighed. "Buck wrote that New York is a place apart. That there's no match for it in any other country."

"Buck who?" Andy asked.

"Pearl S. A writer. She won a Pulitzer."

"Didn't know that. Truly did not." He laughed out loud, mimicking the words she'd said earlier.

Andy apologized that he had to drop her as soon as they got to Manhattan but that was the best he could offer. "I'd stay and help you, I mean I'm not sure where you want to go. Except my sister, well, you know, she's only expecting me. Sorry, kid."

"It's okay. Really." Loretta didn't think it was a bad thing.

Manhattan or where else? She had no idea. She was petrified. Plain scared. But she was relieved, too. Being her own welcome committee made sense. She didn't want to share her arrival with Andy and his muscle car. This moment of destiny was hers alone.

"You meet some good people along the way?" he asked.

"I did. I made a friend. Named Drew. Got me to Omaha. I sure hope I'll see him again someday. And a super semi driver. Took me a long haul."

"Really? I thought they weren't allowed to pick up anybody."

"They're not. But he saw me at a rest stop. I was really draggin' and I think he plain took pity. Even let me sleep in the cab behind the seat. That was cool."

"What about the rest of the way? Anybody try to screw with ya?"

"Hmm, well." Loretta again turned to the river. A week ago felt like another lifetime. She remembered a man who never looked her in the eye. She'd known almost right away when she got in his car that she'd made a bad call. "Just one guy. Outside of Kansas City. Had some kind of car locks that he controlled. He tried—"

"Tried what?" Andy threw his cigarette out the window and hit his fist on the steering wheel.

"I think he was going to try something, but I didn't let him. Said I had to use the restroom at the Circle K. That's where I got away from him. The man at the register helped me."

"No kiddin'?"

"Yep, hid me in the back." Loretta did her best not to show the fear she knew would cross her face thinking of the guy. He'd slammed through the convenience store, threatened the clerk. Loretta had ducked behind the counter, her hand gripping her pocketknife in case. When the clerk started dialing 911, the guy took off. The clerk, a seriously kind man, let her sit for a while.

"You need this," he'd said and gave her a Shasta and a warm apple hand pie.

The man even offered to call his wife to take her to their house, but Loretta said no, anxious to get far from the scene that had rammed nightmarish ranch memories back to the forefront of her brain. She'd made a hurried return to the highway and found a young woman to hitchhike with for a spell, which was, she had to remind herself, what Drew had made her promise to do. Traveling in pairs was highly recommended.

"I gotta give you credit. You're sure something." Andy seemed impressed for a guy who was adept at appearing too cool to give away his thoughts.

"I hope so. This city looks bigger than I expected. Like huge!"

"You'll make it, kid. I'd bet on it." Andy leaned toward the passenger window when Loretta got out of the flashy Ford at a street corner in the middle of the city she didn't know. "I'm one hundred percent sure. And, trust me, my bets always pay off."

"Thanks, Andy. I appreciate the ride. Nice car, by the way. A two-door. That's a plus, you know." It was her turn to mimic his words. She stopped curbside and burst out laughing. Her hand went to her neck. Her eyes gave him a smile of gratitude. "By the way, *you're* one of the good people I met, too."

"Well, that's a high compliment," Andy said, pleased despite his cool-guy smirk.

She carefully shut the muscle car's door and began to walk down Broadway. Loretta didn't have any idea where she was or exactly what step she'd take next. She'd promised to call Ms. Del once she found the AYH—American Youth Hostels—on Amsterdam Avenue, where her teacher had once stayed. The teacher would in turn call Aunt Tammy. A phone tree they'd set up. She'd promised Elsie a letter the minute she could sit somewhere and write. Elsie would send her a sketch, she was sure. But Loretta wasn't in a hurry to lock this moment of arrival into the leaves of her personal book. Today was a big deal.

She'd made it. She'd made it. To New York City! With over seven million people.

Loretta was in a city so large she might easily disappear into the crowd of folks she watched exit beneath a sign that said Subway 1, 2, 3. She'd never been on a train and this was the most blue-jean-awesome, strawberry-red-Slurpie, and peachy-scented-Charlie-perfume day she could have asked for.

The street sign a few corners later said Sixty-Ninth Street. She was completely alone and nothing could have comforted her more. Loretta took slow intoxicated steps until she found an empty bench outside a deli with orange neon letters that blinked C-O-F-F-E-E on and off, next to a dry cleaner's and a pizza place with a Sharpie-written sign taped to the window that said BEST SLICES IN THE CITY.

She stared many directions, back and forth, across the street and farther on, not knowing anything about where she was. A thought came to her clear as watching pronghorns outside her bedroom window. With more clarity than she'd maybe ever had before, a fleeting feeling winged its way through her mind and left a tiny little planting, not yet a bud, but a seed that one day she might live in this neighborhood.

Or maybe she dared to hope she could.

Her hands trembled at the idea, that such high-as-the-sky possibilities could inhabit her brain. She dropped her backpack between her feet and scooched to the rear of the bench. Hugged her camouflage jacket tight around her waist. Shivered from her pensive excitement that mingled with the late summer temperatures outside. Loretta lowered her head so no one passing would see her face. And tears began to drop from her eyes.

It was a good cry. Good! An alone cry she needed.

She bit her lips, shook her hair behind her shoulders, curled deeper into herself, and sadly, but also happily, she cried some more. Prayed, yes prayed, that someday the nightmarish memories of her bruises, the rusted nail, the permanent rip through the skin of her neck, and her awful terrifying final day on the ranch would pass. That she'd be able to declare her own sins and give voice to what had happened. Dear God, could the feel of a rifle's cold, metal trigger be replaced by something, by anything of comfort?

"Please," she whispered and pulled her knees tight to her chest.

Tears poured down Loretta's cheeks, to her jacket, to her lap, and fell onto her jeans. Alone on the bench, she rocked, and cried, and rocked. She wiped her eyes with her faded army jacket sleeve on the bench where she sat with her backpack stored below. She turned her head away from what she'd learn over time was the Upper West Side where the sun had begun to end its day. To the east, she watched the flicker of the deli's orange neon sign flash across the sidewalk. She gazed at an intersection that led to another and another farther on. Red light. Yellow light. Green. This would be her home now. Her new beginning. New York City.

All that lay to the west was behind her. At last.

TWENTY-FOUR

New York City

"It's time." Annie, no longer cautious, stepped into the meeting room. Loretta had told her to take charge of the agenda and she was ready.

"Is it? Really?" Loretta found herself uncertain, scared in a fashion that the sound of her solid western bootheels might hide. How many of her August birthdays had passed for her to be ready, how much had she prepared, and had it been enough?

"I can stall." Annie touched the mole near her lips.

"No, no. Can't do that. Or can we?" Loretta tossed back her head, wondered about the recent appearance of gray in her hair, perhaps more since morning. The three women laughed.

"Up to you," Annie said. She'd know her boss was not serious. She opened the binder she carried with her, checked the agenda. There was far too much at stake on this minute-by-minute every-detail-covered sort of day.

"Right. Except it's gonna matter. It's got to." Loretta said this so succinctly she suddenly remembered hearing about making things matter from Joey, the man who made her coffee at the deli near Union Square when she'd attended this very college.

"I should go. Get a seat." Maggie reached for her leather bag slouched on the floor. Threw her notepad and phone inside. Her hand rested on a turquoise button on her blouse, close to her heart, a pause to offer her own applause for what Loretta had survived, the so-very-much the woman had accomplished, the sure victories that were yet to come her way.

"Do you mind? I need a moment." Loretta offered the smile that often began in her eyes and served to calm even her fiercest adversaries—most of whom eventually became her fans.

"Of course, for sure. May I ask one more question?"

"Sure."

"Will you ever go back?"

"To the ranch?" Loretta knew this was an important question. Nonetheless, she needed to breathe, to pause, to find the strength to share another of her secrets.

"Yes." Maggie stood by, quiet.

"Here's the thing. The honest truth is I go back there every day."

"I get that. I do. Thank you, Loretta. I better head to the auditorium."

"Wait." Loretta stopped her. "There's a meeting room. Down the hall. The Compass team is huddled there. You should meet them. Drew. Others. Feel free to say hello."

"Drew? Def Leppard Drew? Care-to-share Drew?"

"Yes, didn't I mention? He works with us."

"What? How?"

"Well, you can ask him."

"You sure it's okay?"

"I am. There's so much more to our story! Annie will take you."

Loretta raised a hand to her scarf. "We need people to know about our work. Those with money, too."

"I better hurry."

"Don't worry. I have a feeling you'll be spending more time with us. And, Annie, don't disappear on me. Show Maggie the way. Give me ten minutes. But then I need *you* for something."

"Got it. I'll be right back, boss." She saluted with her cell phone.

"Oy." Loretta shook her head. If anything, Annie was more in charge of everything at Compass than she was.

The journalist turned back from the doorway. An odd moment. This had gone beyond being an interview. The two could well be friends who'd hug and give good wishes and say *let's have a drink after*. But one was a writer with no jurisdiction over the final outcome of Loretta's story. The other a woman who'd stood on so many precipices, who'd thought countless times that this was it, this would be the day everything begins, only to find that each beginning circumspectly led to the next.

Loretta tapped her phone to call Clarke. She was surprised he didn't answer. Not surprised but she was afraid. What-ifs exploded in her mind. What if William had disappeared? What if he was in New York? What if, what if. She walked to the window on the opposite side of the room. Stared at the street below. Every muscle in her body was pinging as sweat rolled down her back.

Loretta's phone flashed.

"Oh, Clarke, thank God it's you."

"Sorry, I was talking to them. I'm really sorry. I didn't mean—"

"No, it's okay. I was having a moment. But I'm okay. Really. So tell me." Loretta braced herself. A couple more what-ifs flew through her head. She took a deep breath.

"They got him, Lor." Clarke paused, and she heard him take a breath of his own. "The sheriff called minutes ago. William will spend the rest of his life in prison."

"Do I need to—?"

"No. Nothing. It's over. I have it in writing. Your part is finished. You made this happen."

"Consequences at last."

"Exactly."

"I've gotta go. It's time." Loretta dropped back onto the couch, with Clarke still on the line. She reached for her glass with a half-inch left of no-longer fizzy water. She felt her body relax, her neck cooled, her hands stopped shaking.

"Can I do anything? Anything at all? Should I come there?"

"No. I know you would. But this. It's on me. Come what may, the women are waiting. To hear from me. I've got to make today matter for them."

"You will." Clarke went quiet. They waited a moment. Their silent hug.

"Later." Loretta remained still for a few seconds longer before they clicked off.

Alone in the meeting room, she punched one more number.

"Elsie?"

"Of course, Loretta girl."

"All okay in Santa Fe? You setting up for your show?"

"I am. I'll send you pictures. But none of that is important today. What's the latest?"

"We did it, Elsie. You and me. We never gave up and today they got him. He's going to prison for verbal, physical, and mental child abuse, sexual molestation, and more. But, oh my."

"Oh my, what?"

"It's like something that's stuck in your eye, and you can't get it out. Lord, it bothers you. You pull on your lid. Think maybe you've screwed up your eye forever. And then suddenly it's gone. It's dramatic. Your eyesight begins to clear. This was the last missing piece."

"Like one little button."

"Exactly. You remember?"

"I'd never forget. Did you reach Ms. Del?"

"I called her last night. She's very proud. Wishes she could have come to our conference but her own kids, school, you know?"

"I do."

"Oh Elsie, my best friend. I sure wish you were here. I gotta go do my talk thing."

"I am there. Remember what you said? We're together always."

"Right." Loretta was sure Elsie wore the half smile, half a question mark grin she'd had for years. "Remember our list?"

"Never forgot it. We got every single thing on it."

"And more." Loretta didn't want to end the call.

"Okay, girl, it's time. Make us proud."

"For sure. Later." Loretta turned off her phone. She had a mixed-up swirl of feelings, felt the same as after having the flu, not 100 percent better, but very close, time to get back to life, yet nervous.

"It's me." Annie closed the door behind her. "What's up?"

"I'm finally ready."

"You heard from Clarke?"

"William is on his way to prison."

"So it's over. At last."

"It is and yet—"

"And yet?"

"You know, Annie"—Loretta drank the last of her water and stood—"Elsie and I had this Freedom List. That's what we called it. That's when I became serious about making lists. As you know, I still am."

"I suspect you're telling me you have more work in mind for us." Annie pointed to the door. It was almost time.

"I am." Loretta smoothed her jeans. Shook her hair away from her face. "Come on. Walk me to the others. Let's get started."

"It's here. The big moment of the conference. How do you feel?" Annie asked.

"For some reason I'm thinking of when I was on the road, the other kids I met, how we were a family." Loretta linked her arm with Annie's.

"Like Drew, I'm sure."

"He's a good one. Our whole team is great."

"You know . . ." Annie stopped walking, turned to face Loretta. "You're sure calm lately. It's different. Good different."

"I've been working hard on that. Breathing more. I've even got a new—"

"Quote?"

"Yep." Loretta full on smiled. "Rosa Parks said that 'knowing what must be done does away with fear.'"

"And—?"

"I'm doing my best to let my fears go. I know what must be done."

Remembering the morning at McDonald's hitchhiking with long, tall Drew, Loretta sometimes painted hers a magical journey. Not a lie as much a moment of Happy Meal whimsy that frosted her memories with pixie dust. Except real magic is but the flip side of darkness—where what is unseen is as deceptively alluring as what is apparent. The delight of a furry bunny emerging from a top hat holds different meaning for a girl who spent her youth raising rabbits and selling them for Easter dinners.

Thus, and mostly, Loretta described her travels on highways as scented with the sweet smell of incense. A sort of glory days within the community of strong, young road warriors she'd joined. Folks who afforded her swift entry without inquisition and uplifted her escape to the great city that would adopt her. She secreted away parts of her journey—bad rides, bum steers, and a car with automatic locks.

To many, Loretta was sure she appeared to have the strength to battle any foes. This was not true. Someday in the future, she wasn't sure when, she'd tell more of her truth, her anxieties, her need for help. For the moment, she'd shared enough, so much of it overwhelmed her and she could barely think what it did to others. Her friends had heard her speak of her past, how she'd both cowered and prevailed. She'd have to explain what that meant; she'd have to tell them how facing off with evil doesn't mean you are fearless.

She'd tell them that it's not easy to take to the road and flee. It's traumatic to cut off the head of a rabbit. Skin its furry body. The blood runs amok in the dirt at your feet. She promised herself she would think of William less often. He would be filed away although that remained a challenge. She speculated that he probably wasn't her father, especially after she opened the envelope from her mother's lawyer. She wasn't yet certain, but it didn't matter. She wasn't of him anymore.

Wearing so much protective armor tired her. It hardened her ability to speak out—except on this important day when Loretta felt blessed with a wellspring of hope and an energy that was near boundless. The button in her hand would remain her personal talisman. The possibilities made her grin. Loretta had no doubt many more wayward girls were finding their way to her. And she would be waiting for them.

"You okay?" Annie tugged on Loretta's arm.

"I am." They strolled down the hall to thank the team. Loretta heard chatter and laughter from the crowded auditorium beyond. They passed one of the conference signs with COMPASS in big letters and a peregrine in flight.

"Your cue is in like three minutes." Annie checked her watch. "You sure about this? No introduction? You're just gonna walk onstage?"

"I am."

"We could have the announcer give your name."

"Nope. As we planned. No introductions. They know me and I know them."

"All right then. A quick word with the team and then I whisk you stage left."

"I'm ready."

In the weeks before the conference, the Compass offices had been crowded with printed materials that would be handed out at the coming events. Their whiteboard was a panoply of lists written with a variety of dry-erase markers: red for to-do stuff, blue the ever-changing speaker schedule; anything in green had to do with funding for the new building's reconstruction.

"I'm running to my appointment." One afternoon, Loretta grabbed her leather satchel, knotted the scarf around her neck, and hurried out. "Gotta go."

"No worries. We've got plenty to do here." Annie, head bent, raised her eyes from a sheaf of color-coded sheets of paper, one for each donor that listed where their name was to appear on conference posters and booklets, as well as in media and PowerPoint presentations.

"You're tired. You should go home." Loretta stopped in the

doorway, set down her bag, took a few steps backward. "I ask too much."

"Yes, that's true." Annie laughed. "And I do it. Sucker that I am for a good cause."

"Oh, Annie. I'm sorry." Loretta hesitated, in a hurry to go, yet committed to never abuse or take advantage. "I'll come back. This evening. I can do that stuff."

"Loretta"—Annie waved her boss off—"don't you know yet? We're in this together. You couldn't stop me if you tried."

"Thank you."

"Thank us." Annie brushed tawny hair over her shoulders and returned to the pile of paperwork. "By the way, remember I'm leaving early, too. Please do not come back. Not tonight. We'll both go home. Agreed?"

"Okay, got it. I promise."

Loretta ran when she heard the bell of their building's ancient elevator. Listened to it whine its way to their floor. Inside, she let her spine lean against the wall and thought how blessed she was to have Annie by her side, to have calm in her life, that investigations had been done and legal statements taken. She hurried to the Washington Square subway station. She'd take a B or C and get to Dr. Kagan's office in plenty of time.

Suddenly a text arrived. Her therapist had an emergency. She was sorry. Could they reschedule? She texted back they could. It was fine. She'd go home. Be there before Clarke for a change. Maybe even relax.

Sitting alone on her couch, Loretta had unlatched her leather satchel. In sweats and comfy socks, she opened the accordion bag. Notes from her recent board meeting sat next to Hillary Clinton's memoir, *Hard Choices*, a birthday gift from Clarke. Great title. She reached for the book then paused, her eyes caught on the large manila envelope that had arrived months before.

"Your mother dropped the charges against you, Lor." Clarke had raced home one night with champagne. "You'll get a letter from her lawyer with some details he's got for you. It's over. Everything's been expunged."

"Truly gone?" she'd asked.

"Yes, it's over."

She slid the envelope from a side pocket. The return address was stamped with the lawyer's name. Herb Muldoon, Attorney-at-Law. Beneath in bold was printed: Legal Services, Insurance, LLCs, Wills, Burial Plots.

"Well, he sure covers everything," she said and slapped the envelope against her thigh, unbent her knees, stretched her legs.

Loretta opened the flap and pulled out a sheaf of papers stapled to another envelope. On top was a letter from Mr. Muldoon.

Dear Loretta,

You may remember me from our church but that was a long time ago. Your mother came to me privately and asked me to contact you in the event of her death. She said to send you these documents and the attached envelope. She also made me promise these three things: First, I was not to tell William of her request, and second that I advise you her death was not your fault, that she knew her thrombosis was taking over, that nothing you did made a difference, that she was glad you ran. Lastly, your mother asked me to be sure you know that she wished she could have shown you better that she cared. She said that maybe what is attached will help you understand.

If I can be of further assistance, please don't hesitate to contact me.

Yours in justice,
Herbert R. Muldoon

Beneath Mr. Muldoon's letter, Loretta found a copy of her mother's death certificate. Attached was the bill of sale for the ranch. William had bought the land and the house from Mama's parents with one clear condition underlined in bold print: ALL FURNITURE AND CONTENTS INCLUDED.

"Saved you from the poorhouse," William used to yell at Mama late at night. Upstairs, Loretta listened, ear to her bedroom door, afraid he'd drag her to the closet, lock her inside if she dared come to Mama's aid.

She never heard her mother say anything in return.

Saved you from the poorhouse; the words shot from his mouth again and again. Now Loretta understood. Her mother had been part of the deal. Lock, stock, and barrel at its best.

Behind the paperwork, Loretta pulled off the envelope stapled to it. Pink stationery with the prettiest stamp that pictured a baby lamb with its mother; the words *American Wool* ran along the bottom, the sky beyond a very light then darker blue.

"Oh, my Lord." Loretta inhaled a deep breath. She blew it out. Inhaled again. "The letter addressed to me. Mama put it here."

No return address. The postmark from a city in a state halfway between there and here. The curlicued uppercase *L* that underlined her whole name—her whole name!—as magical as that day when the yellow school bus had dropped her off after school.

"Ain't anybody gonna meet ya?" the driver had asked.

"Meet me?" Loretta had been bewildered. Her parents never came to the road for her, never held her hand, walked her in, or asked about her day. To be met would be a bad omen. And it had been.

She turned over the pink envelope starched stiff by time. More than crisp to her touch. She worried, took extra care, could not risk inflicting a rip or tear in the small letter that was addressed to her.

To Loretta!

The thrill of the moment as prescient as the benefit of hindsight. Her hand quivered. She slid a finger under the flap. Joy burst within her when she felt a folded piece of paper on which someone had written her a letter.

"Hmm," she murmured and read the note that had the most glorious cursive handwriting she'd ever seen. The word *Dear* preceded another perfect *Loretta*.

Written by a woman who wrote "I am your mother's sister."

Her mother's sister?

"Married and we have a daughter a little older than you. Your mother declared if her baby was a girl she'd baptize her with the name Loretta. I'm glad she did. Wish we'd met you before my parents lost the ranch."

Before?

"Can you imagine" followed by "never knew the man who bought it" and "I hope we can see you all one day. Would love to meet you."

Never knew William?

Signed, "Fondly, Aunt Becky."

A PS that said, "My address is above, please write me."

"I have an aunt?" Loretta held the pink stationery close to her face. Read the words again.

How the hell is that possible? They never knew him?

Does that mean . . . ?

What does that mean?

Loretta's heart raced.

Before they lost the ranch? Before?

That would mean before William.

They never knew him? Yet this woman, this sister to Mama, knew Loretta existed. Knew she existed before, before the ranch was sold to a man the sister had never met.

An Aunt Becky?

Before? Never knew? The words popped prairie dog style inside her head.

"He's not my father," she whispered. "I'd bet on it. Never was." Her words a litany, a choir of big sky peregrines not forgotten, a benediction of tears flooded her eyes.

Loretta had once asked *Why me?*, and here, right before her, was the answer. The bill of sale was clear. Her mother, the ranch, and its faded lodgepole pine cabin, a two-bedroom with a fenced yard where dogs ran near wooden beds of radishes, cabbage, beets, and carrots, had been included.

A wooden bed with a rusted nail that scarred Loretta for life.

Sold to a man who no God would bless. Loretta raised her hands to her lips. Covered her eyes. More tears fell. Decades far behind in the rearview mirror faded into nothingness. No matter what she'd eventually find out, on this day she was sure she was not of him. He not of her. There are moments when God lets women decide their chosen truth. She knew hers. Her destiny was self-ordained. Her life was her own.

TWENTY-FIVE

Speech to the Compass Conference for Women

I'm Loretta and I'm here to talk about us. Just us. Who we are, who we will be, our lives, our choices, the consequences we deserve, and who we want to be. How to wake each morning, make our beds, accept our pasts, and carry on. That's hard, isn't it?

No one understands what we have experienced. Unless they've been through it like Ashley, Crystal, Dominique, Andi, Rita, Elsie, Jennifer, Faith, Sarah, Jessy, Tea, Kitty, Naomi, Jamika, Stephanie, Sabine, Gayle, Caroline, Rebecca, Tanya, and many, many more of you here today. Or like me.

Are you asked what you experienced? As if it is in one of those prewrapped gift boxes on TV—where the lid is garnished with shiny paper and a big bow. The cover is lifted, and the fancy wrap stays intact. No ripping required.

Except that doesn't work for us. Our bruises, pains, our wounds, our experiences cannot be put into a box for later. A box cannot store the abuse we've known. It's similar to those who praise our recovery, who tell us that we are strong and brave.

"Oh God, what you've been through," some say, and I'll admit to you—I wonder if they believe me. They don't know what happened to me. They can't.

Do you have an "I'm okay" face? I do. I call upon my I'm okay smile at least once a day. It is on my face even when people believe in me too much. I'm not okay. I need help. All women who struggle do. I need empathy. I need compassion. I need to know how to control my fears and anxieties . . . although I'm getting better at that. Perhaps we should lobby for a federal office of anxiety management. How's that sound?

And then there are people who want to say it couldn't have been that bad. Who ask, "Did that really happen? Are you sure? Maybe you're being dramatic." That's a tough one to hear. I promise you, we are not being dramatic. I'm here today to end all this. Today we stop berating ourselves, wondering what we could have done differently, whether what happened was our own fault. It wasn't.

I say this remembering how the man who raised me used to howl his truth into my face, his finger jabbing at me, his arm poised to attack, his words a double dare should I think to defy him. His abuse was real. I did nothing to deserve his venom.

I see each of you in front of me . . . and I know why you are here.

Our experiences can never be put in a box because they are the circuitry with which we are wired. Yet, despite whatever abuse was delivered onto us, today it becomes our power. If you hear one thing from me, please let it be this. You are strong and capable. Do we forgive our aggressors? No, I don't think so. But what matters is that we let go of any unjust guilt we carry. That we absolve ourselves of our pasts and build our lives.

Today is a new beginning. Compass will offer you more services, more education, more assistance. We are happy to announce that our incredible new center is almost ready. An entire building within blocks of this college. Due to the righteous generosity of a small group of formerly wayward women, we will have in-house programs, an office for employment, legal aid, a scholarship fund, and more. Yes, righteous generosity! Let us know what you need, and we will help. We must act. And we must take charge of our future.

A great teacher taught me that within the swords we want to carry, it is better to find the words that become our truth. Words we've hidden too long. Words that are our strength. The words that give us hope. Speak up. Own your destiny. Today, we choose life.

A Year Later

They parked the rental car near the yard where dogs no longer barked. Beyond was an expanse of prairie that backed up to nothing. It was the nothingness Loretta remembered.

"Well, a last look," Loretta said. She took strong steps, determined. Her hair breezed over the shoulders of her corduroy blazer; she played with a loose button in one pocket. A bitter day welcomed them. Earth-encrusted snow lingered. Loretta opened the door.

"So this is it?" Clarke asked. He scanned the perimeter, checking, on watch.

Loretta's shoulders twitched. The ranch's silence was as uncomfortable as a playlist of wolf howls and fox moans. Empty, yet there was a stench she recognized.

"Yes," she said. "This is it. William and Mama's house."

Loretta walked a few feet into Mama's kitchen. She glanced at the double-gauge standing guard by the door. She wouldn't touch it. William's oilskin slicker hung idle on a nearby hook. His black

western hat sneered at her from the shelf above. The elderly scent
of onions and bacon was burnt into the walls of the musty room.

Clarke stood quiet. She'd let him come with, after discussions
about how her being alone was fraught. With what? They weren't
certain. She handled the attacks better these days, hadn't stumbled in the subway in a long time.

Loretta ran a finger along the edge of the oak kitchen table,
her burgundy nails foreign in these parts. She might have been in
a furniture store where it was preordained that nothing would be
chosen. Clarke sat on a bench to one side, took off his blue Mets
cap, and scratched at his forehead. Loretta knew he felt the same
as when a client called him to a home where something unpardon-
able had happened.

"Sorry," she offered. "This place. So very—"

"Don't be sorry," Clarke said.

"Right." At the foot of the stairs that led to her childhood
bedroom, Loretta stopped, slapped her hands on her Levi's, and
swung around on her bootheels. The sight of the kitchen mot-
tled her skin with itches and childhood memories. William in his
chair at the table. His hand on the green ledger the day he told her
he'd kept a log. Such an insidious sin.

Loretta remembered Mama by the potbellied stove. Her
stained pink-green-red plaid apron tight—how her chest heaved—
her brow dotted with perspiration. Mama's tired feet, the flesh
of her legs thick and layered upon layer until she had no ankles
at all.

You didn't think you'd be goin' anywhere, did you, daughter?

Loretta again felt the cringe in her heart, how her breath had
gasped away, oxygen stolen from her that morning when William
told her she'd be in charge of the residents.

"Need help?" Clarke asked.

"Don't worry. I've got this," she said.

Loretta stared to the front room with the red horsehair couch where William had wooed the parents of bad girls who were in fact good, wonderful, freedom-loving young women whose parents were enticed by his lectures about sinnery and learning right behavior.

"Stay here. I've got to get something," Loretta said with her hand on the banister.

"You sure I shouldn't go with? In case?"

"I'm sure."

Loretta headed upstairs to the door that Mama had often locked with a key. She twisted the knob. The room was unchanged. Her lonesome twin bed. Loretta touched the dresser and pulled out the top drawer. Inside, her forbidden-to-wear Rolling Stones tee folded on top of a STOP FOOLISH SINNERY version from William's private label.

"Well, that should go up in flames," she said and reached beneath both. Found the relic she'd left behind—a very dried-out bag of Twizzlers. The licorice proof she'd once been a teenager with a teen's yearnings, not every moment a dread.

She stepped to the ladderback chair painted with bluebells, some yellow, that had belonged to the grandmother she'd never known. Aunt Becky told her it was probably for the best. She stopped at her makeshift desk and leaned close to the window hoping to sight a pronghorn galloping across the land.

"I'm here," she said to her prairie outside. A cloud surfed by— far aloft in the big blue sky. "I'm going to save you, or at least give you a chance."

Loretta reached beneath the desk. To the right she found the manila envelope taped to the underside. Her fingers tingled—a chill of relief pulsed when she held it close.

She sat on her bed. Dust flew. The scratchy army blanket smelled of tired mothballs. The butterscotch-colored envelope, which had meant everything to her, awaited. She flipped it over. Her hand caressed the flap, the golden clasp.

"Mine," she said and dropped onto her side, knees bent to her chest. Loretta rested her head on the near-flat childhood pillow. Let her hair fall in front of her eyes. With the envelope tight in her grasp, her breaths came quick, the anxieties she'd come to accept, her arms hugged tighter, her eyes checked each corner of the room.

"One, two, three"—she counted the way she'd learned in therapy. "Are you safe?" she asked herself. "Yes." "Is there danger?" She knew there wasn't. She'd found what she came for.

The light outside genuflected. Daytime preparing for evening. She felt a sad happiness. Not delight. Not revenge. She thought of her list, things not to forget. A couple items she needed from the kitchen. She carried the ladderback chair downstairs.

"That comin' with us?" Clarke asked, eager to assist.

"I'd like to take it home."

"I'll take care of it." Clarke set it by the door. His Mets cap alone on the table.

"Thank you." Her gratitude covered much more than the chair.

"No need." He touched her hand and grabbed his hat. "I'll put it in the car. Get everything ready."

She slipped the manila envelope into her satchel and walked to the counter. Pulled at the handle of a drawer. It was stuck but gave way. Inside was a Bic pen. Three rubber bands. She found what she wanted. The ledger in which William had itemized what she'd cost them: baby food, toddler clothes, meals, so many meals, soap, a puffy jacket, a used backpack.

Loretta took quiet steps to the potbellied stove. Mama's place. Mama's tired pink-green-red plaid apron slumped from a nail in the wall. She hesitated. Her hand lifted to the scarf on her neck. She reached for the apron. It felt wrong; intrusive. Like a child opening a mother's purse. A space she wasn't allowed to explore. Her hand searched deep inside the apron's pockets. A couple of buttons were there. Her mother had rescued them. She'd gathered them, stored them in her own pocket. Had Mama saved them for her?

Loretta set her satchel on the back seat of the silver rental car. Left the ledger on the hood. Clarke pulled on work gloves. She knew he was relieved to have something to do. He opened the trunk. Inside were six gas cans he'd filled at the Flying J near town.

"Don't worry," he told her. "I double-checked. The G&A cleared out the attic."

"Payback"—she offered a tiny laugh—"for my pocketknife and compass."

"Yes. Now, I've got this part." Clarke picked up one of the gas cans.

"I'll do it, too. I need to," she said.

"You sure?"

"Yep. Got to."

"And then we are outta here." He followed her lead. They trudged left and right pouring gas along the foundation of the decrepit wood buildings, then to the office at the rear of the bunkhouse where residents had been forced to bend to William's demands.

Loretta reached into her left pocket for a box of Diamond wood matches. Uncertainties reminisced in her head. Mama might well be standing in the doorway. A worn dish towel thrown over her shoulder, the incongruities of her mothering a nest of prickly thistles.

"Hey, you," Clarke called from the path.

She heard a series of clunks. Clarke tossed the last of the gas cans into a vegetable bed. Loretta didn't move. The darkness not quite fully descended.

"I can—" Clarke offered.

"I'm doin' this," Loretta told him. She gave him her tender smile tinged with her ingrained understanding that a person can only be truly happy if they've known pain.

"You okay?" he asked.

"I think so." Being okay came in stages for her. At any given moment Loretta felt assured. The next was as if the whites of William's eyes leered near hers.

"You don't have to be."

"I know. Thanks for reminding me. Except"—she stared into the distance, the highest mountaintop barely visible, such a beckoning spirit in the almost night sky—"this is important."

"Yes, it is."

"My devoir. You know?"

Their eyes roamed west to east, surveyed the dilapidated remains of the ranch that had never thrived.

"Something that must be acted upon. I know."

"Right," she said.

Loretta grabbed the ledger and walked closer to the house. Her hair a precious mess from the earlier breeze. Dirt stuck to her heels. The prairie quiet.

"Best time for a fire," she announced and inhaled deep. Felt both weak and strong. At this moment, on the land where she'd been born, quiet tears creeked down her face and trickled into her scarf.

"It's over," she told the big sky above. "I'm done here. You don't own me."

Loretta pulled out a match.

Pop! Followed by a small *whoosh.*

She saw Mama's face. Her sagging eyes wider than ever. Blood streaming. A stagger. Mama waved her arm same as batting away a gnat. Her mouth muttered, "Go."

Loretta had run.

She lit the match. Held it in the air. A small flame in the almost night of day. Loretta threw it at William and Mama's house. Fire leapt and soared. She lit another and tossed it into a vegetable bed, the one with the nail, where she'd rested her boot on the wooden frame, so sure-footed she'd not heard William's approach that awful night so long ago.

Into the fire went the ledger along with her debt.

Next, she ripped off the scarf that hid the scar that had never truly healed.

She flung it. Watched the fire coil its edges until the scarf shriveled and was gone.

"Loretta—" Clarke called to her.

She needed another minute. She had to see the house burn, the bunkhouse begin its descent. The prison where girls were sent to live. Where their families left them to learn how very sinnerly they were.

"They were not sinners," she called out. "Not them. Not me. Not any of us."

Flames jostled begging her eyes' attention.

"I know one thing—" Loretta paused to watch the fire shudder and drift. The hint of her mother's sorry love her only inheritance. "I know this is another beginning."

The horizon line was no longer beyond her reach. Soon, the instant would come when the setting sun bid good night to earth.

"Look!" She pointed to the darkening sky.

Clarke walked close to her.

"It's Venus. The evening star." Loretta began to whistle, something he had never before heard her do.

"I see it," he said.

"That one's mine," she announced. The treaty of her past, present, and future at last ratified.

"Of course."

"They're coming." Loretta heard the sirens of the fire brigade approaching.

"It was set. They'll handle it," Clarke told her.

"And—" Loretta said, sweating, knowing she'd found some semblance of relief.

"And what?"

Loretta lodged her eyes on the beyond, the nothingness.

"A new prairie will grow."

Postscript

Representative Adam Schiff (CA) introduced H.R.3024, the Stop Child Abuse in Residential Programs for Teens Act, in 2017. It was referred to the House Committee on Education and the Workforce by the House of Representatives, where it has remained. The Stop Institutional Child Abuse Act, SICAA, recently sponsored by Congressman Ro Khanna (CA) and Senator Jeff Merkley (OR), seeks to establish a Youth in Congregate Care Bill of Rights to ensure those institutionalized have, among other things, access to clean drinking water and nutritional meals as these are not currently guaranteed.

As of 2021, residential programs specializing in the troubled-teen industry with possible questionable practices have been identified in Arizona, California, Georgia, Idaho, Florida, Massachusetts, Mississippi, Missouri, Montana, New Hampshire, North Carolina, Oregon, South Carolina, Tennessee, Texas, Utah, Vermont, West Virginia, and Wyoming.

Paris Hilton appeared in a Utah court in February 2021 giving testimony against Provo Canyon School. She has accused their staff of inflicting emotional, physical, and psychological abuse on her during her stay as a teenager. In March 2021, Utah's governor Spencer Cox signed the first bill in fifteen years enacting more oversight and limits on the use of restraints, drugs, and isolation rooms in youth treatment programs in the state. Ms. Hilton stated in an October 2021 Opinion piece in the *Washington Post*, "The 'troubled teen industry' needs reform so kids can avoid the abuse I endured." In 2022, she continued to call upon Congress and President Biden to enact the bill of rights for teens in congregate care.

Why I Wrote This Book

I think many books are written to answer an author's own questions. This was certainly the case for me. *The Home for Wayward Girls* helped me explore the tragedy many young people, including my own sister, experienced as teenagers. My ideas for this story bumped around in my head for some time until I was traveling out west a few years ago. Down a small country road, I saw a sign for a "home for girls."

Twisting about in the passenger seat, I tried to see more, to grasp what was there, but all I could make out was a distant building and I was left confused and disturbed. I found it hard to believe that in the twenty-first century there would be such a place. Thus began the research that inspired this book. Much of what I found was eerily similar to my own sister's story years before.

I was raised in a family of seven. My parents, two brothers, two sisters, and I basically lived at a crowded kitchen table—the living room was for adults only—in a small brick home on the South Side of Chicago. My parents didn't have a lot, but they were dedicated to supporting our family and giving us what we needed in our lives.

One morning, I was headed out to the 103rd Street bus to go to high school. My sister, whom I'll call "the swimmer," should have been right behind me. But the girl with chlorine-green hair refused to get out of bed that day and then many more. While we thought she was just being difficult, we learned over the years that it was depression that was plaguing her. Our sister was a Division 1 trophy-winning swimmer, with a high IQ, and college scholarships in the offing. But something was wrong. She stayed in bed, stopped seeing friends, and became distant from us. There were times we thought she would be okay but more when she wasn't. Sadly, she spent much of the rest of her life in and out of residential programs in Illinois.

Often my siblings and I would visit the swimmer in whatever program my parents with no health insurance were able to afford. Each institution promised rehabilitation, and most every time we went to see her, my sister complained about how she or others were being treated. We hugged her, raised our eyes to each other, believed (possibly incorrectly) that she was making things up, that it couldn't be so bad, and that the nice staff we met knew what they were doing. However, now, in retrospect, I wonder what we didn't know. I remember her talking about food deprivation, that they had to be silent at times, and that snacks were used as rewards for good behavior. As I wrote *The Home for Wayward Girls*, fragments of conversations with my sister returned. I began asking what I might have done differently.

One thing I discovered is that the Troubled Teen Industry is a big business; it includes residential and wilderness programs, mostly in locations outside of the public eye. I was stunned to read that in 2021, the American Bar Association estimated that there are more than 100,000 teenagers in these programs, which

receive $23 billion dollars* in public funding. There is little or
no oversight and young people of all genders cite examples of
abuse. I know these stories because many people post them on
social media—and there are Reddit groups devoted to the topic
of controversial homes. I've learned that activists have appeared
in state houses and in Washington, DC, to call for regulation.
Some of the groups working on behalf of abused children and
troubled teens include Breaking Code Silence, the Beau Biden
Foundation, the Unsilenced Project, and Survivors of Institutional Abuse (SIA).

Recollections of teen survivors can be found online. A quick
search on YouTube offers videos. I once watched a young woman
talk at length about being dropped off at a program somewhere in
Florida. From what I recall, her parents' decision was mainly based
on mildly wild teen behavior. She was left there for the entirety
of what would have been her remaining years in high school. She
spoke about the use of silence as punishment, meager food, and
that being allowed to speak to other girls was a privilege awarded

---

* See: https://www.americanbar.org/groups/litigation/committees/childrens
-rights/practice/2021/5-facts-about-the-troubled-teen-industry/#:~:text
=The%20%E2%80%9Ctroubled%20teen%E2%80%9D%20industry%20is%20
a%20big%20business.,operate%20as%20for%2Dprofit%20organizations

https://www.breakingcodesilence.org/

https://www.beaubidenfoundation.org/

https://www.unsilenced.org/

https://sia-now.org/index.html

https://www.reddit.com/r/troubledteens/

https://www.usatoday.com/story/entertainment/celebrities/2021/02/09
/paris-hilton-testifies-alleged-abuse-utah-boarding-school/4446908001/

https://www.nbcnews.com/news/us-news/paris-hilton-bill-troubled-teen
-facilities-rcna3349

for conforming to their rules. The more I learned, the more certain I was that I had to complete *The Home for Wayward Girls*.

My sister died after years in a long-term facility. It is too late for my family to know what her life might have been in different times with different caretakers. It is my hope that *The Home for Wayward Girls* will shine a light on programs in existence now and open the door for many teenagers who deserve the chance to grow up without fear and indignity.

Acknowledgments

I procrastinated before writing these pages of thanks. I had notes on chits of paper around my house with names not to forget, some under a refrigerator magnet, others on an end table, and I hope I've gathered them all. In an earlier draft, I wrote "Words cannot express . . ." to which my sister wisely asked, "You don't have the words? But you're a writer." Her message was correct, of course, and so here it is.

My sincere appreciation to Sara Nelson, vice president and executive editor, and HarperCollins Publishers for believing in me and in Loretta's story. My deepest gratitude to the kindest of agents, Cynthia Manson, who had faith in me before others and reminded me often that destiny was but a day away. Thanks to the HarperCollins team, Laurie McGee for great copyedits; Allison Hargraves for the incredible proofreading; and to Edie Astley, Stacey Fischkelta, Jen Overstreet, Olivia McGiff, et al.

A huge shout-out to survivors, families, and the activists rallying for regulation of teen residential programs. I hope they know many of us are supporting their efforts. My thanks to every reader for taking time to get to know Loretta.

My respect and thanks to everyone at the Sarah Lawrence

College MFA program who gave to me without pause, especially Brian Morton and Paige Ackerson-Kiely, and for kind assistance, Alba Coronel. I was fortunate to begin graduate school in a class taught by author Carolyn Ferrell, who told me she'd always be there for me, and she has been. To my adviser and most trusted mentor, author Joan Silber, your patience, wisdom, and kindness inspire me to this day. You taught me to slow down and focus; to write the stories I wanted to tell. The manner with which you place your finger on the exact spot on a page that needs work is magnificent. Such gifts, and I thank you.

There are teachers who were guiding me before I knew I had anywhere to go. At Antioch University Los Angeles, my thanks to those who urged me to take the writer's journey: Ed Frankel, whose belief in me was pivotal; Deborah Lott; Caley O'Dwyer; Alistair McCartney; and the inimitable Jim Krusoe at nearby Santa Monica College, the first who told me I could write.

Thank you to the *Capital Gazette* and editor Rick Hutzell for publishing my essay about my brother Jay, and for understanding a sailor's last wishes. Thank you to the Witkins for so much and to photographer Christine Petrella for taking just the right author photo for this book.

Thank you to the Writing Institute at Sarah Lawrence College, my fellow teachers, and my awesome novel and memoir students. Writers would struggle far more without the support of organizations like the Bronx Council on the Arts, Ragdale, Community of Writers in the High Sierra, and Writers in Paradise at Eckerd College. I am grateful for the scholarships they gave me and the unfettered opportunities I had to write within some very special retreat settings.

I've had the good fortune to befriend the most generous of readers. Thank you, Kimberley Lim, editor, for assisting me in completing this book, and to my writing friends who counseled me to stay the course. I'd have been lost without my closest writing partners, authors Patricia Dunn and Jimin Han, who held my hand, uplifted me, and would have carried me over the finish line if needed. This book wouldn't have been completed without the invaluable help of my friends and writers Rachel Aydt, John Mitchell Morris, Monica Comas, as well as Kate Brandt, Gloria Hatrick, Deborah Laufer, Alexandra Soiseth, Dr. Maria Maldonado, who rescued me in numerous ways; and Barbara Josselsohn, Jennifer Manocherian, the incredibly giving Amy Oman, Alice Campbell Romano, Jane Gordon Julien, Robbie Oxnard Bent, Suzanne Weiss, Jane Glucksman, Cathy Donovan, Andrea Sidor, writer Stacey Rubin, and Swiss writer Constanze Frei.

Love and thanks to my BFFs who cheered me on: the inimitable and loving Fern (mazel tov!); Anita, the best reader I know, who reviews books before the Sunday papers can; my protest partner for life, Susan; my soul sister Lisa L.; my close-as-family friends Austin and Connie; my dearest cousin Cris and the Altosinos; and my friends Jeanette, Wendy, Sweet, Lupita, Cherie, Bella, Nancy, and Matt, Claudia, Joyce F., Katie and Cory, Monica L., Todd, Patricia Glynn, John C-B.; my many British Airways colleagues including Sandy, Sakko, Chris C., Bet, Jodee, Judi, Nancy H., Karen H., Brigitte, Ingrid, ML, Mark, Daniel, Debbie. Yo! to Pecos. Thanks to Myrna, Susan, Claire, and my tennis pals at Seton Park. Cheers to all the daughters of Fairfield Avenue, the Beverly Arts Center, and Mother McAuley High School, where I am grateful to have learned to always try to do better.

My parents were readers. I miss them more, not less, as I get older. They taught us to respect and cherish books. Every three weeks, Mom took us to the Mount Greenwood Branch of the Chicago Public Library where we anxiously sought new titles. Special thanks also to the Culver City Julian Dixon Library near Los Angeles; Ken Pienkos, MSLS, MFA, at AULA; the New York Public Library; and to the many librarians who never tire of unending questions from people like me.

I've had the honor to roam this country and globe with my beautiful daughters. My eldest reminds me that love is by far the best answer, and my youngest helps me laugh more often than cry. Both put up with my wanderlust; they packed bags to hit the road with me and mustered adventurous spirits despite any challenges we encountered. *Romey and Michele* will long be a favorite of ours for many reasons. *I love you, daughters, forever and more.*

I owe so much to the Smat and Kagan families, especially my brother's wife, Kathy, a true sister who tends to us like her special garden; and my sister's husband, Rick, who is such a good brother to me that I can't remember a time when he wasn't there for me without question. Thank you to Zoë whose "go for it" optimism is an inspiration, and to Jen for living her dreams.

My sister, Joanne, is my best friend and has been by my side since we were kids. She has helped me through very tough challenges, is generous beyond measure, and has an amazing intuitive ability to know when to calm me down and remind me to believe in myself—thank you from my heart, Jo. My brother Tom's faith in my endeavors has never faltered even when he's trying very hard not to offer more practical options—you're the best, bro. It's just us three now, but I wish the five of us could grab a booth at Fox's Pizza on Western Avenue and order a large thin crust.

My entire family has loved me unconditionally throughout the twists and turns in my life. The work of writing was often a solitary journey for me, but I treasure the ballast and even keel given me by my family, who never ever suggested I give up or stop. Love you all.

About the Author

Marcia Bradley earned her MFA from Sarah Lawrence College after receiving her BA from Antioch University Los Angeles. She was awarded a Bronx Council on the Arts/New York City Department of Cultural Affairs BRIO Award for Fiction and has been published in *Two Hawks Quarterly, Hippocampus Magazine, Drunk Monkeys, Eclectica,* the *Capital Gazette,* and in *The Writing Disorder,* which graciously published an early story about Loretta. A natural-born wanderer, Marcia grew up in Chicago and moved to Santa Monica where she raised her daughters, with whom she then migrated coast to coast. She teaches at Sarah Lawrence College and lives in the Bronx, New York . . . for now.

https://marciabradley.com/

Reading Group Guide

1. Loretta has a connection to nature and wildlife at the ranch. What do you think the falcon, the logo for Loretta's foundation, represents?

2. The author says only that the ranch is located "west of the Rockies." Why do you think there isn't an exact location? How does the remote prairie permit William's harsh treatment of the residents?

3. Loretta describes watching her physical bruises fade and describes her scars as a road map documenting William's abuse. Will it be possible to overcome her childhood trauma?

4. Adult Loretta suffers from trauma and anxiety. Will she ever feel safe?

5. Loretta's therapist pushes adult Loretta to unearth a happy memory from her childhood. Loretta insists there weren't any. Can there be good memories among the terrible ones?

6. Consider William's punishment: "Silent Cloud." Why is this social isolation so feared by the girls? Does social isolation inflict more anguish than physical abuse?

7. Consider Mama: Does she bear the same culpability as her husband, William? Is Mama a victim?

8. Do you think Mama loves Loretta?

9. Do you believe working with runaways and abused women is a good fit for adult Loretta, given her experiences?

10. Loretta doesn't wear a ring. She states, "I don't like identifications of any sort. . . ." What do you think she means by this?

11. Do you agree with adult Loretta's decision to burn the ranch? Is it possible to "erase" the past? What do you think she should do with the ranch?

12. What role did Ms. Del play in changing the course of Loretta's life? Did a teacher impact your life?

13. Does the title *The Home for Wayward Girls* suit the novel? What would you name the book?